FIRST COMES LOVE

A Grumpy Boss Surprise Baby Romance

MORE BOOKS BY ASHLEE PRICE

https://www.ashleepriceromanceauthor.com/

PROLOGUE

Greyson

What's better than winning the lottery?

Hitting jackpot when you didn't even realize you'd bought a ticket.

And this woman— this Harley Davison— has jackpot written all over her.

Thin yet strong athletic body. A dipped-in waist I instinctively want to put my hands around. A generous mauve-lipped smile that slays me. Green eyes with a brand of amusement I'm not quite sure I get but want to. Even her gap-toothed teeth and every golden wave on her head seem to beam.

I rip my gaze off her, force it onto her hands. Lithe rosy-skinned, small-boned things, they flit and fidget, as if small birds that want to be cooped up in this over-air-conditioned office as little as I do.

"I'm Harley," she says.

Her voice has an exotic flare to it—Australia? New Zealand?—one that her clothing—red-gold brocade blazer, black on black pinstriped pants— only accentuates.

Just another quick glance and a whole number of 'exotic' things I'd like to do to her flash through my head.

Focus, Greyson.

But it's too late. Another smile of hers and I'm done for.

Why she's here, what I'm supposed to be doing, what this interaction is even for, all falls away.

I have to grip the arm rests of my seat to physically keep me in place. No more glances for me, who knows what would happen.

All I know is that I, impossibly, unaccountably, incredibly, with an intensity that's almost painful—want her.

CHAPTER 1

Greyson

One Day Earlier

Here we go again.

Another day at the office, in a position most people would kill for—Storm Media President.

Below the second-level balcony I'm standing on, the open-concept, plant-friendly configuration of cubicles buzzes with eager-anxious activity. Around me wafts the vanilla scent from the air freshener that our janitor, Gladys, installed last night. Across my neck, prickling where I grazed the skin with my razor this morning, is the slight whish of the energy-efficient fans.

I pause, appreciating all the productivity in competent motion, even if I'm not a part of it. One office down from mine, Landon has his head down, slogging away at the mess of the books Dad left us.

I should get back to the office too.

Ah, yes: the office. Still haven't managed to successfully call it 'my' office. Probably because it isn't.

It's Dad's, from its memorabilia-strewn walls down to its desk—his luggage for the first trip that got him backers, back when Storm Media was just a dream in an overly ambitious college kid's head. The place even smells like him: some sort of spruce—weird, since he never was one to spend an afternoon in nature that could be spent building up the company.

Every time Emerson saunters in here, his first comment is how this is a museum, and his second a question on when I'm going to 'clean it up'. Truth is, I don't know. I don't think I want to. With Dad gone, it's one of the few things I have left of him.

Seems like every day I'm getting angrier, more restless, pacing the floor of my office like a trapped panther.

Anyway. Time to get started on…

I scowl at my reflection in the laptop screen before turning it on.

That's just it. My assistant's on vacation, and even then, Madeline has been admittedly muddled at what exactly I'm supposed to do now that I'm president. Somehow, Dad managed to be busier than anyone I knew, and yet his files and instructions leave out one major point: on what?

Everyone knows he was a great man for raising morale—but exactly how many times are you supposed to saunter around telling people to 'keep it up, you're doing great'? What else did he do?

Build and conquer, always, his voice echoes in my head. I reach for my phone, stopping myself just in time. I'm not the producer for StormTV anymore, no matter how much I want to be. My place is here now, even if we all know I'm no Collin Storm.

I wander to the door, then out. I know, without thinking consciously of it, where I'm headed. Where I always go when I lack inspiration, or when I just need a break from it all. Better that than me snapping at some clueless intern, which I've been doing more than I'd like to admit these past few weeks.

Makes me feel like a slacker, strolling off with everyone else hard at work, but I did pull several all-nighters last week to get through all the company's day-to-day minutiae, plus get caught up on all the press conferences and tell the reporters, "Yes, sorry, we still don't know how it happened," when what I really wanted to say was, "No, I don't know how Dad died and I wouldn't tell you if I did, you bloodsucking leeches."

Outside, the air is fresh after a rain, although I see no signs of it. A few blocks, and I'm there.

Ulric looks up first, smiling his one-toothed smile. "Lookee who the cat dragged in."

That's another thing I like about being here, under the McGuinty Overpass: Ulric and the others don't care who I am or what I do. Sure, they may tease me about my fancy suit from time to time, but at the end of the day, I'm just the same as them, another guy working on a wood project. A wood project that, once it's finished, should provide shelter for around 20 homeless men.

"How's it coming along, boys?" I ask.

Harry pops his head out of the tent to knock two bottles together. "Ain't get shit done when you aren't here, ya know."

"Now..." Marlow protests, pausing between two cigarettes to wag an admonishing wrinkled finger. "We did adjust it, now."

I chuckle, walking over. "No worries."

The structure is about three quarters done, a bunch of pine boards and nails that don't go far in their current state yet are still better than what these poor guys are living in now: old, stinking tents that are one rip away from being a pile of useless fabric.

The bag of tools is where I left it, so I get to work, hammering away at the boards, losing myself in the bliss of being actually useful.

"Imagine seeing you here," a familiar voice purrs.

I keep on hammering away, hoping beyond hope that she'll go away.

But Amelia Cavendish only switches which hip she has her hand on. "You going to make me stand here all day?"

"I'm busy."

"And I told you, I can help."

I pause, already knowing this is going nowhere. "Amelia."

She bites her lip. "I could help with... moral support?"

I shake my head. "Not in the mood."

"Maybe I like charity work too, ever consider? God, you're such a conceited prick."

I look at her, deadpan. I don't mention how the only times she's been here are when I have, conveniently because this area is visible from her office window. Nor do I mention how our fling a few months back is done, how we have virtually nothing else in common. I don't need to.

"Amelia, this has to stop," I tell her.

"Fine," she hisses, tossing her Coke can to the side.

The boys have the decency to hold in their chuckling until she's several feet away.

"Fuck you, Greyson Storm!" she yells over them as she storms off.

"Guys," I say over their hooting laughter now, "can't you..."

"We didn't say anything," Harry protests. "Just like you said!"

Last time, after Ulric's innocent 'nice skirt' compliment had Amelia threatening to sue, I'd suggested to the guys that it might be easier to keep it down until she, inevitably, left.

My phone goes off.

It's Madeline. "Greyson, thank God." She sounds terrible, like she's just finished running a 10K and has a runny nose to boot.

"You OK?" I ask.

By the sound of it, my assistant might need a vacation to recover from her vacation to Costa Rica. She was just supposed to go to Corcovado National Park's rainforest to make sure all was running smoothly after we lost contact for a few days, but...

"No, no I'm not, actually. Everyone here has the dengue fever. I... uh... I have it too."

"Shit. Where is everyone? Did they manage to make it to the hospital? Are you OK?"

"I'm fine, don't have it too bad, just this fever and a bit of vomiting. As for the others, they've booked the next flight out of here. Decker walked out yesterday."

"Shit." Suddenly realizing that I've been pacing, I stop dead in my tracks. I knew that guy was off the first second I met him, just passed off my uneasiness as wanting to be in the producer chair myself. "So StormTV has no crew."

"Well—" Another low groan. "Yes. I'm so sorry, Mr. Storm."

A sick urge to laugh twists in me. "Thank you, Madeline," I'm able to make myself say. "Is there anything you need?"

"No, I'm fine, really. Thank you."

She speaks with a careful clip, but I can still hear the anxiety in her voice.

"Don't worry," I tell her, with more assurance than I feel. "I'll get this sorted out. I'll have a new crew there in days. As for you, you get home and rest as long as you need."

"Good luck, boss. Let me know if there's anything I can do."

"You just concentrate on getting better. Thanks again."

I freeze, staring off into space.

Shit.

First Dad dying, and now this. StormTV is a major moneymaker for Storm Media. Without it…

I don't let myself finish that sentence.

"That bad?" Ulric asks.

"Yeah, I… I'm sorry, boys, I have to go."

Harry grins lopsidedly. "Don't be all sorry. We'll be here when you have time."

On my way back to the office, I call up Landon, tell him, "We have a problem."

**

They're all waiting in my office when I get there.

"You're lucky I felt like a stroll downtown," Emerson says, running a hand through his golden hair, blue eyes narrowed. "Otherwise you'd have had to wait a good hour until I was done practicing."

Noah snorts, intones in a caveman voice, "Piano love. Piano life."

We crack up, even Emerson. "Not all of us can be business superstars."

Although truth is that Emerson turned down the Storm position Dad handed to him, decided to go out in left field and try to become a concert pianist of all things.

"I'm no business superstar," I grumble. "I'm just the guy who got thrown into the president position."

My brothers all like to pretend that being cooped up here in this office is my calling or something. Like dealing with all the shit Dad left behind is just a blessing.

"Same here," Landon says, his muscled arms tensed as he rubs at his light-brown-haired temples. "Minus the president part. It's not like I have some undying love for poring over figures from five years back."

Nolan gives him a sympathetic pat. Landon really did get the short end of the stick for this one. As hard as running this company seems without Dad, making sense of the books which Dad self-admittedly 'played by his own rules' is damn near impossible.

"Anyway," I say. "We've got a problem."

"Catastrophe," Nolan agrees morosely.

I don't call my brothers in for many business meetings, but when I do, they know it's serious. All it took was a one-text summary of what had happened, and they were here within minutes.

"What are our options?" Landon asks.

Emerson crosses his arms across his chest, his fingers absently drumming out some chords from some piano piece. "Hire a new crew, obviously."

"What's to stop the same thing from happening again?" I say. "The rainforest in Corcovado National Park is no walk in the park, and Decker came with all the right credentials."

"He was an ass," Nolan says simply.

"An ass you all wanted to hire," I remind him. "You ignored my reservations."

"It doesn't matter," Landon states. "We'll just have to choose better next time."

"I plan to," I say.

All eyes swivel my way.

"Greyson," Emerson begins, "You're not seriously suggesting—"

"Actually, I am," I say. "What better way to ensure that we don't run into the same difficulties again? That, and getting each crew member vaccinated."

"I don't like it," Landon says simply. "You're supposed to be the president. You can't just go gallivanting off here, there and everywhere, just like…" He trails off, scowling.

"Just like Dad used to?" I point out. "Too bad. I'm going."

Three cool pairs of eyes greet me. I have to get my temper in check if this is going to fly, even if I am pissed. I didn't want to be president, but if I am, there should be some perks attached to it. One of them being that I get to decide what I do, when I want.

Which technically I can, but I'd rather not deal with three pissy brothers while I'm gone.

Taking a breath, I force my tone into a neutral one. "C'mon, admit it, me being there will speed everything along and make everything that much easier."

"Not to mention that you get to return to your dream job," Emerson grumbles.

I eye him. "That so bad?"

My brothers scowl. Clearly they agree already, and don't like one bit of it.

"Admit it," I say, "This is a win-win."

"It could be," Nolan says. "Although that doesn't solve everything. We still need a new crew ASAP."

I grin. And there it is, just what I was looking for: agreement, implicit if not explicit.

I get out my phone. "On it."

One Day Later…

"I still don't see why we all had to be here." Nolan gives his long light brown hair-ed head an irritable shake as he chomps on some cashews.

"Agreed." Emerson's on his phone, glaring at it as if it's to blame. "My knowledge of business practices is exactly zilch."

"You know I value your opinions," I tell them. Besides, it's not like sitting around interviewing endless candidates is exactly my idea of a great time either. If I suffer, it's only fair they do too. "Anyway, it's time."

The next few hours in my office pass in a blur of faces and names, takeout food, first impressions, quick discussions and split-second decisions.

After what must be all of the hires, I'm already out of my chair, ready to leave, no questions asked, when Landon stops me. "We still don't have a cinematographer, and we've got four hopefuls out there."

Shit.

I mentally set aside my long hot shower for another hour. "Alright, send them in." Might as well get this over with.

The first woman barks more angry questions at me than I have for her. By the end, I'm ready to fling my clipboard at her head, except she leaves first.

The next woman walks in as I'm sipping my water. I look up and freeze.

"Hello," she says. "I'm Harley."

"Hello," I force myself to say, while I try and fail to tear my eyes off the showstopper that's just walked in.

Keep your head in the game, Greyson.

But it's too late. One smile of hers and I'm done for. Those turned-up mauve lips light up her entire face, make her green eyes crinkle in the corners, her freckled nose crinkle too; even her gap-toothed teeth and every golden hair on her head seem to beam.

Everything else falls away.

All I know is that I want her. I want her bad.

Landon clears his throat, and I brace myself against the chair. Attractive or not, we still have an interview to give. With any luck, she'll flub it and the choice will be easy. On the other hand, I just want to get these interviews finished and get out of here.

"Why do you want this position?" I ask, swiping a brief glance at her.

"I love cinematography and I've loved your work from the start. Evergreen Avenue, then that special on flamingoes, plus the show where they were all cooped up in the cabin, I've watched every one of them dozens of times. Opportunities like this don't come every day—sometimes they don't even come every lifetime."

My back teeth grind together. Alright, she's good, I'll give her that.

Landon shoves a resume under my nose and I scan it briefly. Harley is just as young as she looks: she's fresh out of college.

"Why do you think you'd be a good fit?" I ask her next.

"I might be new, but I know my stuff. I was top in my class at USC School of Cinematic Arts, and even now on my days off I'm always learning and practicing. I love what I do. Oh, and I don't quit. Ever."

The intensity in her tone makes me look up. I swallow.

Her face is even more driven, which makes her look even sexier. And the way she's acing all these questions... fuck.

"You have any questions for us?" Noah asks.

He likes that one, claims it's the only half-interesting question, thanks to some terrified man who started crying two hours back and then basically ran away.

"What do you want?"

She looks straight at me. My mouth falls open. She can't possibly...

Catching my eye, her mouth falls open too. She recovers herself quickly, though.

"I mean, for the job—what are you looking for?"

"You," Emerson says, then chuckles. At my glare, he coughs. "Joking, of course. I'll let my big business whiz brothers answer this one."

"Thanks." Landon's ironic look is no less harsh than my glare was. "We are looking for someone who's passionate in what they do, a team player, someone who isn't afraid to get a bit dirty."

An awkward silence settles as I force myself not to look her way. A bit dirty—he has to use this phrase with our hottest applicant yet, when I'm already having trouble concentrating? Seriously?

And I thought today couldn't get more frustrating.

"Meaning," I cut in, forcing unwanted images of Harley, bent over my knees right here and now out of my head, "the rainforest can be dangerous, even to the experienced. There's disease, rabid animals, shitty weather, the works."

Her chin lifts. "I can handle it."

Then, all innocence as she looks to me, "After all, you're going, aren't you?"

"Where did you hear that?" I ask.

A half-shrug. "One of the women you interviewed earlier mentioned it to us while walking out."

My brothers scowl, while I have difficulty holding my smile back. They probably planned to try to talk me out of the decision later, but me stepping in as producer is looking like more and more of a certainty.

This Harley isn't just hot, she's on the ball. Way too young for me, but I'll be too busy in the producer's chair to be distracted anyway. About fucking time I get to do something I like for a change, too.

"Alright, you're in," I say.

My brothers heave a relieved sigh—clearly, I'm not the only one who's fed up with all the interviews.

"Great!" she says.

We shake hands, her fingers looking even smaller entwined with mine, although her firm handshake is no pushover. Electricity zaps through my fingers. I push it down.

Not the time.

"We're happy to have you as part of Storm Media," I recite the spiel Dad developed who-knows how many years back. Repeating it now feels stupid and trite, especially considering what I suspect about Dad, but it's all I've got, so I go with it: "For us, being punctual, true to our word and a real team are the most important things. But for us, team means something a bit different. We like to work as equals—at least in the suggestion and idea sense. So, if there's anything you think we could do differently or better, just tell us."

"Really?" Harley tilts her head at me.

"Really," I say, looking to the door.

I'm too tired and horny for this. This is not the normal response the spiel gets.

She bites her lip. "Well, if being punctual is the most important thing for you, then you should hold to it. My interview time was…" she glances at her phone, "scheduled an hour ago. I get it that you guys are in a time crunch, but then maybe you should change your tenets?"

What. The actual fuck.

My brothers crack up.

"Oh, this one's got fire, big brother," Nolan says, sauntering out.

Fire that I'd like to test out myself, somewhere private.

I swallow back the thought. "You're right, of course." I bare her my most businessy smile. "See you tomorrow, bright and early. And on time."

She tucks a wavy blonde strand behind her ear. "See you."

CHAPTER 2

Harley

"Yes, Hannah, I really am on the plane to Costa Rica." I frown, even though Hannah is thousands of miles away, probably chowing down the falafel I left by the sounds of it, and can't see my frown at any rate. "You were there while I was frantically packing, remember?"

"Maybe I'm just trying to block it from my memory." She cackles. "The sight of you yelling at nothing while you tried to fit half your closet into a tote the size of my boot was unenjoyable to say the least."

"Not unenjoyable enough to avoid you filming some of it to show me later," I remind her. "Remind me again why I thought living together was a good idea?"

I'm just messing with her, and Hannah knows it.

"Because we're two peas in one wild pod," she continues breezily, "Besides, what else are cousins for?"

"I don't know, moral support? Once a year family gatherings and nothing more?"

"We've never been that kind of cousins, and you know it."

I sigh. "And thank God for it, but seriously, Han, I'm freaking right now." I look around, lowering my voice even though I don't see anyone sitting nearby. "I'm on a fancy-ass plane on my way to Costa Rica to work with Greyson Storm on StormTV."

"I still can't believe he just let your punctuality jab slide."

"He did ask for suggestions."

"Har. On your first day—literally seconds after you'd been hired? In most places, that would be career suicide."

"Well, I'm still here, aren't I?" I say, with a bit more confidence than I feel.

"He probably thought you were hot," Hannah says easily.

I throw another stealthy look around before declaring, "Top executives like Mr. Storm do not hire someone just because they're hot! Not for a job like this. Maybe for some kind of secretary or ass-kissing position."

Hannah sighs. "Ah, professional ass-kisser. Has a nice ring to it, doesn't it?"

We crack up. "Honestly, though, this is a great opportunity. I know that I'm ready, but I'm still nervous."

"Good," Hannah says. "Welcome to the real world."

I frown, playing with a fishtail braid I keep doing and undoing. "I do get nervous, you know. Just not for minor things."

"Being nervous for the first date with the Most Handsome Man Alive is not a minor thing." I can hear the ice in Hannah's voice, even though she's now happily dating Roger, AKA the Most Handsome Man Alive.

"Sorry," I say. "Different things freak us out, I think."

"Have you ever gotten freaked out over a guy?" she asks.

"Nope, not since James stood me up for that Grade Eight dance, and I don't plan to start now. Anyway, how's Anchovy doing?" I'm surprised I forgot about my cute little fat ferret for this long.

"Escaping every other hour, sneaking into Giselle's and pissing her off," Hannah informs me.

"Our dearly beloved neighbor hasn't moved out yet?"

"She'll never move out. She exists to spite us."

"Well, you did get promoted over her. And didn't Anchovy shit all over her Peruvian rug that one time she tried smacking him with a broom?"

We crack up, although I yawn mid-way through. "Think I should get some sleep. I basically got none last night."

"I know, I was there. But yeah—you have a good sleep. We'll talk soon. Good luck with your awesome new job and sexy new boss. If you decide to jump his bones, I want details!"

"Han!" I hiss, but, laughing, she's already hung up.

"Jump his bones," I mutter to myself ruefully.

Although the thought had crossed my mind, even during the interview itself—Greyson Storm is six feet four inches of dark-haired sculpted gorgeousness—I'm here for the job. Sex would just get in the way.

I close my eyes and slow my breathing. Now, if I could just get a good few hours of shut-eye...

I open them to a hand on my shoulder. It's Greyson. "Mind if I sit here?"

"Yeah?" I say.

A smile plays at the corner of his lips. "You sure?"

"Yes."

"Good."

Although I'm less sure as soon as he's beside me. He smells... attractive, and I'm not a scent girl. Neither did I think a guy smelling like pine would be at all a turn-on, but here I am, biting at the inside of my lip to avoid practically drooling over his alluring scent.

Then there's how he's sitting, legs sprawled lazily so that they touch mine. His voice is equally lazy as he speaks to me, although he doesn't as much as look my way. "You sure you're up to this?"

Something tells me he's not talking about the job.

"What are you doing?" I ask, craning my neck.

I don't see anyone nearby, and the overhead lights are down, meaning most people are probably asleep, but still…

Next thing I know, his hand has slid over casually, his voice a murmur: "What you want me to."

His fingers slowly trace the outline of my thighs, up and down, up and down.

I sink back into my seat, don't manage to fully swallow back the groan coming out of my throat. Oh, it feels good alright.

But are we really doing this?

A sidelong glance catches his, and he just smirks. I smirk on back. Fuck this guy, new boss/Greyson Storm or no.

If he wants to play this game, we'll play it.

My hand grabs for his cock, finds it hard.

My eyes meet his with a challenge—How do you like it now?

His other hand grabs mine, while his thigh-resting one strokes up, higher and higher, applying more and more pressure, until he presses the firm pads of his fingers into… there.

Fuck. Yeah, I'm wet.

I don't bother fighting his other hand as it moves mine away from his cock. What he's doing now, where he's touching me, feels too damn good.

Although something flits at the edge of my consciousness, half-remembered, yet still annoyingly important.

"What about…" I begin.

He presses a finger to my lips. "Shh."

His other fingers slip under my velour track pants and press into the wet of my panties.

I arch my back as a moan rolls out of my throat. My eyes flutter shut. Goddamn does it feel good.

His fingers press and swirl and dip under the wet satin. Until they're all under, playing with my opening, until they're…

"Oh, fuck," I mutter.

Inside me. He flits his finger in and out expertly, and I can feel myself getting close. The problem is my groans: they keep getting louder. I can't keep this up unless…

He presses the heel of his other palm into my mouth as he places his lips on my ear. "That's it, baby, come for me. I want to see you moan my name."

Already my body is spasming, pleasure exploding through me as his fingers slap into me as hard and fast as ever.

"Greyson!" I shrill muffled into his palm as my orgasm crests and takes over, my whole body shaking.

And still he's not finished. As he fingers me with a fury, it occurs to me that I'm dreaming, that this can't be real, that it doesn't matter, that with pleasure like this, the only thing that matters is…

His palm lifts and I wail, "Fuck yes, Greyson!" as I come.

The plane jolts and my eyes snap open.

"Sorry about that, ladies and gentlemen," the chirpy voice overhead says. "Just encountering some minor turbulence. We should be back to our smooth flight in a few minutes."

I'm barely paying attention. The main thing is that I'm alone. Flushed and horny, but alone. The dream was just that—a dream.

Thank God. Although it was crazy hot, I'm not about to get finger-banged on some airplane when anybody could walk by at any time.

Hearing footsteps, my spine stiffens. But it's just Horatio, the flight attendant. As I relax back into my seat, Greyson strides up. He looks like he's slept as little as I have, with his adorably rumpled dark hair and dark under-eye circles, and yet he looks different from when I saw him last. Less frustrated, obviously, but there's something else in his dark eyes. Excitement?

"Few more hours and we're there," he says. "You're new, so if there's anything you need clarified or don't feel comfortable doing, tell me. Even if it means you have to go home and we need to find a new cinematographer, I don't want to pressure you into anything, especially with the rainforest being as dangerous as it is. Those shots we gave everyone before the flight can't protect us from everything."

I eye him. Is this guy trying to let me go already?

"Got it," I say. "But unless we're eating pineapples for every meal, I should be fine."

His serious expression cracks with the beginnings of a smile. "Least favorite food?"

I nod. "That and pickles."

At this, his eyebrows fly up. "But pickles are—"

"Horrible?"

"Not at all."

"Slimy and gross?"

"What pickles have you been having?"

I smile at him. "The only kind there are—the gross kind."

"No, pickles are…" he trails off, probably just realizing that he's arguing with his employee about pickles, of all things. "Also, I just got word that our plans have changed. The plane won't be able to land as close to the camp as expected, so it's going to be a bit of a hike there. And not an easy hike, either. You OK with that?"

"Definitely. I've always wanted to see the rainforest anyway."

"Not like this, you haven't." Greyson's face darkens. "There's poisonous snakes, disease-ridden mosquitoes, and sometimes more rain than you can believe."

He studies my face, but if he's looking for fear, he isn't going to find it.

"Look," I say. "I'm no expert trekker, but I have done my fair share of hiking and I know enough not to pet the cute, furry monkey that may or may not have rabies. Anyway, like I said, this opportunity is too important to me to pass up because of some scary snake."

"OK. Good." He stands there for a minute, finally saying, "Sleep well."

"You too."

I'm only able to relax once he's out of sight. Needless to say, it's pretty awkward seeing your boss literally minutes after you've had a sexy dream about him. Especially when you prefer the dream him to the real him.

A sigh rolls out of my lips. "Dream on, sister." Then I chuckle. That's something Han always says.

Although in this case, it definitely suits. Greyson Storm is my boss, and quite a bit older. Men like him always have boring girlfriends/wives anyway, ones they are ridiculously devoted to. Then there's the simple fact that I can't afford to screw up this job, no matter how hot my boss is, or how, despite his guarded ways, his eyes rested on me a bit too long for someone who's uninterested...

At any rate, any way you look at it, Har-Grey is not going to happen.

CHAPTER 3

Greyson

And here we are. Fucking finally.

Getting everyone the vaccines took way longer than expected. As did convincing Samantha that no, the vaccine would not give her and her future children and her future children's children autism, Asperger's and polio.

Fuck's sake. I didn't sign up for this.

I count off the crew as they exit the plane: there's Manuel, Samantha, Jorge and... no Harley.

Great, another delay.

Back on the plane, I find her, passed out in her seat.

I'm about to give her a good shake, when I pause.

Even asleep, she's damn hot: full lips parted ever so slightly, blonde waves the definition of bedhead, her mustard button-up showing just the right amount of tan skin to give me a hard-on.

Forget it.

She's 21, too young and my employee.

The thought makes me grit my teeth with annoyance. I haven't been this attracted to anyone in a while, but too fucking bad.

I don't hook up with employees. Ever.

I'm no Emerson, who uses periodic office flings as proof he's trying to show an interest in the business.

Giving Harley's shoulder a light shake only makes her shift and murmur sleepily without opening her eyes. When I shake her harder, her eyes snap open.

"Hello?" she murmurs.

"Hi."

She blinks uncomprehendingly at me, and I tell her, "We're here. On time, too."

She chuckles as she gathers herself up, a half-folded book on her belly. "Guess I deserved that."

"Maybe." I can't help but smile, like an idiot. Something about being around her makes me feel lightheaded, stupid. Focus.

I gesture to the book she's stowing away in her messenger bag. "Any good?"

Harley shrugs, then nods. "Using the adjective 'good' for Dostoevsky doesn't seem at all right. He's a master, and yet his books are depressing as hell."

"Wasn't his life, too?" I ask. "He had a gambling problem."

Harley pauses, looking at me as if with new eyes. "Whoa. OK."

"OK what?"

"Handsome and well-read. I like it."

Jesus, what that voice does to me...

No way am I about to admit that I only knew that Dostoevsky fact because I did a project on the guy in Grade 11.

"Sorry, boss." She rises, biting her lip as she sidles past me. "I shouldn't have said the handsome part. Anyway, I'm taken. By my job."

"Yeah." I manage to force out a chuckle through my gritted teeth. "Of course."

I frown at her back, but when she turns my way, pausing, her expression is impossible to read. "Time to go?"

I rip my gaze off where it's unconsciously fallen—her lips—and jerk my head in some semblance of a nod. "Yeah."

And then she goes, leaving me to glare at the seat she was in.

What the actual fuck? Who gives a fuck about Dostoevsky? Harley is off limits. End of story.

I pry open my fingers, which have been unconsciously squeezing my frustration into the plane seat.

My phone buzzes with a message, and looking at it only deepens my scowl.

Banged her yet? is Nolan's latest message.

Dude, I type back. We just landed. Have some respect.

So you like her then, is his whip-fast response.

Go fuck yourself.

Whoa. Most times you're cool with jokes? Busty Britney, anyone?

I shove my phone back in my pocket. Trust Nolan to screw things even further.

Yes, maybe back in the day we had our jokes about my intern Busty Britney and how she'd bake me a different muffin every day (carrot, banana, bran, cranberry, peach, a baffling amount of others), but this is different. I'm president now.

Nolan's voice, unbidden, sounds in my head: You know Dad would go for it.

I stride off the plane and out. I've wasted enough time as it is.

Although there's one thing I do know and I know it well: as much as I love and respect Dad, he's the last person I ever want to become or even emulate.

Yet, as I survey the waiting crew, all round nervous eyes and hopeful faces, I wish I could emulate Collin Storm's charisma, at least a bit. He'd know just what to say to get everyone all hyped and confident for this upcoming difficult hike to the camp. Whereas the only thing I can think of right now is some trite (was it Kanye?) saying about how "what doesn't kill you makes you stronger."

Out here, the air is muggy, the sky is dark and I can practically feel the mosquitoes preparing for the feast of a week. Fan-fucking-tastic.

No sooner have I opened my mouth than I hear movement to my left. Taking out a flashlight, I point its beam at the foliage. But it's a solid wall of plants and trees and…

The movement is nearing—and fast. The others are whispering and clamoring away, while Harley, who's already off to the side, just looks to me and asks, "Greyson?"

"It's OK," I say, "It's just—"

"Raaaaaaa!" a creature roars as it crashes out of the trees as I lunge towards it to protect the others.

Seeing our expressions, Russel, on all fours now from his jungle launch, throws back his golden dreadlocked sombrero-topped head and lets out a loud belly-laugh. "You all look like you've been chased by a killer woolly mammoth."

I don't even try to laugh. "Not the time. We've had a long flight."

Although it is good to see him. A surprise, too. When Madeline told me about everyone leaving, I just assumed that that included Russel, madman that he is. How he manages to be the stunt coordinator, lighting director, and boom operator, and still be as energetic and happy as a sunbathing goat is beyond me, but it works for me. I could use some unfounded enthusiasm right now.

But as he nears me, Russel's face drops. "You want good news or bad news first?"

"Good news," I tell him.

"Well." He smiles. "Good news is that you made it here in one piece." He nods. "Yeah, OK, now that that's done with... on to the bad news. First off, the entire crew left with virtually no useable footage and most of the camera equipment. Second, I'm pretty sure I stumbled on a nest of fer-de-lance snakes on my way here—you know, the deadly poisonous ones. Third, weather forecast says rain, rain, and more rain for the next two weeks, but hey, we are in a rainforest, am I right? Fourth, the old campsite got ransacked by monkeys, so we'll have to go set up another one, deeper in the jungle where there's more mosquitoes. Five, we still haven't really figured out how almost everyone got dengue last time." He stands there, still catching his breath, hands on his hips as he eyes us from behind his coke-bottle glasses. "So, we gonna get going or what?"

"I..." Am literally at a loss for words. After Madeline's call, I hadn't expected a smooth ride, but arriving here to find out that we're expected to trek through a deadly snake-infested, dengue-filled rainforest and shoot a successful show with a fraction of the equipment and staff we need is as close to worst case scenario as you can get.

I turn to the rest of the crew, who look like they've been told they have terminal cancer and the apocalypse is in two minutes.

"So..." I trail off. I swallow back the urge to march right back on the plane and tell the pilot to take us back. "This isn't going to be easy, I'm not going to lie to you. All of us might not even make it." I glance at Russel. "Russel probably hasn't even told us all the bad news, either."

"I sure haven't," Russel chirps.

I resist the urge to grab him by his obnoxious lei shirt and give him a good shake. Right now, I have to reassure the others somehow.

But as my gaze scans the others and lands on Harley, something occurs to me. I may be a veteran of grueling treks like these, but this crew isn't. The crew that was got dengue and got so discouraged by this place that they were forced to leave. And now I'm asking a less-experienced crew to succeed where they failed? And Harley... damn it, she may be determined, but even hearing about it, she has no real idea what she's getting herself into.

"Honestly," I tell everyone. "Going home may be the best thing. Or finding a better spot—Russel, do you know of any viable places for StormTV to have an alternative special?"

At this, he brightens, ripping his sombrero off and giving it a flourishing shake. "Well, my dear Mr. Storm, let me tell you. Playa Grande beach has sands like liquid gold, an ocean view like a postcard, and Guaro Sour like Heaven itself."

"A beach," I say dully.

While there would certainly be fewer hazards at a beach, there would also be no special. No drama. The whole damn point of StormTV is to capture great shots in genuinely interesting and perilous conditions. Maybe not this perilous, but still. I'm fairly certain there's no sharks at this beach, and there's only so much you can play up a crab bite.

"You've got to be kidding me." Harley's arms are crossed, her glare and raised eyebrows saying it all. Her tone is all business. "This is StormTV, not Baywatch. Or is all the adventure on the show always BS?"

"No, not at all." It takes all my self-control to keep my voice cool. "I just can't in good conscience put a bunch of underqualified people in harm's way."

"You're not forcing anyone," Harley argues. "And I don't know about the others, but this is exactly what I signed up for: trying my luck against dangerous odds in nature."

"Still." I shut up as she strides towards me, her jaw set. She looks like she's about to slap me... or kiss me. I'm angry enough to do the same: catch her slapping hand, kiss her.

She stops a foot from me, less. Close enough to slap or kiss. But she only leans in to hiss, "I didn't come here for the opportunity of a lifetime, only to throw it away because things aren't perfect."

"You don't know what you're getting into," I hiss back. "And I'd remind you who you're talking to. Your boss."

Her chin rises, then wavers. "Sorry. I... my point is: I do know what I'm getting into. I'm here for StormTV with Greyson Storm, the supposedly notorious daredevil, no-holds-barred producer who lets nothing get in the way of a good show. Nothing."

Her words echo in my head annoyingly. Notorious daredevil, no-holds-barred producer... nothing get in the way of a good show... Nothing.

"You're out of line," I finally snap.

Harley may be hot and mouthy, and I may even be getting the beginnings of a hard-on right now, but at the end of the day, I'm the boss and she's just someone I hired yesterday.

"Thought you said this was a place of suggestions, a team," she snaps, although she takes a step back and folds her arms across her chest.

"Lip-service and you know it." I'm mad, suddenly, really mad. Mad enough to say what I really think and not just blab Good Boss 101 BS. Harley's right, and it pisses me the hell off.

Backing down from a challenge? This isn't me. But with her there... it's scrambled my brain. If anything were to happen to any of the crew, I'd feel responsible. "Fine." I turn to the others. "Your decision: Stay or go?"

Silence.

Harley raises her hand, eyes on me. "Stay."

Russel half-raises his hand. "Beach?"

"You mean 'go'," I tell him, then turn to the others. "What about the rest of you?"

Sighing, Jorge raises his hand. "What can I say, I've never been known for my wise choices. I'll stay."

"Stay," Manuel squeaks.

Samantha gives Harley a death glare as she intones, "Stay."

"Alright." I nod. Who knows whether what's on my face is a relieved smile or an ugly grimace. Only time will tell whether this was a worthwhile risk or the biggest fuck-up of my career. No point in overthinking it now. "We're staying. But I'm not about to go stumbling back into the rainforest without a detailed game plan, tight schedule or no. Russel, tomorrow you'll plot out the path you took to get here, everything you know about what's in there, and we'll figure out our trail. Tonight, and maybe tomorrow night even, we'll camp here. Alright everyone, let's move."

And just like that, everyone disperses into a flurry of activity. Not that I can blame them. I did get in a quick nap on the plane, but I'm dead tired and still pissy as hell. Hearing about so many difficulties isn't exactly an upper.

"Greyson, my man, have I got the thing for you." Russel's gesturing me forward with what may or may not be a come-hither gesture.

"Not now," I tell him. "Got to help set up tents." I've already about had it with his jolly attitude. We may all die in here if we screw up. Doesn't he get it?

I start with helping Jorge, then end up helping the others as well.

While everyone in this crew claimed they had 'camping' experience on their resumes, I know enough to realize that means anything from roasting marshmallows in the microwave one time to actual tent setting up. Plus, there's something meditative about the repetitive staking of the tent, assembling the poles, attaching the rain fly. And I need anything I can get to calm me, right now.

Once the tents are set up, Russel leads me over to what looks like an outhouse.

"My dude," he says, "You have to check this out."

"Don't call me that," I say, then pause, peering inside. "Is that...?"

"A shower." Russel lets out a low, self-satisfied whistle. "Hell yeah, it is."

"But... how?"

Russel reaches in, and next thing I know, hot water is spilling down my arm.

"Don't ask how," he whispers with a gleam in his eye. "Just say yes."

"Yes?" I say.

But Russel's already walking off, with a wave. "Thank me later."

"Russel, seriously though. How?"

"You're welcome!" his far-off voice calls.

"Russel!"

Silence.

I glare at the shower. Might as well. After all the flurried activity—half of the crew really were as incompetent as I expected—I'm definitely sweaty. But a shower... now? In the middle of the rainforest?

"Why the hell not?" I mutter to myself, pulling off my clothes and climbing in. "Might be the last one I get for a while."

Admittedly, once inside, the hot beads rolling down my body feel amazing. My eyes close as I soak in just how good this feels. Maybe this whole expedition is destined to be a fuck-up, but at least right now this hot water feels like bliss. I'll have to tell Harley and the others that—

My cock stiffens.

Fuck, Harley...

Even her standing up to me, while it pissed me off, it also turned me on more, somehow. Fuck. I need to get her out of my head, off my mind. If I'm going to get any work done, I can't be thinking about how much better she'd look out of her clothes, how I'd like to teach her a lesson in manners bent over my knee.

I lean my forehead against the wooden shower wall. This needs to stop. We have less than two weeks to shoot this thing. I can't let myself be distracted like this.

Maybe if I just got it over with…

My hands close around my cock and start to run up and down my hard-on.

Maybe I just need to get her out of my system, rub one out to her and be done with it. Good riddance.

Some grumbling voice begins an objection in the far corner of my mind, but I'm already five steps ahead.

I can almost see her now, stepping into the shower with me. Her taut curves coated with wet, slick, her lips locking with mine. I can almost feel the suppleness of her tits, the firmness of her ass under my fingertips.

"Greyson," she kisses into my ear, and that exotic roll of her voice makes me shove myself inside her.

She feels good and tight and perfect and we clutch at each other, smack into each other, our bodies throwing us more and farther and closer and… yes!

As I come, my eyes snap open.

Jesus, that was fast. Sure, Harley is hot, but… I shake my head.

Doesn't matter now, it's done. Now, I should finally be able to get some peace.

CHAPTER 4

Harley

Bong-gong-gong… bong-gong-gong…

My eyes open in a glare, settle on a scaly green lizard with black almonds of eyes.

"Damn gong lizard," I mutter sleepily.

The lizard scurries away.

Hold on—what the hell is a lizard doing in here? I sit up fast, and, squinting into the sun, remember.

Getting the job, going on the plane, setting up camp.

What the hell was up with that gong, though? And somehow some lizard got into my tent too.

I scan the canvas to see a big-ass hole in the side.

Great, just wonderful.

I text Hannah: A ripped tent, seriously?

—Ooh. Was wondering when you were gonna notice.

You didn't think to tell me?

—You had twenty minutes to get to the airport. I didn't think it was the time.

Well I just woke up to a big ol' lizard looking at me, so thanks for that.

—Really?? That's so cool!

I toss my phone into my haphazardly packed duffel bag. Last night, in my sleepy stupor, all I managed to find was a strange profusion of bras, but now with the sun out I have higher hopes for finding my toothbrush and soap. Before I do, though, a tempting scent of roasted yumminess draws me out of the tent.

"Just in time," Russel says cheerily, beside the gong he must've sounded earlier. "Manuel's making roasted plantains."

"A family recipe," the tanned man says, waving a chubby hand. "I'm Manuel."

"Harley," I say.

In our harried arrival last night, I barely said more than two words to anyone other than Greyson, let alone exchanged names.

The corners of Manuel's dark eyes crinkle. "Harley. Like the motorcycle?"

"The very same." I don't sigh, because Manuel looks so genuinely delighted, even though I've heard the comment about a zillion times. "Want to know what's even better? My last name is Davis."

At this, Manuel throws his head back and hoots with laughter. Russel gives him a happy pat. "My man, if your plantains are as good as your laugh, we are going to have one happy morning."

"We'll have one happy morning once Greyson tells us what's happening," a woman in a tight rhinestone tank top declares in a nasal voice, striding up with what looks to me to be exaggerated hip sashaying. But maybe I just need some coffee.

"Don't worry, Samantha." Russel sips at some brownish liquid that definitely isn't coffee and smells suspiciously like whiskey as he nods to the newcomer. "I know Greyson. The man knows his stuff. Once we form a game plan, we'll be golden."

"Oh, I know that." The woman plops on a log opposite me and shoots me a significant, bitchy look. "I don't go questioning my boss."

I open my mouth just as Manuel says, "Plantains ready!"

I close it, my belly giving a joyful grumble. No way do I want to put off breakfast just to tell off some bitchy coworker. Maybe she just needs coffee too.

As the others gather, Greyson joins us too, in a slightly tight shirt that sets off his lean body even more.

I peel my eyes away.

Don't.

"Oh, hey!" Samantha's by his side in a millisecond. "I just wanted to say how brave you were last night—and how honest and just, like, virtuous you were, letting us decide for ourselves whether we should stay."

Greyson only has eyes for the plantains, though. "Thanks," he says distractedly.

His gaze wanders to me, freezes, then snaps away like a live wire.

Yep, either he hates me or wants me.

Why not both? Hannah's smug voice in my head asks.

I sigh.

Han doesn't get it. Maybe Greyson is hot and smart and sexy, but this job is my dream. My literal dream from when I was a kid and used to film my beanie babies spinning on the overhead fan before they were plopped in random places (wooden bed, cluttered desk, book-filled shelf) in my bedroom. All through university, even through the classes with the notoriously horrible professors, I persevered because I knew it was worth it. Because when I get behind the camera, everything else fades away. Time doesn't slow down or speed up, it ceases to exist. Everything is pure flow, magic, creation. And I love it. I can't get enough of it. And if I actually managed to make a go of it, to make this work, to have this—my love—be my career too? Well, there'd be nothing better in the world.

Even if Greyson has been my film idol for years, and is even hotter in person.

I go and get some plantains on a plate too, although I have barely eaten one bite before someone approaches.

"Hey, can we talk." It's Greyson, plantain-piled board still untouched as he stands before me, his eyes carrying even less of a question than his words.

Samantha thankfully huffs off to chow down her plantains in bitchy silence.

"Sure," I say, following him a bit of a ways off so we can talk with some privacy.

"About yesterday," he says, awkwardly. "I wanted to thank you."

"Really?"

"No. I wanted to tell you not to embarrass me in front of the others again. But then I realized I was being an ass, just how..." He pauses, his mouth working as if he was about to say something different. "Just how I didn't want to be, going into this. Maybe all that about suggestions and being a team is lip-service for StormTV, but I think we might actually need it here." He runs a hand through his dark hair, scowling. "I'm not used to working like this, to be perfectly honest. All my regulars are out with dengue, my assistant too, and…"—these last words come as if physically pulled out of him, as if he's as surprised by them as I am—"you were right."

"Wow, I…" Greyson Storm is thanking me for being a pushy bitch last night? I'll take it. Half of it was probably just my sleep-deprived grumpiness talking, that and pure old stubbornness, but still.

"Thanks," I tell him. "Although if I told you that you have a stain on your collar?"

His scowl deepens. "Don't push it."

"Fair." I bite my lip, but can't help smiling.

Open to criticism? Check.

Willing to own his mistakes? Check.

Not a pushover? Check.

Be still, my rapidly beating heart.

"So, about this game plan…" I begin.

"Nothing set in stone yet," he says. "Although I do have some ideas."

"Oh?"

He takes a bite of the plantain, exhales in pleasure.

"It is good," I agree, taking a bite of my own.

"Don't tell me," he says, after he's chewed and swallowed. "You have some ideas too."

"Not many," I admit. "After all, I'm just a rookie. I may know my way around a camera, but I don't have my head so much up my ass that I actually think I know much about trekking through a rainforest."

He chuckles. "But?"

"Well, what were you thinking?"

"We're in a major time crunch." Without thinking, he reaches forward and brushes a crumb off my cheek. I swallow. Without missing a beat, he continues, "The show was supposed to be ready already. We've got two weeks, but it will most likely take half that much, at least, to get to the old camp, near the swamp where all the American crocodiles are. What I was thinking was that those don't have to be the focus of the entire show. They can be the climax, but…"

Something throbs in me as I zone out. Dear Lord. I'm so attracted to this man that even hearing him say the word 'climax' sets me off. I would roll my eyes at myself if Greyson wasn't standing right in front of me, eyeing me expectantly.

Oh. Crap.

Eyeing me expectantly because he just told me what he was thinking, which I asked for and also stupidly zoned out of at the end.

"Sorry, what was that last part?"

Greyson chuckles, pats me. "It's fine. I'm dead tired too. Just eat your plantains and leave the worrying to me."

"Hey," I say, though he's a few steps away. "Seriously, what did you say?"

Let him leave, a voice in my head warns me.

But there's something else in me, angry and hot and eager. And just curious. I do want to know.

"Just that I have to talk about the logistics of all this to Russel, but if it's possible, best thing would be to film some scenes on our way to the camp, too. Takes the pressure off of getting a ton of good shots all within a few days of each other."

"Good idea," I say.

"Good," he says.

"Good," I say.

I swallow back a groan at my own lameness.

Harley, it's official: you are an idiot.

"OK." He clears his throat, was clearly done with this conversation minutes ago. He holds out a hand. "Thanks again. Happy to have you on the team."

"I'm more of a hugger," I say breezily. Next thing I know my arms are around him, and his are around me, and it feels… outstanding.

Yep, now I know what those Harlequin novels mean when they talk about being 'weak in the knees'.

I inhale his pine scent and have to practically choke back my utterly pleased exhale. Nothing like a horny exhale to ruin your whole cool vibe in front of your boss.

And his arms feel even more substantial than they look. Like there isn't a safer place in the world.

Too soon, he's drawing away, hardly looking at me—did he enjoy that as much as I did? Was that a stupid idea?

"See you, Harley—oh." He pauses again. "Almost forgot." He hands me a nifty-looking flashlight. "Take this."

I eye it, but don't move. "Don't you need a flashlight too?"

"Russel has a bunch of extras. I heard you stumbling around last night with your phone flashlight. You could use this."

"Oh." Good thing it's so hot out that my cheeks are probably flushed anyway. "How did you know that was me?"

Greyson's smile is off; he probably feels odd admitting it. "Figured no one else would say 'drat!'"

I laugh. "Blame my high school years in England, I guess."

"Oh. Is that where your..."

"Accent came from?" I say. "Maybe. I mean, my mom always loved to sing instead of talk to us, and I had Russian, Spanish and Indian nannies growing up, so that might've done it, too."

"Ah, OK."

Is he feeling it too, this strange current that seems to keep drawing us back into conversation again and again, like a magnet?

He holds out the flashlight closer to me. "I mean it. Take it."

I grab it. "Alright. Would be nice for my phone to have some life so I can talk to my cousin Hannah anyway."

Like lightning, his hand goes into his pocket. "I have a power bank too, if you need to charge your phone."

I laugh. "At this rate, we'll be here all day with you repacking my bag and supplies for me."

"I—"

"Greyson!" Russel calls. "This game plan won't draft itself!"

"I'd better go." He smiles apologetically, starts heading away, although his head is still turned my way, his eyes never leaving mine.

"See ya," I say.

"See ya," he says, finally looking away.

I can only stare at his back as he walks away, finally sitting down right where I stood. If this looks weird or antisocial or whatever, too freaking bad. I need to get my head around what just happened.

What the hell just happened?

Did I just have the easiest conversation with the man that I swore I would under no circumstances sleep with?

Did he just act like a gentleman several times?

I switch the flashlight on and off, shining its beam onto a patch of shade, toggling through the different modes. Way better than my phone flashlight, way way better than my phone flashlight, eons away from my phone flashlight.

As I finally remember to bite into my plantains, I can only reflect that one thing is for sure: this is going to be one hell of a trip, in more ways than one.

CHAPTER 5

Greyson

"Not that I blame you for being distracted," Russel says convivially, stirring something that looks like a mix between manure and stew, "But Miss PrettyPants is going to be having a rough time if we don't figure out how to voyage through the jungle in one piece.

"Miss PrettyPants," I say, deadpan.

How is it morning and I'm already annoyed with the guy? Is Russel hinting at what I think he is? At least he had the tact to save this conversation until now, when it's just us, but still.

"Yeah," he continues, "Your fit little blonde friend. She's nice to look at, but she won't be as nice if she gets eaten by a grumpy mother puma."

"Not funny," I growl, surprised to find that I'm almost halfway to smacking him with the board I'm eating on.

What the hell is up with me? Yes, the conditions are shit, and yes, I've been becoming a bitter old grump in the past few months with everything going on, but I'm here now, finally doing what I love: producing. Or should be soon, at any rate.

"Hold on—there's pumas here too?" I ask.

"Ah, did I forget to mention?" Russel waves his hand dismissively. "No matter."

I practically choke on the plantain I'm eating and once again have to resist the urge to give him a good hard board smack. "No matter?"

"Well." Russel tips his head. "Yes, and no. As long as she doesn't have any babies around, we should be fine."

Do not smack him with the board, Greyson.

Instead, I clench my fists as I grate out, "And if there are?"

Russel makes a face. "I suppose we'll just have to run for our bloody lives, then."

"Shit."

"It's not all bad." Russel's smile is almost reassuring as he takes a sip of his manure-stew. "Taste this."

Despite my frustration, I take a sip, and find myself smiling too. "OK, so you've managed to cook an edible stew, and warned me about pumas. Let's talk strategy now."

"Strategy." Russel wiggles his bushy golden eyebrows. "I like the way you say it." His face sobers up as he leans in to peer at me, hard. "Since what we decide here may or may not decide the fate of not only our lives but the lives of those with us." A wave of his hand. "But no matter. With my expertise and your... Storm blood, we are destined for success."

I would glare at him if I wasn't still reeling from his rapid-fire change of attitude. "Your only faith in me is because I'm a Storm?"

"Nah, I've seen you in the field, I know you know your shit by now. Although the Storm name is good luck, yes?"

"In some ways," I say. "But what about an actual plan? You must have a map of this rainforest, know some locals we can consult."

"Oh yes, map." With the hand not spooning stew into his mouth, Russel riffles through his patchwork messenger bag. "Here."

One look and the small shard of hope forming in me evaporates. "You call this a map?"

Russel fans himself with the map napkin, wearing a vaguely offended expression. "It's better than nothing."

This would be funny if it wasn't real life. "You've drawn a blob and labeled it 'rainforest'."

Russel sniffed. "If you've got a better idea, please do share."

And so passes the next few hours: I propose ideas, dig for information, and get increasingly pissed off at every turn. There are no locals to help us, no decent maps to consult. Clearly, the only reason Russel even called me over to discuss what to do is because he doesn't want to be held responsible when this all goes to shit.

Finally, after an infuriating back and forth, and such frustration that I'm actually driven to wolf down some of Russel's cold mystery stew, I put my foot down.

"We're going back the way Russel came," I tell everyone.

"He remembers?" Samantha asks dubiously.

"I did have to do quite a bit of slashing to get here," Russel says with a sniff back at her.

"Beaches are sounding more and more enticing," Jorge mutters, almost under his breath.

Clearly, everyone else has picked up on the mood of uncertainty among the leadership. Better not to mention that we have no usable maps.

Seeing Harley's pointed look—Wasn't this supposed to be a team?—I clear my throat. "Any questions?"

"Yes," Manuel says, raising his hand tentatively.

"Yes?" I ask him.

"What if... we fall off his trail."

"Good point, almost forgot." I reach into my pack and fish out the spool of ribbon I threw in at the last minute. "We'll be tying this on trees every so often as we go. That should help. Although I don't expect to use it."

"Besides," Russel cuts in, "my path-finding skills are out of this world. I can get us back to the big fat alligators before you can say 'big fat alligator'."

Samantha grumbles something that sounds like 'big fat alligator' and the others exchange uncertain smiles. Only Harley looks ready. Time to take this show on the road.

"Right. Any questions? No?" I smile at everyone with more confidence than I feel. "Then let's get trekking."

As we walk, I try to believe my own words. Even though, after everything, I've come up with a plan that could've been brainstormed in five minutes: Go back the way Russel came, following the tramped-out, slashed-down path through the forest. And hoping it's still there.

"I did survive my way here," Russel keeps reminding me with a winning grin as we continue along, as if this is supposed to be the greatest endorsement in the world.

We trek for a good few hours amidst the muggy jungle, following Russel's clumsy zig-zagging path, before setting up camp.

This time, we quickly set up our tents almost side by side. Afterwards, we sit around the fire roasting the last of the marshmallows.

"Anyone know any good ghost stories?" Harley suggests.

"Now's probably not the time for ghost stories," Samantha grumbles, nursing a new scrape.

She ignored my suggestions to stay behind with the others and rushed so much to keep up that she tripped over an unnoticed lump of dirt.

"What, afraid of a ghost hippo?" Russel teases.

"No, just a real hippo," Samantha snaps back.

"There are no hippos here," I point out. "Only in Africa."

As if she didn't hear, Samantha's eager gaze swivels my way. "Why don't you tell us one of your great stories?"

"Great stories?" I ask.

"Yeah, you know—you're Greyson Storm, you must have some crazy stories to tell."

"Well..."

Truth is, I do, and lots of them. But most of them involve near-death experiences in similarly difficult climates, and something tells me that's not going to be a crowd-pleaser right about now. And talking myself up always makes me feel like a huge tool anyway.

Without a word, Harley rises and walks off.

"Buddy system?" Manuel asks, looking after her.

"She probably wants to pee and doesn't want me coming along," Samantha says officiously.

In the flickering firelight, Russel's eyes look downright humorous. "Why ever not? You are such a pleasant individual."

I resist the urge to laugh—or get up. Harley shouldn't be out there alone, whatever the reason. More than that, I want to talk to her. I barely said two words to her while we were trekking today.

Mostly since I was up front and she was behind, joking with Manuel and Jorge, but...

Focus, Greyson.

I grab myself another few marshmallows. It's probably good that I haven't picked up where I left off with Harley. Jerking off to her was supposed to get her out of my head. Doesn't look like it worked.

Only a few more minutes of diminishing chit-chat and everyone else is dispersing to their tents. A long, hard day of trekking will do that to you, even if it weren't for the murderous hordes of mosquitoes coming out now.

My tent is at the end, and I've just gotten in and laid down when I smell something that has me jolting upright in my sleeping bag.

Smoke.

I wait a few seconds to be sure, then rise. My tent is the farthest from the fire, so the new smell probably isn't from there. As for another source...

Poking my head out allows me to make out a grand total of nothing in the pitch black. But once I get out and start walking, I'm able to follow the smell quietly, a minute or two into the rainforest, until...

For fuck's sake.

It's Harley, sitting on a mossy log, looking out into the darkness. In the moonlight, she's as beautiful as I've seen her—long legs crossed, hair spilling over her shoulders.

"What the hell are you doing?" I hiss.

She freezes, then turns to smile at me. "Caught me."

I sniff the air again. "That's pot, isn't it?"

Another lazy smile. "Yep."

"You can't be doing that."

As I approach, she looks genuinely curious. "Why not?"

Anger spikes in me, sudden and unreasonable and hot. "You could get yourself killed!"

I'm surprised at the vehemence of my own voice.

The curl of her lip corners is pure amusement. "Didn't know it bothered you so much, Mr. Storm."

"Of course it... what kind of boss do you take me for?"

"Honestly?" She looks at me head-on. "A talented one. Other than that, I... don't know."

I find myself going to sit down beside her. "I don't pretend to know you, either. But I thought you were better than this."

"Better than what?"

"Endangering yourself and the camp needlessly."

"How am I endangering the camp? Afraid a snake will be drawn to the mouthwatering scent of la ganja?"

I want to laugh, but stop myself. "Harley."

"What?"

"Fine. Endangering yourself, then. Being out here alone would be dangerous even if you were sober."

Eyes on me, she slowly lifts the joint to her lips, takes a puff. Like a challenge. A sexy one that's damn near irresistible.

My eyes on her lips now, what I even came here for is slowly rolling away, like the smoke from her lips, dissipating in the clear air.

"Is it that big of a deal?" she asks lightly, "Camp is literally a minute away if anything happens."

"If you're here, you're my responsibility. And if anything happened to you..." Once again, I fall silent, surprised at how I'm talking. None of the cool all-business tone I've gotten more and more practiced at using. The words I'm saying sound too... real.

Her chuckle is throaty and infuriating at once. "Nothing's going to happen to me, promise. It's a perfectly safe way to chill out—I can prove it to you."

As she holds out the joint to me, her gaze holds a different sort of challenge.

I take the joint without thinking, take a puff.

"See?" she says. "Not so bad."

"Here's a deal: I join you if you promise this is the last of this. If the others find out, it could look bad. The company could get bad press too, if this got out."

Mid-puff, she giggles. "You already joined me, boss."

"Don't call me that."

Even with my stern glare, she just giggles some more. Then, finally, she places a hand on her heart. "Alright, I promise." She extends her pinky finger. "Want me to pinky swear too?"

The prospect of touching her makes me swallow, although I don't so much as look at her tempting outstretched pinky, just tell her, "Good."

After the next puff, I begin to feel the effects. The weight resting on my shoulders slackens, loosens.

My fingertips run absently along the bark, enjoying the intricacies of the different textures, grooves and dips and smooth patches amidst the soft fluff of moss. I keep my gaze straight ahead, into the impenetrable blackness of the forest. As if I don't know full well what I long to actually run my fingers over, feel the grooves and softness and give and...

Greyson.

I can smell her, too, like some tempting jungle fruit I don't know the name for yet.

We pass the joint back and forth, our fingers brushing, every touch akin to an electrical shock. I'd leave except she seems so... relaxed. If something was happening she wouldn't be so relaxed, right?

Right?

My head is clogged with her, what I have to do, what I can't do.

At some point, the sides of our legs touch. And though I know I have to move, I can't seem to get the message to my legs.

Once the joint goes out, her head droops onto my shoulder, rests there. I force my eyes not to look at her, to see if she's enjoying this added contact as much as I am. Fuck me. I'm the hardest I've ever been without watching porn. This is fucking stupid.

She lets out a little sigh. "I am sorry, you know."

I don't say anything, but she goes on as if I did. "OK, you may have had a point. Maybe it was a bit reckless and disrespectful, smoking just now, out here alone. I just couldn't help myself."

I swallow. Couldn't help myself. Before, I wouldn't say I knew the feeling, but now...

Get out, leave, my thoughts are snapping.

And... I can't move.

She's still speaking, her voice easy and resonant in the night. "I just—stress is so unnecessary, the way I see it. At least for me. We push and push and push to get things, and when we get them, we just push some more." She chuckles at herself. "Sorry, getting all metaphysical there. What I mean is: pot helps me relax, enjoy myself more. Not that I wasn't before, just, you're a big deal, and I'm new, and I actually think you're really cool in person, which a lot of these big deal people aren't, which makes it all worse, and..."

That's it.

My lips find hers, and as soon as they do, it's clear: she was just talking to fill the space before this. There never could've been anything else but this.

As thought ebbs away as our lips meet and remeet and swirl and twist with absolute perfection, I find myself thinking of those words. How she was right.

For the first time in what seems like months, as I kiss her, my mind is going blessedly blank, relaxed with nothing more than pure enjoyment.

CHAPTER 6

Harley

Oh, yes.

Fantasy has nothing on reality, as far as kissing Greyson is concerned. His lips are the perfect balance between giving and taking, which for me means a whole lot more taking. They lead mine in a dance his tongue soon joins in.

He tastes like the sausages we had for dinner, and smells like that maddening pine. Half a minute of kissing and I'm wet already, and we've barely begun.

The pot strengthens every sense: makes his fingers combing down my back nearly maddening, his lips on my throat ecstasy. This would be glorious without the pot—Greyson knows what he's doing, that's for sure—but with, it's almost unbearable.

Our fingers explore each other, my shoulders, arms, sides, hips tingling pleasure with his touch. His body is lean but fit, ridged with compact muscles I bring my lips onto. The shirt's getting in the way, though.

"Hmm," I say, catching his eye.

We undo his button-up together, chuckling at how difficult it is, when all we want to do is touch each other, feel.

We're doing a whole lot of that right now. He runs his fingers through my waves, then, suddenly, grabs and brings the side of my head to his lips. Pain mingles with pleasure as he laps at my ear.

"You're fucking gorgeous."

It's part accusation, part worship. When I pull back to tease him with a "Thanks, boss," his growl yanks me right back to him.

"Don't call me that."

I twist a kiss onto his lips, then pull back, taking his lip partway with me to eye him tauntingly, "Or what?"

Greyson's hands settle on my ass, then pull back—"Or I'll do this"—and spank me. "Or this." They knead the fat there.

I groan into the side of his face. God, it feels good.

Our fingers entwine as our bodies move together, rub together, flow as one. Our lips can't get enough of each other—kisses last several minutes, even every slight pause seems unbearable. His fingers drawing away to skate under my top is only part of the kiss. Part of the onward flow that's impossible to stop or even slow.

Another kiss—and his fingers lightly trace the outlines of my bra.

Another kiss—and his fingers press into my bra harder.

Another kiss—and his fingers smear my bra into my breasts, and the pleasure is so intense that I groan again.

He growls with pleasure. "That's it."

The next kiss, he rips off my shirt, then my bra, his fingers delighting in the softness of my breasts. His stroking touch has me moaning again as he lowers his lips to my breasts.

My fingers grab hold of his hair as he kisses circles around my nipple, using the slightest touch of teeth, until he lands on my nipple and sucks it.

My crotch is thrashing into his, feeling his hard-on. I'm aching for him.

As his lips move to my other breast, we scramble to undo his pants, half-laughing half-panting as we fumble with the button then the zipper. He bites down on my breast and I cry out. Once again, pain slaps pleasure to new heights.

Next thing I know, his hard-on is closer than ever before as my pussy rubs against him.

My hands go to both sides of his face as we kiss. His fingers press into the wet spot on my panties, directly onto my clit.

He smirks at how I'm practically panting now. "Yeah?"

"Yeah," I groan.

We kiss the rest of our clothes off, our bodies clasping and re-clasping, his cock easing into me further and further until—he shoves himself inside of me and I gasp, pleasure rocketing through me.

"It feels so... fucking good," I moan.

"Fucking good," he groans back, flexing in me.

For a good minute, neither of us move, enjoying just how tight he is inside of me.

Then, he slams his lips onto me and pulls himself partway out again. At first, Greyson fucks me slow and sensually, every penetration a mini-ecstasy. I come once, but Greyson's hard-on is as rock-solid as ever. Slowly, he builds his pace, in and out, hard and harder, fast and faster, until out bodies are slamming together and I can't think of anything but more, more, more—I need it—I need it.

And I'm screaming into his palm: "More—fuck me—yes—more—please—ugh—yes!"

And I'm coming over and over again, as he spills into me, and our bodies spasm together.

Afterwards, I tremble I don't know how long. After that: warmth, the soothing up and down of his chest, silence.

CHAPTER 7

Greyson

I wake up hard. Still tired, too, and dreaming.

No way in hell can this be real. In the golden light of the sunrise, in my arms, Harley is nothing short of a goddess. Her lightly freckled toned curves are perfection, while her slightly parted lips are just begging for a kiss.

I give it to her.

It really is a dream, because her eyes flutter half-open and she murmurs, "More?"

I slip right inside her.

Our bodies move together in sleepy memory. Utter rightness. Still half-asleep, we kiss our way from one position to the next: her on top, breasts jiggling gorgeously as she rides me, me behind her, the view of her ass exquisite as I ram her doggy-style. When she comes, I hold her tightly, enjoying all her little groans and shaking, then I fuck her some more. I come once, yet my hard-on springs back up almost immediately.

She's that sexy, and I guess this is a dream, after all. She has the softest skin imaginable, and some kind of fruity scent that somehow makes me hornier. As we hold and fuck each other, I lose track of how many times either of us comes; the only passage of time is the movement of the sun in the sky.

Until a caw makes me look up. I gape at a toucan, peering at us jauntily, its colorful beak open in a laugh. I'm about to yell at it and shoo it away when I hear Harley laugh. Catching her merry eye, I can't help but crack up too.

That's when it hits me.

"This isn't a dream."

"No?" Harley rises and stretches, offering me a magnificent view of her fine ass. "I think it is, in a manner of speaking."

In a manner of speaking...

Still dazed, I watch her put on her clothes. She doesn't rush it, only smirks at me every so often, as if enjoying how I can't bear to peel my gaze away.

Goddamn is she beautiful. The kind of beautiful the bright clear light only outlines in greater clarity.

Once she's finished, she pauses. "What did I say—it was good, right?"

"What?"

Calling what sexual magic just happened between us—because that's what it was, nothing less than fucking magic—the hottest, craziest, wildest, in a word—best—sex that I'd ever had—calling that 'good' seems absurd.

A chuckle. "The pot. It was good, yeah?"

"Yeah," I grumble, my voice gravelly in the morning, "but you still can't do it here again."

Harley makes a face. "I only brought one joint anyway, Mr. Storm. I'm not some pothead. But I'll be seeing you?"

She's already off a few paces before it occurs to me to respond. "Don't call me that!"

She just laughs. "See ya!"

I glare blankly at the horizon, the sun already beating down mercilessly. We're in a clearing now, but hopefully the trek won't be as hot as I am here.

What the fuck just happened?

A series of caws has me direct my glare at the fat toucan perched on the leafy ceiba tree overhead.

How did I go from staying in control to losing it all? How could I fuck up so badly?

Only... was it that much of a fuck-up? Harley seemed cool about it, and the sex was spectacular. As long as we don't get caught, we should...

"Fuck!" I hiss, remembering myself.

Ass-naked, less than a minute's walk from the camp. Have I lost my dumbass mind?

I leap up and begin throwing on my clothes as fast as I can, muttering curses at myself. Luckily, no one ventures over, and by the time I get back to camp, people are just starting to get up.

Russel, of course, is still perched by the fire, wearing what looks to be a Hawaiian lei-covered toga, working away at a mashed conglomeration of food that I probably don't want to know about. "Howdy, Greyson. Aren't you looking like a mango in a banana field this fine morning."

I don't know what his weird saying means. I don't want to know what it means.

I yawn and stretch, hoping it's believable. "What time is it?"

"Little late," Russel says smoothly, with a wink. "10:15."

I frown. "That is late. Very late."

"It is," he agrees cheerfully.

Something about people who are overly cheerful in the morning, especially after bad news, has always pissed me off. Right now I'd like to upend that stupid food mush on Russel's stupid head.

Instead, I take a breath, then grumble, "Good everyone got some extra sleep since we'll be pushing it hard today. Though that's it for the sleeping in—we have to get going."

Russel nods sagely, giving his strange dish a smack with his spatula.

I feel like a bit of a hypocrite calling to the others still in their tents, "Let's go guys! We should be trekking in 30, so let's get eating and packing up."

Especially since it was my lazy ass that slept in too. Still. No reason to hold everything up even longer.

I go off to check my phone quickly before helping with the packing up.

I'm surprised it still even works, but I did pay an extra hundred with my phone company to ensure uninterrupted service. After all, I am still the president of Storm Media.

Although there doesn't seem to be anything work-wise, I do have a few texts from Landon.

How's it going so far? No good updates about the tax records—I'm stumped.

I scowl as I type out a quick response: All good, you've got this. Both lies, but now isn't the time to unload just how off-plan this has gone so far.

My back teeth grind together with frustration. My suggestions to hire a financial advisor or a plain old accountant were unanimously dismissed by my brothers. They were convinced whoever we hired would discover major monetary infractions on Dad's part, maybe even fraud. And Landon was sure he would be able to make the books balance.

But now... it's not looking good. Landon's making as shitty progress as I predicted. If Dad really was fudging the books, I don't see how Landon will be able to fix it, aside from committing fraud himself. For all that I'm the big brother and the boss, my younger brothers listen to me precious little.

I make sure to tie a ribbon at the edge of the path to mark our way. Everyone has helped out with the ribbon tying, although it's an annoying delay when you've been trekking for hours and are dead tired. Still, it's a wise precaution.

It takes another, louder call to get the others straggling out of their tents. First is Manuel, wrapped in mosquito netting and yawning sleepily. Jorge looks better, beelining for the food and eating the strange mash that Russel calls 'My Special Recipe' with vigor. Samantha is next, smiling and giving me a little wave before digging in herself.

I scowl in the direction of Harley's tent. Still not out. Maybe just sleeping off last night, but maybe she... No, she better not have gone off by herself again. Even in broad daylight with all your senses about you, it's dangerous.

Speaking of senses... I stretch my arms experimentally and a grin slides onto my face. That pot really wasn't a big deal. It seemed strong at the time, but now I feel pretty damn good. No hangover.

Not that I believe any of the Reefer Madness earth-shattering bogus reports some authorities gave on pot. But I've always avoided drugs instinctively, preferring the clear highs of working out, or just taking a good hike. Plus, I saw what partying too hard did to Dad, not to mention that Emerson had a crazy run of it for a while, too.

But last night was… fun. Too fun.

Mid-scan of the surrounding trees for Harley again, I stop myself. Get it together, Greyson. She'll come out when she's ready. No point in waiting around like an idiot. Even if we should get going.

It's only after I tuck into the food (which is actually good, tasting like sweet potato, lime and lamb) and we're all starting to pack up, that Harley finally comes out.

She smiles at me, and something that I hadn't even realized was tensed in me lets up. I smile back.

Is that it—no awkwardness? Good. I've got enough to deal with without a (maybe rightfully) pissy employee.

"Not hungry?" I ask her.

"Already ate," she says.

There's a stray smear of food on her lower lip I have to stop myself from brushing away. Or mentioning. You don't look at your cinematographer's lips. Period.

Over the next few minutes, the group packs up our stuff quickly enough. Then, it's trekking time.

Trekking is a mixed bag. On the one hand, we keep up a fairly regular pace, and the others follow my direction virtually seamlessly when it comes to shooting. We even remember to get in a few good ribbon ties on trees as we go along. On the other hand, there's Russel, who is unpredictable and impulsive in the best of times, and now, in the worst of times, is downright infuriating. He'll change direction mid-pace, stop and stare around blankly for minutes at a time, and sometimes urge us on faster in a harried shrill with no discernible reason whatsoever. I have to stop myself from yelling at him so many times I lose track. Finally, I have to tell him off.

Unfortunately, the effects of my "Get yourself together, Russel. Most important thing is that we keep going" only last a few minutes. Next thing I know, he's stopped dead, glaring suspiciously at a knobby tree.

"Hey," Harley says, coming up beside me.

"Hey," I say.

"This sucks, eh?" she asks, frowning in Russel's direction as he starts tapping different trees, apparently for guidance.

"Yeah, Russel is—"

"A complete psycho?" Harley offers.

I chuckle. "Yeah."

She giggles. "At least we got some good shots of those crazy blue beetles. Next time he pulls a long stop, I'm going to try to catch some more. Looks like they have a whole extended family reunion going on 'round here."

"That's... a really good idea," I say.

I smile at her. This one feels different from the ones I've been giving the crew whenever Russel has stopped. Those are like some mask or duty I have to assume. This one feels real.

Maybe because I'm not nearly as pissed off anymore.

"Finding my old path isn't easy, you know," Russel grumbles now in explanation. "Sorting out these memories is a muddle. You know, where I saw the deadly snakes, where I fell into a hidden ravine and almost broke my leg, where there were these delicious tiny bananas that I don't know how I lived without before... that kind of stuff."

Do. Not. Yell. At. Your. Guide.

Something tells me Russel wouldn't take well to be reamed out. I've seen him cry before and it isn't pretty.

I grit my teeth together, grate out, "Reassuring."

Thanks to him, I've started eyeing nearby holes in the ground with suspicion.

Although I can't deny that Harley is right—Russel's haphazard start-stop pace is good for capturing interesting shots. When Harley and I aren't working on having her capture an odd-shaped tree, or two sloths hanging lazily from a palm, I'm having her catch a seemingly endless trail of fire-ants marching along the forest floor, up a tree trunk into a hole, then out the other side.

She's quick, too—no complaints when I give her seconds of warning to get set up and shooting.

I already know the video editor is going to have a fun time editing this one—lots of choppy shots, a deadline of a day or even less—but that isn't my problem. My job is to get the best footage I can, and I intend to do just that.

It gives me a second wind, too, an escape from Russel's incompetence. It gets me in the zone and working. Reminds me why I signed up to do this thing in the first place. Getting behind the camera, right in on the action, putting ideas into practice before my very eyes, it's magic.

By the end of the first day, as the shadows on the ground grow long and eventually fuse, there's soon no denying it: it's time to turn in.

Samantha plops down gratefully, but Russel sighs, scanning the forest around us suspiciously.

"What?" I ask him.

"If we'd only gone an hour longer," he mutters.

"It's dark out," Samantha says flatly.

"I have already tripped many times," Manuel adds tentatively.

"They're right," I tell Russel, "We keep on going and we'll lose someone. Maybe you."

"Oh, it's nothing." Russel is mopping off his forehead with a Mario-print bandana. "Only the snakes."

"Which ones?"

In the moonlight, his teeth glint as he shows an ominous smile. "The fer-de-lance."

The poisonous ones. Fucking great. "You saw them here?"

"Around here, I think. Told you, memory's a muddle since I was hepped up on adrenaline and whiskey." He sighs regretfully. "If only the whiskey hadn't run out."

If only I didn't have an idiot for a guide, a joke for a map and... yeah, whiskey would be nice right about now.

"What does it look like?" Harley asks. "The snake, I mean."

"Grey or brown, has a triangular head with diamonds."

"Right, avoid diamond-head snakes," Harley mutters, half to herself.

"Not just those snakes," Russel says, cheerful for some reason now. I see him light a pipe and then I understand.

"There's other dangerous ones?" I ask sharply.

He should've warned us about all this at the start, so we could've made a better informed decision. Especially since he was the one who was dying to go to the beach.

But there's no point in bitching about it now. What's done is done.

"Tons." Still that cheerful tone that makes me want to shake him. "There's the eyelash viper snake, and it's yellow, green, red or brown. The coral snake is striped. Very, very bad, if you get bitten."

Before I can snap at him, Harley sums it up: "So just avoid all snakes at all costs."

"Basically," Russel agrees, taking a whiff of his pipe.

"Snakes should avoid our camp as long as we're loud enough for them to know that we're here," I point out. If I'm going to snap at Russel, better if the others aren't around, especially Harley. No point in worrying them needlessly. "Jorge, didn't you bring a small speaker that can be hooked up to your phone?"

"Er—yes?" Jorge says, tipping his dark curly-haired head. He was the one with the largest duffel bag by far, after having spent half his interview stubbornly insisting on his right to bring 'what I want, where I want'.

"Perfect," I say. "Set them up with whatever music you want. That should help. I'll do a quick trek around to make sure we don't stumble on anything either."

Which is how we come to be listening Pink Floyd's The Dark Side of the Moon a few minutes later as we set up our tents. I make sure to set mine up well away from Harley's—no fucking way do I want a repeat of last time.

Although when I see her struggling with getting her tent upright, I have to go over and help. Russel beats me to it, though.

"We'll figure it out together," he says, with a wink at me.

I stand there for a minute, frozen with sudden rage.

Asshat.

I make myself turn away. No, it's good. The less I am around Harley, the better.

Although it takes effort to ungrit my teeth and walk away. And to pry the image of her, leaning over to grab a tent rod, and showing a tantalizing hint of cleavage too, out of my mind.

CHAPTER 8

Harley

After the long and action-packed day we had, I assumed I would've fallen asleep like a babe. Instead, I'm lying on my back, staring up at the black stretch of canvas that is my tent's ceiling.

For the first time, I let myself think about what happened last night.

Last night, Greyson and I. Our bodies moving together as seamlessly as if the whole thing was choreographed. Although nothing so unexpected and good and impulsive and wild could have been choreographed like that.

And now... now, so what? Why overthink it? I've had flings before and enjoyed them for what they were, pleasurable dalliances that were necessarily fleeting.

Only, a fling with the guy who has admittedly been my celebrity crush for years...

I sit up and check my phone. Hannah hasn't texted, of course. She told me herself that she didn't want to bother me during what might be the most important job assignment of my life. I was supposed to text her.

And now... what do I even say? I wish I could call her, but it's awfully late. And what would I even tell her? That I hooked up with my boss and he's actually really cool?

No.

I get up and make for the tent entrance. No point in sitting here obsessing over him like a Twilight-obsessed preteen. Dark Side of the Moon is still playing quietly outside—I don't need to venture far to clear my head.

I slip on my sandals and slip out, being sure to close the tent door behind me. No way do I want to wake up as one giant mosquito bite.

It happened to one girl I went to camp with—she got so obliterated by mosquitoes that her face was swollen and unrecognizable and she had to go home.

I give myself a shake. Enough putting it off—time to go.

Outside, the air is crisp and the kind of cool that I love. No mosquitoes, at least that I can see or hear. Who knows, maybe they're having a giant feeding frenzy right this second.

I zip up my hoodie all the way to the top, wander over to the fire.

Someone else is there already, though.

"Can't sleep?" Greyson asks softly, although his gaze is on the fire.

"Nope," I say.

Now he swings a gaze over, an assessing, intense gaze that would have goose bumps erupting up and down my arms if they weren't there already. "Glad you didn't decide to wander much further."

As he squares his shoulders in a protective stance, something rebellious and irritated twists in me. "I still can, you know."

"Harley—"

"You can't babysit me the whole time I'm here."

Silence, only not really. The fire crackles, a far-off animal hoots.

Then, finally, "Is that what you think I've been doing?"

"A bit," I admit.

And I actually kinda like it, I don't admit.

"Sorry," he says, rising. "If you want me to leave you alone..."

"I don't," I say.

He pauses. "What do you want, then?"

I pause. I know full well, but I don't want to say it, let alone admit it to myself.

Though I do: "Stay. Sit beside me."

He doesn't move.

"Greyson—" I begin.

He sits beside me, agonizingly close enough to touch, but not touching.

"This whole trip has been a shitshow," he admits. "Thanks for being cool with it."

I chuckle. "Honestly, I think it's gone fine. We got a few great shots today, even with Russel leading us God-knows-where."

Greyson chuckles too. "He's an odd guy, Russel."

"Yeah," is all I can think to say to that.

I yawn, then lean my head on his shoulder. It feels good, sturdy, familiar.

His shoulder tenses. "Harley—"

"You're not going to let me sleep?" I tease.

"It's not that."

And suddenly, I'm mad, stupidly pointlessly mad. I snap my head up and, inches away, glare at him. "What is it, then?"

"I..." The rest of his words melt away as his gaze catches mine. It's strained and angry and, more than anything else, full of want.

"Do it," I breathe.

He doesn't ask what. We both know what.

He waits a half-beat too long. I rise.

I don't want men who don't know what they want. He's my boss anyway. This was stupid. I've been stupid.

"Fine. Night Greyson."

"Harley."

I start walking.

"Harley, wait, I—"

His hand catches my arm.

"What?" I say, too loud and too angry, probably. But my heart is slamming in my chest, and I'm tired of all this almost, this back and forth, this pretending to be normal, when what happened last night was anything but.

"This," he says simply.

Our lips meet, and then suddenly, overwhelmingly, everything is OK again.

**

Light, too much…

"Ugh…" I groan, although there's no one to hear it, or care.

I'm back in my own tent, still sleepily trying to make sense of this awake thing. My body feels nice, buzzy.

I remember.

"This," Greyson said, as his lips finally met mine.

And then, with the fire watching, and The Dark Side of the Moon playing, around a corner to be out of sight of the others, against a tree, we did it again. The best stress releaser imaginable. Although it was so much more than that.

Or was it?

I rise and start getting on my clothes. Probably not the smartest thing, sleeping naked in the rainforest, even if I do have a damn good double-lined sleeping bag.

I check my phone and find a barrage of worried messages from Hannah. After texting her late last night, I completely forgot to check or respond after.

My first message was a bit foreboding, I'll admit: Major problem here.

After, Hannah's messages got progressively more worried:

Oh damn, what??

Harley, you can NOT send a message like that and not explain!

Harley?

HARLEY FRANCIS DAVIS RESPOND NOW

Harley, I'm serious, I'm super worried about you and now you go and send that message, what is going on? Do you need me to come get you?

And, finally: I hate you. Just so you know.

I have to smile as I read. That's Han for you, worrywart to the extreme. After her first date with the Most Handsome Man Alive, she spent a good four hours agonizing over what outfit to wear for the second one, then finally chose one ten minutes before rushing out of the house.

Sorry Han, I text her back. Fell asleep.

Her text comes back almost instantaneously. God bless modern technology.

—Oh, so you are alive, then?

Just about, I respond. The trekking is hard and apparently there are lethal snakes around. But there's something else.

—You totally did it, didn't you? Did your boss man.

Yep, I did the boss man.

—!!! Was it amazing? Or nah.

Amazing x1000. That's the problem.

—What? You want to do it again? Or did people find out already?

God, no. No one knows. And kind of. We already did it again.

—!!! You she-devil

—So wait, what's the problem?

I don't know. Sent the text late last night.

—Liar.

OK. Just... he actually seems cool.

—Hmm. You like him?

Maybe. It's not a big deal. Anyway, gotta go.

Russel's distinctive voice is calling, "Harleyyyyy!" Better I go out before he wakes the entire rainforest.

—Harley. You totally like him.

I don't even know him, I still respond. We just have sex and he helps me with my tent and supplies sometimes.

—Harley Storm. Has a nice ring to it?

STOP. Love you, BYE!

I put my phone away, my mouth still deciding whether to smile or scowl. Han is perpetually trying to convince me I've met my Prince Charming in whatever guy I happen to be dating at the time. And 10/10 times she's been wrong.

It's not her fault, really. I think she just wants to be able to double date with me, my guy and the Most Handsome Man Alive.

Anyway. I have some food to eat. And camera shots of rainforest coolness to catch.

CHAPTER 9

Greyson

After a quick breakfast of some stale cereal Russel had squirreled away in his pack, we all set out again.

It seems like barely five minutes have passed before Russel falls back so that we're walking side by side, the others several paces behind us.

"So," he says.

"So," I say.

He's giving me an annoyingly significant look that could mean anything—from him spotting a nest of thousands of lethal spiders, to him wanting praise for whatever breakfast was this morning.

He sniffs. "I won't be the first to bring it up."

"Good."

Whatever Russel's getting at, I'm really not in the mood. Our trekking isn't off to a great start. Manuel's already got a minor stomach bug, while Harley insisted on being the last one in our line, thus the most vulnerable.

Speaking of Harley...

Another look back finds her as fine as the other five times I checked. This time, though, she catches me, and quirks a brow.

Dipshit idea, Greyson.

But it's just being a good boss, making sure my whole crew stays safe. Even if I've been checking way more than usual.

Russel is chuckling, and suddenly I can't stand it anymore. "What, Russel?"

Russel rubs his chin, a merry twinkle in his eye. "I know what's been happening out in the bush."

OK, now I'm full-on pissed.

"Careful," I hiss. I manage to keep my angry tone low, as low as Russel's has been.

"If you want to bang Miss PrettyPants, it's no concern of mine," he says breezily, "Just, be careful."

"Watch your tone," I growl.

Russel only shrugs.

Then again, he hasn't out and said that he knows for sure that we've slept together. Maybe if I just keep my mouth shut... As long as he doesn't out and ask me. I've always hated lying—and been as bad at it as Dad was good.

"Work relationships can get messy." Russel's gaze has a faraway look as he says this. "Believe me, none know better than myself." His head droops a little, as he murmurs, half to himself, "Her name was Esme, and we were going to spend our lives together."

"Let's just get to the next camp in one piece," I say.

Over the next few hours, we barely stop to eat, let alone get any usable shots of the surrounding rainforest. Probably because this part of the rainforest is thick, so thick that it's easy to tell where Russel passed through—it's the only possible way to go.

A sigh of relief rolls out of me once we finally step out into a clearing.

"Looks like this is a perfect place for a pit stop," I tell the crew.

Russel groans, but I hardly notice.

This place is...

"Beautiful," Samantha breathes behind me.

Which just about sums it up. Somehow, we've stumbled on a near-hidden waterfall, with crystal-clear waters and exotic yellow and red flowers bordering it.

"No, no, no, no!" Russel's muttering furiously, starting to pace.

"What?" I ask.

"This isn't right." He shakes his head despondently. "Not right at all. I didn't pass any waterfall on my way here."

"You want to take a look around while we rest?" I ask him.

"Indeed." Already Russel's striding off, talking over his shoulder. "Not to worry. I'll figure this out. Just give me an hour, maybe two."

The others are already setting their bags down and nearing the water, while Harley... is nowhere to be seen.

Shit.

I scan the trees around us furiously, but there's no sign of her. When was the last time I saw her? Ten minutes ago? Twenty?

"Jorge," I say, "Seen Harley?"

Jorge points past the waterfall. "Think she went that way. Took the cameras too—said she could maybe get some good shots there."

"Oh. I'll go see if she needs any help."

I head that way, unable to reconcile the angry constriction in my chest—I told her not to wander far from camp—with how reluctantly impressed I am. She's doing exactly what I would've done, if I'd thought that far ahead.

As I near, the tension in my shoulders grows. If anything happens to her...

But as soon as I see her, the tension only increases.

Harley has stripped down to her panties and is wading in the water, video camera propped on her shoulder.

"Hey," I say.

She pauses, grins over her shoulder. "Looks great, doesn't it?"

"Yeah," I say, unable to admit that I can barely notice our surroundings with her ass in full view.

Though not for long as she advances further into the water.

She gestures to something ahead. "I know people love scary alligators. But cute alligators have their appeal, too."

That's when I see it, what she's advancing towards—its small, army-green, scaly head just visible on the surface of the water: a baby alligator.

Fuck.

"Harley," I say sharply, advancing too and scanning the nearby waters tensely. If there's a baby, the mother should be nearby.

"Shh," she says, eyes never leaving the prize.

"I don't like this."

Not one fucking bit.

"I'll be careful. Promise."

"Fine," I grate out, ripping off my shorts and hurrying after her. "A close-up shot..." I stop mid-sentence. A close-up shot of the tiny crocodile's snout—have I lost my mind? No lapsing into producer mode. Not now. "Just get what you can."

As she advances, I go until I'm right behind her, my body lightly pressing hers. No fucking way am I letting her even one step away from me. If anything happens, I'll be here.

If I had my way, we'd be putting as much distance as we could between us and the baby alligator, but I know better than to try to order Harley to do anything she doesn't want to.

Despite the overwhelming awareness of her body against mine, I keep my gaze scanning around us, poised and alert. If anything dangerous approaches, I want to be the first to know.

"Would you look at that," Harley breathes quietly as she shoots. The little creature paddles towards us, pauses, blinks its small-pupiled yellow eyes, then paddles away.

Harley makes to follow, but I don't like how far the pea green waters snake through the trees, how the gloom could hide any number of creatures.

"That's enough for now," I tell her, even though the producer in me is screaming for more, better footage.

"But—"

"I mean it."

Hearing in my voice that I'm not about to let up on this, Harley sighs. She turns off the camera and turns to me. When her green eyes meet mine, they carry a mischievous glint. "What's the matter—don't want your cinematographer getting eaten?"

"Something like that."

She throws an ironic hand to her chest. "I'm touched."

"You should be. Most cinematographers, I don't care one way or another."

We crack up, and she grabs my hand. "Come on—the small falls can't be dangerous."

Next thing I know, we're splashing onto the rocky floor under a small pattering falls, laughing. Harley pulls me back under the stream with her, so it's falling directly on us.

Leaning in close, water splashing over her face, she murmurs, "It's better this way."

Her arms wrap around my neck, and our lips find each other.

It is better: her lips, mine, moving together, our tongues, the water. But what's best is her in my arms, how perfectly her waist fits in my hands. How right as fuck it all feels.

Our hands run along each other's bodies like the water, like relearning every curve and swoop and fall, memorizing it.

Fuck, do I want her.

I'm as hard as ever, and the slick perfection of her breasts under my fingers is maddening. I cup her face, kissing her, kissing her—never have I cared that much about kissing, but kissing her is on a plane of its own. Our mouths, our tongues, us, we just... work together.

My hands slip under her ass and I hoist her up and over, press her into the rock wall of the waterfall.

The water streaming on us has stopped, but we've only started. Our lips twist as our hands scramble to rip off the layers separating us, delight in the wet soft flesh beneath. Her breasts are two perfect handfuls I knead and knead. Almost meditatively, except I'm getting hornier, and my self-control is edging away.

Anyone could round that corner at any minute, she's my employee—and I don't give a flying fuck. All I know now is that I want her—here, now.

She's naked in my arms, and going down on her knees and... oh, fuck yes. Her warm tongue encircles my erection, and a pleased growl rolls out of me.

She's on her knees now, lapping all around my dick, taking her sweet time, enjoying it. It's so good I have to lean back on the rock wall for stability. The sight of her—eyes closed, the slightest curl of a smile on her face—would be enough to get me rock-hard. But how intent she is, how skillful—hand pumping and lips up-down gliding and tongue swirling all in tandem—it's enough to bring me to the edge already.

As if it wasn't clear just how much she's enjoying herself already, she looks me in the eye, and, cock still in her mouth, smiles. And then she slurps me down all the way. Until the head of my cock rams the back of her throat.

"Fuck, Harley," I groan.

And then she does it again. And again, and again. I'm losing the last of my control now. I've never come this fast before, but there's no choice anymore. Not the way she's slurping me, all the way to the back of her throat, harder and faster and groaning a little herself from the enjoyment of it, until I can't take it anymore and my orgasm bursts out of me and she slurps all that down, too.

Both of us sink onto the rock floor, her face tucked into the crook of my arm.

I hold her tightly, unthinkingly.

It feels goddamn good.

I smooth back her hair and listen to the waterfall, streaming the same as ever.

Before long, my lips are drawn back to hers, then her neck, her breast, then down, down over her navel, and lower, until they find the wettest place of all. I kiss and lap at her trembling thighs, light kisses, then harder kisses, with the slightest of teeth.

Goddamn is it hot. She's groaning already.

Slowly, my kisses draw closer… and closer… and closer… until my finger slips inside her, and her whole body breaks into tiny spasms.

"Ooh…" she says, and it's music to my ears.

I dip further into her wetness and begin pumping as I pick up my kissing, drawing closer to her clit, little by little.

Now she's trembling and can't stop as she groans, "Greyson."

I fucking love the sound of my name on her horny lips.

My fingers pump her quickly and lightly, until my lips circle her clit. Her back arched, groan after groan rolls out of her.

I'm rock-hard myself. This is hot as fuck.

Once my lips land on her clit, my finger starts pumping faster than ever. Her groans grow louder and pick up pitch.

I'm lapping at her, swirling my tongue all over her, while my finger pumps her fast and hard and merciless. In and out, round and round. I kiss her clit, and lick it, and finger her pussy. Now she's shaking harder than ever, groaning, "Greyson, Greyson, oh yes, yes, yes!" until she shrills "Uh!" and loses it, her whole body trembling into beautiful spasms.

But I'm not finished. Not yet.

I keep my finger pumping, my lips kissing, a bit softer, helping her ride the climax until she's coming a second time—"Greyson, no, oh, yes! Oh, more!"—and then a third—"Fucking uh, that's it!" Until she collapses in my arms.

As I hold her tight, no thoughts come. All there is, is the perfect feel of her body in my arms.

"Greyson," she says urgently at some point.

And then I hear it, the calling voices:

"Greysonnn!"

"Harleyyyy!"

Fuck.

We scramble up, then for our clothes. As I fumble them on, my mind is reeling.

How the fucking fuck did I let things get this far, so close to the others? I'm supposed to be the producer, for Christ's fucking sake! I'm supposed to be in charge. What kind of shithead leader goes off to fuck his cinematographer, leaving the rest of the crew to fend for themselves in an unfamiliar rainforest?

Not the kind I'd be proud to be.

Harley, now dressed, looks a bit ruffled but otherwise unflustered. Fixing me with a grin, she states, "You're good."

"You're great," I have to admit. "But—"

She nods. "I don't want the others finding out about this either. No worries. We're just having some fun."

And with that, she goes to where she set down the camera, hefts it on her shoulder, and strides off in the direction of the voices.

What I can't understand, as I watch her walk away, is why I don't feel at all relieved by what she said.

CHAPTER 10

Harley

Of course it was Samantha who called the 'urgent search party' to find us. With the assumption that, naturally, I was the one who'd led poor Greyson into a near-death experience. I almost want to out and tell her that the only near-death experience we had was one without clothes, but I couldn't do that to Greyson. Or myself.

I still haven't figured out whether our affair getting out would be really bad for my career, or really, really bad for my career. Would directors and producers really scoff at working with a cinematographer who liked to have fun? Although that would not be the case at all. I didn't mean for things to get out of hand with Greyson, just, every time I was around him, they did.

Anyway.

"You were getting a good shot," Samantha says skeptically, glaring at me, then looking to Greyson, her glare softening immediately.

Clearly, she's just jealous, and as much as I'd like to tell her to go shove it, we still have a long-ass time stuck out here together.

Manuel and Jorge are avoiding looking at us, clearly realizing that something's going on too.

"Exactly," I tell Samantha, showing her the camera screen and the little alligator footage. It's a stellar shot—a clear, close-up view of his little scaly head—and by how her scowl deepens, she knows it too.

"Whatever," she says, turning to Greyson. "How long did Russel say he needs again?"

"A while, but it's probably not a good idea letting him wander too far," Greyson says, heading for the trees. "I'll go find him now. Wait here until I get back."

Although he doesn't look at me, I can tell his words are directed at me. It's a bit cute, how he worries. Though he's probably right. I do need to be more careful.

I accept a granola bar from Jorge, then retreat to my tent. Inside, chomping away at the peanut butter-chocolatey goodness (Han and I always used to call granola bars 'glorified chocolate bars'), I check my phone. Hannah's sent me a video that cracks me up immediately: it's of the Most Handsome Man Alive fast asleep, snoring with his mouth open. At the end, the video pans over to her quietly chortling face. I find myself watching the video several times before finally tearing my gaze away.

Obviously, it's funny, it's just... there's something else. Something in Hannah's eyes that isn't just sheer amusement. Love.

I've seen that look before. Seen where it's led to.

Something twists in me. Mom and Dad, in the photograph they used to have hanging over the fireplace, hippie wedding attire on, eyes on each other, they had that look. And yet, where they ended up was so far gone...

Dad, away from home more nights than not, his face red and his eyes unseeing when he was home, blowing up at the stupidest things. Mom, barricading herself in her room, though the thick oak-panel door couldn't muffle her sobbing... And it wasn't just the years of it, the two going on three, until they finally broke up.

If that had been all of it, if they'd been able to bounce back after it, maybe then whenever I heard about or saw love I wouldn't get an instinctive shiver. But they didn't. Mom was still popping the same pills she'd been proscribed a few months after their separation, and Dad was as much of a functional alcoholic as ever.

That's what love does to people.

I take a contemplative bite of my granola bar, chew some.

Maybe not always, but a lot of the time. Either love fizzles out and you become the bored couple that nitpick everything the other does or the love inverts, turns into something so hateful and ugly and monstrous that it's unbelievable that what's left behind even came from the word.

But Hannah and her guy, you can see it. She's happier with him, he with her. They make each other better people.

But is it worth the risk?

Tossing the wrapper in my bag, I rise.

Whatever the answer to that question, there's no point moping around in here. It doesn't matter anyway. Greyson is my boss. End of story.

As soon as I stick my head outside the tent, I realize it's been longer than I thought. Already the sun is setting, the shadows growing long. The others have set up a fire and are sitting round its crackling warmth. Greyson is back with Russel, who's glowering into the fire, with an almost-full bag of marshmallows pressed to his chest.

"Hey," I say, approaching them. "What's up? Did you find which way we have to go to find your path again?"

He throws a couple of marshmallows in his mouth and, cheeks poofed ludicrously, grumbles, "No. No idea how we got here. No idea how to get back."

"We'll all check together tomorrow," Greyson firmly, in the tone of having said this before. "Any rate, we've already got a great bunch of shots."

"But the alligators!" Russel exclaims, throwing both arms out in his fervor and dropping the marshmallow bag in the process. "The big, terrible, gnawing murderers of beasts, what of them? This special was supposed to be great. It was supposed to be about them."

"You were supposed to know how to get back to the camp," Greyson growls.

Then, catching my ingratiating smile, he takes a breath.

"The show was supposed to be finished and sent to post-production over a week ago," he says. "But here we are. As much as I want to capture those alligators, I'm not about to sacrifice everything to do it. Anyway, Harley's right: people do love babies, and she got some good footage today."

"Only a few minutes of it," I say, although my heart is hop-skipping with his praise.

If a few years ago, you'd have told me that I'd be working with Greyson Storm—hell, hooking up with Greyson Storm—I would've thought you were crazy.

Samantha sniffs loudly. Manuel hands me a sausage. Meanwhile, Russel is eyeing Greyson with what looks to be admiration. "Taking charge like that—you know, you are your father's son."

Greyson grunts noncommittally.

Russel seizes the marshmallow bag, grabs some, and declares, "What! It's a compliment!"

Greyson's looking at the fire, doesn't seem to see anything else. "In some ways."

"Oh?"

"I won't badmouth the dead," Greyson says flatly.

"Oh," Russel says, "But he was a good father?"

"Yeah," Greyson says. "He was that."

Russel rubs his hands together contemplatively. "And a good businessman?"

"Depends on your definition of good."

"But he did what he had to, yes? Paid the price."

The silence after his words stretches so long that it seems like Greyson isn't going to respond at all, until he finally murmurs, "Some prices aren't worth paying."

"Maybe," Russel says, after a pause of his own. "But in your personal life, your brothers and you are like him, no? All grown men and perpetual bachelors."

Greyson shrugs.

"Come now!" Russel exclaims. "Remember, I have partied with you in LA! I've seen the beautiful, work-of-art beauties you all have enjoyed, I—"

"Russel," Greyson says curtly, "Shut up."

As if remembering the rest of us for the first time in a while, Russel casts a musing look around. "Ah. Yes. OK, boss."

As I eat the rest of my sausage, and roast and eat another, and chat with Manuel and Jorge about their own backgrounds (Manuel is from Spain, and Jorge grew up on a remote farm in BC), I can't get a weird twist out of my belly. A weird twist that came right after Russel's words.

Oh well.

**

The next morning, we set out bright and early. Russel doesn't find the path, but we do stumble on a mother puma and her cubs. As we are slowly creeping away, with Greyson coolly hissing instructions to us and Russel blubbering about how he doesn't want to die, I manage to get a good shot of the mother puma hissing ferociously at us, probably puma for: "Come any closer and I'll bite off your face."

By the time we choose our campsite, Greyson's decided that we have enough footage to head on back, alligators or no. He's also successfully avoided being alone with me for the entire day, while also making sure I don't wander as much as two feet away from the others without him noticing.

Which isn't as much of a burden as it sounds, considering we trekked a good eight hours, on and off, and I'm dead tired.

It's a nice kind of tiredness, though, one that doesn't allow any extraneous thought other than a sluggish awareness of itself and how many times I've yawned lately.

The others are busy getting dinner started, while Greyson and I are fetching firewood, when suddenly Greyson freezes.

"Hey—" I begin.

He shushes me, points.

A few feet away from us, a weird grey-brown creature is eyeing us uncertainly, its curled snout twitching.

"Camera," Greyson hisses. "Slowly."

I'm on it in seconds that feel like hours. And to think I was beginning to wonder if hauling around this heavy-ass thing 24/7 was worth it.

"Don't move, though," Greyson mutters, as if reading my mind for my next thought.

Not that I was about to bound at the thing with camera flailing, but it would be nice if I didn't have to rely on my unreliable zoom-in function.

"Sweep a shot over it, nice and slow," he says, "Then get the baby tapir in the woods a bit ahead."

As he's saying it, I'm already doing it, swallowing back my gasp of surprise that there's another equally weird and actually cute little creature a few steps back from the first.

"Now, I'm going to hold out this leafy branch and..." To my surprise, the tapir slowly advances to nibble on Greyson's extended leafy branch.

"You should probably also get..." he sounds awkward as he trails off, but I know exactly what he's getting at. I capture of shot of his pleasantly surprised face.

"Greyson!" Russel calls from behind us.

As the tapir races away, Greyson instructs me, "Get it," and I am, and I'm laughing. We're laughing.

"Coming!" Greyson calls back, although he doesn't move.

I grin at him. "That was..." I feel like hugging him, even though the tapir scene probably won't even be a main shot in the show, maybe won't even be included in the final version. It's more how seamlessly we work together.

Next thing I know, he's swept me up in his arms and spun me around. "That was amazing, you were..."

He sets me back on my feet, a sheepish look amidst the excitement on his face.

I find I can't quite meet his eye, can't trust myself not to kiss him if I do. "I can see why they call you a legend. You were so in the zone, like you knew exactly what that tapir was going to do before it even did."

"Baird's Tapir," he explains. "It's mainly nocturnal, so we lucked out, but... it was perfect. We just went with it."

I stifle a little prickle of joy at his 'we'.

"I'm no legend, though," he continues, although he can't manage to wipe that big goofy smile off his face. "I just... this is what I love. This..." He trails off, gestures around him then shrugs helplessly.

I nod. I get it. It's the same thing I feel when I get behind the camera: a loss of time, a flow, a perfection.

"Thank you," he says, his hands going to my shoulders. His face looks different than I've seen it, as if some undefinable sort of tension has loosened. "This is what I came here for."

"Really?" I can't help but ask. "To catch shots of weird tapirs?"

"No, to catch great shots and work with great people." His mouth quirks to the side. "From a business point of view, I'm just here to get the job done, but..."

"What's the point if you don't love it?" I finish, hyper-aware of how his hands are still resting on my shoulders, how I don't want them to leave. "But you do. We do."

And how we both get it is so satisfying that we stand there for a bit longer. Seconds, minutes, who knows. All I know is that we break apart and head back to the camp only when the next "Greyson!" comes and the spell is broken.

CHAPTER 11

Greyson

That night, I can't sleep. I roll back and forth in my sleeping bag. I flip my pillow, smack my pillow, get rid of my pillow. But I can't.

Something's buzzing inside of me.

Something I haven't felt since... the last time I sat in the producer's chair.

Getting up, I sit with my sleeping bag bunched all around me and scowl at nothing.

Finally, I get out and look around me and see...

"Wow," I whisper, my neck craned up.

I hadn't even realized we'd reached a clearing until now. It's not a full clearing, but enough that trees aren't blocking the overhead view completely. With the result of a view that has me staring.

Before I know quite what I'm doing, I'm going over to Harley's tent and, crouched at the door flap, whispering, "Harley?"

Nothing.

Good.

What was I thinking, coming over here to wake her? Sure, she should see this, but us alone at night isn't a good idea.

"Ay?" comes back a murmur just as I'm turning away.

Shuffling, then an unzipping and her adorably rumpled head pops out. "Something wrong?"

Her eyes are still half-closed, her lips curled in a sleepy smile.

I grind my feet into the ground to avoid lunging there and kissing that smile bigger, rumpling that hair more. "Nothing important."

A blink, then her eyes narrow my way. "Then why... wake up?"

Fuck, do I want her. Instead, I turn away. "I'll tell you in the morning."

More unzipping, more shuffling, and next thing I know she's beside me.

"Do you ever listen to anyone?" I ask her wryly.

"Yeah, sometimes," she says.

"Oh?"

"I used to listen to my parents, until I realized they were just flawed people."

Surprised, I glance at her and she grimaces. "Sorry. I'm tired and a bit dopey. Kind of a depressing thing to say."

"It's true, though," I admit. "It's a sad day when you realize they aren't the omnipotent beings you once thought they were."

"But necessary," she agrees, "to becoming an adult. That and owning your shit. Like, even if they did screw you up, it's your responsibility to unscrew yourself."

I laugh and inwardly curse myself at the same time. God, she's so cool and fresh and honest and yet... why in the fuck do I have to get a boner when she says the word 'screw'?

"So, how's that going for you?" I find myself asking. "Unscrewing yourself."

"It's a process."

Silence, then she says, "Hey, as much as I like wandering through potentially treacherous rainforests with no aim in sight, what are we doing?"

I freeze, and this time curse out loud.

You fuckwad. This is no way for a producer to act, and maybe even endangering Harley too?

Luckily, I've been leading us in wide circles around the still smoldering campfire, so we aren't too far off.

"Shit, sorry, I..."

I trail off. I'm not about to admit that being around her messes with my head in a way I've never experienced before. That it's almost like being in the producer's chair, a clarity, a loss of time, a focus, a desire to stay in the state as long as humanly possible.

Get it together, Greyson.

I make a mental note to call up Nolan. He's always been good at sorting out my brothers whenever they think they've found 'the one'.

I point up overhead. "Thought you should see these."

"Oh, I..." She falls silent as she sees what I see. Seeing them through her eyes, it's like seeing them for the first time.

A mind-shattering amount of stars. The kind of view you expect to see in the middle of the desert maybe, or in some high-res image in a nature museum exhibit. Not just randomly trekking and happening to look up.

There's big stars, small stars, spread-out dots of stars, constellations of stars.

"It makes you think." Her voice is soft and clear in the night, like an auditory star. Our hands have found each other's, hers cool and fitting right in mine. "Who else has seen stars like these? Peoples all throughout history, maybe even beings on other planets. Even me, as a kid, I was so self-absorbed, I didn't give a shit about stars or stuff like that, so whenever I did see them, I didn't really see them, if you know what I mean?"

I can feel her gaze on me. And I do know, but putting it into words, what I hadn't even consciously realized but now know, seemed impossible.

What other things were right in front of me, obvious and beautiful now, yet that I couldn't see for all the world?

All I know is that her hand feels right in mine and that this now, whatever it is, I don't want it to stop.

"It's a good shot," she says, after a time, her hand drawing out of mine." I'll go get my camera."

My hand is cold with hers gone.

The next few minutes pass as part of the flow: I direct and she responds, the two of us working like two limbs of the same beast, like a connected mind. By the time she's captured the shots, I don't need to look back on the footage to know that she's captured a winner.

After, all there is left to do is take one more look at the ceiling of beauty we've been sleeping under unknowingly all this time.

"So," she says.

"So," I say.

My body is itchy with her closeness, my arms empty with how she should be in them. I wet my lips and twist myself towards my tent.

"We should get to bed." I force all emotion out of my voice.

I want her. I want her with a wildness that's unfamiliar, a tenderness that feels dangerous.

"We should," she agrees.

She doesn't move. I don't move.

Get the hell out of here.

Kiss her, take her, you know you want to.

My thoughts fight each other, until I stride ahead, not daring to look back, not even daring to say a word because autopilot and my want would take over.

She catches my arm. "Greyson."

I spin her into my arms, and all self-control falls away.

Our lips meet and what follows follows. Behind a big ceiba tree, in sight of the camp, yet far enough away, we make love for the first time.

It isn't sex. It isn't hot or fast or rough. It's slow and sensual and building. It's part of the night and watched by the night. And if I didn't know better, I'd think that this was what love feels like.

Afterwards, we're curled up in each other's arms.

"We can't keep doing this," she says, half to herself.

I don't answer, because I don't have the slightest clue what to say.

CHAPTER 12

Harley

I wake up with a jolt. I'm back in my own sleeping bag, but how? After last night with Greyson…

I let out a little groan. Last night with Greyson.

Not that it wasn't good, ungodly so. Just that it's starting to feel like we're creeping into dangerous ground. New ground. Ground where I actually care about the guy and wonder what he's thinking. Like now—what is he thinking?

"Get real," I mutter to myself, forcing myself into a somewhat sitting position.

Number 1: It doesn't matter what he's thinking.

Number 2: He's probably thinking about food. Or something that has exactly nothing to do with me, at any rate.

Maybe a generalization, but anytime Dad made one of his invariable fuck-ups or forgettings (forgetting my mom's birthday for the fourth time, after multiple reminders on her part, was what precipitated the fight that ended up in them divorced), it was due in some esoteric way, to food.

'Dinner with clients', 'Had to stop in for a bite because I was starving', 'They had a sale on these delicious nacho chips I saw on the way home and I had to get some'; these were the doomsday ticks of my childhood.

But I digress.

Number 3: How in the hell did I even get in my sleeping bag?

I strain my memory, wincing already in the expectation of some walk of shame or being caught, but unless I'm suffering from major amnesia... we didn't.

Checking my phone finds the answer.

Carried you to your tent last night—Greyson

How he even got my number I'm not sure, nor do I care. I wince, wondering if I was full-on snoring at that point, the way Hannah always moans about.

I pause and prick up my ears, but I can't hear anyone by the campfire yet. Nor do I have any desire to go out there.

The past few days, Samantha's dirty looks have gone full-on volcanic, with her grumpy sighs and 'go-die' glares being caused more often than not by absolutely nothing at all.

Thanks, I text back.

His reply comes back lightning-fast:

—Noticed your sleeping bag isn't in the greatest shape, want mine?

It's not that bad, I reply. Nothing a good sew won't fix.

Greyson does have a point. I'm pretty sure some weird mouse or opossum snuck into my tent the night I went on my ill-advised pot romp and chewed up the corner of my sleeping bag. Some mornings I wake up with my toe caught in the hole, but it's more funny than annoying, and anyway, Greyson is a lot bigger than me and my sleeping bag might just be a skirt on him.

A real solution would be just to share his, an unwanted voice purrs in the back of my mind. I shove it aside.

I check my phone to find his response already there: I mean it.

What—don't want me filing an abuse suit against Storm co? ;)

—Something like that.

—Seriously, Harley.

Seriously, Greyson. We have about two more days. And I'm a grown and capable adult.

—Don't make me come over there and convince you.

I freeze. What the hell is he getting at, exactly?

Next second, my phone is ringing.

"I mean it," he growls.

"Whoa, did you not get any sleep or something?" I tease.

"No, actually. And listen, I've got enough on my plate without worrying about you."

"Well, sorry. I'm not forcing you to worry about me over a stupid sleeping bag, OK? So just forget it."

Silence, then a measured exhale. "Will you just take the goddamn sleeping bag?"

"Will you just drop it? I don't get what the problem is."

"I..." Another silence. "You know what, you're right. Not a big deal. It's not like you're my..." A cough. "How did you sleep?"

Despite myself, I find myself biting back a smile. "Good, thanks for asking."

"I saved some food for you out there. Russel was dead-set on feeding it to some parrots, but once I threatened him with burning his sombrero, he backed off."

I laugh. "Oh, what a relief. Guess I should go have some now, then?"

"Right, yeah, I... don't even know why we're talking on the phone when we can be talking in person."

"Your leadership gets better every day."

"Careful," he says, a serious note in his light voice.

"Got it, boss," I say, "See ya!"

He's halfway through "Don't call me—" when I hang up.

I sit cross-legged, fluttering my knees up and down a bit, like I used to do in gymnastics.

God, I feel silly and goofy and stupid, and... Maybe I do know why he preferred talking on the phone. Maybe it's the same for him as for me: it's easier to control myself when I don't have to see him, when the visceral magnet-pull of him is dulled a bit. Just a bit, though.

Outside, everyone else is packing up. I feel a guilty twinge that I shove down. It's not like they woke me up or anything. If they wanted me up and going, they just had to ask.

"Ooh," I say to Greyson, bare-chested and approaching as I spot what awaits me by the fire, "cinnamon toast crunch, my fav."

"Even after his parrot idea was shot down, Russel swore he was saving it for his trip-end victory snack. He even tried getting us to eat some mushrooms that he was 60% sure weren't poisonous, but I put my foot down."

I open my mouth, still stretched in a goofy smile, waiting for something witty, or at least decent to come out. Instead, all that does is: "You're good at that."

He chuckles, then his face darkens. "With some things."

I swallow. Just eat, Harley.

Then hopefully my brain will start functioning decently again. All I know now is that without a shirt Greyson looks hot as hell.

"So," I say, once my bowl is filled. I look around again to be sure that we're alone.

"So," he says.

"Is that our thing?" I wonder aloud, "The so game?"

"I so hoped we were better than that."

We laugh and laugh, and I can't stop laughing, even though I know full well the joke wouldn't be nearly as funny if anyone other than Greyson said it.

"Aren't you two just peas in a pod," Russel says companionably as he treks by with, for whatever reason, a fishing pole clasped against his shoulder.

Greyson and I exchange a look once he's gone.

"About last night," he says, careful to keep his voice low. "I have to apologize."

I eye him blankly. "About?"

"You know what. I've been beyond inappropriate."

"Oh, I'm sorry." I'm surprised to hear my voice so biting and curt. "I didn't realize that there was just one person in this thing, that I have no say whatsoever."

"But I'm your boss. I'm the one who has the power, which means I should—"

"Oh Greyson?" I cut in.

"Yeah."

I point at a heavy-looking rock a few steps away. "Can you get that for me?"

"Sure," he says, headed that way within seconds.

A twinge of guilt goes through me as I see him hauling it back with extreme effort, sweat rolling off his face. By the time he plonks it down in front of me, I'm wearing a sweet smile.

"Thanks. You were saying about who had the power?"

Greyson's jaw falls open. "But... you... I..."

I rise, then lean in to hiss in his face. "Don't you go acting like this is all on you. I'm a grown woman. Maybe you're my boss, but you've never once forced me or coerced me into anything. I do what I want. And I wanted you, so I did you."

Greyson gapes at me.

Suddenly, here in the itchy forest with a big ant scuttling over my bare feet and Greyson staring at me like I'm suddenly speaking Mandarin and growing a goatee, is the last place I want to be.

I hurry into my tent, and take my cereal with me.

CHAPTER 13

Greyson

I gape after her departing form.

What... just happened?

My breathing is still a bit labored from hauling over that insanely heavy rock.

I feel how the cartoon characters do when they smack their forehead. Like a complete idiot. So much for making things right with Harley.

I had just wanted to... I don't know. Whenever I've heard about relationships on set, especially between older, established guys and younger new girls, I've always been disgusted.

That was how my parents met, and I saw how long and well it lasted after us kids. And what it did to my mom afterwards. I've always sworn I'd never be one of those men, that I'd be better than that, and now...

Fuck.

I head over to my duffel bag, set beside my packed-up tent. Jorge, Manuel and Samantha are probably still at that somewhat-decent pool of water they found, washing up.

Which means I have some time to do what I wanted: call up Nolan.

"What a pleasure," he says, as he picks up. "Especially after our last conversation."

"Last time you were acting like an ass, and I told you so," I reply smoothly.

"So, you did go for it," he says boredly.

I say nothing.

He laughs. "That big of a deal?"

"I'm not Dad," I say simply.

"And no one's accusing you of being. You're just human, Grey."

"Yeah, and I'm supposed to be the producer."

"It's normal. Seriously, chill. Is this what you called me for?"

"No, I…"

I pause, resisting the urge to chuck the phone in pointless rage. Who knows why I called him—maybe just for someone else to talk to, other than the crew?

"Good news is the show's been shot," I tell him. "We're on our way back, could be on a plane as soon as tomorrow."

"Wow. You made it all the way back to the camp already and got some footage of those psycho alligators? How were they? Did they kill anyone?"

"Thanks for your concern. But no. We had no map and Russel is even more of an incompetent alcoholic than he was before, but we still got a few scenes of other wildlife and nature. Harley's talented."

"Oh, I'll bet." His tone sets my teeth on edge.

"You watch your mouth."

"Whoa." I can almost see his long light hair bobbing as he throws his arms up in a conciliatory comedian's gesture. "Anyone with eyes could see that she had the hots for you. And you said—"

"Doesn't matter what I said. I don't want this getting out, OK? Not even to the other brothers."

"Well, Landon often feels like he has to tell Madeline, and seeing as Madeline is well-meaning but a notorious gossip... that would be a hard no. But Emerson doesn't even have any friends, what can it hurt?"

"Nolan—"

"Why do you never trust me? I'm just trying to—"

"Fuck's sake, Nolan!"

Silence, then, his voice, finally sobered up. "Shit. You really like this girl, don't you?"

"Stop fucking around."

"I'm not. Shit, Greyson. This is bad, really bad."

"Forget I said anything. We're just having some fun."

"Right. Well, make sure you keep it that way." Nolan's voice sounds odd, strained. He never was a good liar.

"I've gotta go," I say, even though there's still no one in sight. "Bye."

I hang up before he can say another word.

Fuck.

Trust fucking Nolan to make something out of nothing.

Then again, what did I expect to get out of him, calling him up for no reason whatsoever?

His voice echoes in my head mockingly: You really like this girl, don't you?

What the fuck does he know, anyway?

So what if even the glancing thought of her now makes me hard, and I have to physically rip my gaze off her tent to avoid going there. So fucking what?

Maybe it's just an animal kind of magnetism, based on how good the sex is. It could be that.

"Has to be," I mutter grimly, as I go to find the others so I won't be alone with Harley.

CHAPTER 14

Harley

"Fuck him," I mutter as I crunch away at my cereal.

What the hell is his problem? We were supposed to be just having fun, and then he has to go and ruin things, for whatever reason.

Unless the reason was that he wanted to end things? What the hell.

I grab my phone, then put it down again. What's the point of texting Han, really? I know what she's going to say.

—Can you blame him for being worried? is what she does say when I do cave and text her.

Yeah, actually. No one forced him into this.

—Come on, Har. How many guys have said no to you?

You're really pulling this on me?

—Yes, I mean no. Obviously, it's shitty.

Why do I feel like there's a 'but' coming?

—But HE'S YOUR BOSS. He's just trying to do the right thing.

I put my phone away after that. Hannah's right, of course. And now there's nothing to do but suck it up.

I just... didn't expect to have to so soon. Or genuinely enjoy myself so much around him. Or find him so goddamn stupidly sexy—

Stop, Harley.

Now that I've finished my cereal, I go out and get packing my tent. After all, sitting around isn't going to make me feel any better.

**

The next few hours, I stay busy not talking, looking at, or even being around Greyson. Which isn't all that hard, seeing as he seems to be trying for the exact same thing.

By the time we get to our new campsite, I'm dead tired.

So I'm barely looking as I stride up to the place where I'll set up my tent.

That is, until I hear the hissing.

"Shit," I groan.

Time grinds to a halt.

Triangular head? Check.

Diamonds on said head? Check.

Grey body? Mother-fucking-check.

Yep, that's a fer-de-lance snake. You know, the lethal one.

Next thing I know, Greyson's leaping in front of me, leg jabbing out at the thing. "Run!"

The snake dives, and I take off. I run as fast and hard as I can. Do snakes chase things? What about Greyson?

"Ah!" I say, as a rock gives way under my feet and I'm pitched forward, straight into a… whoa…

Something cracks into the center of my skull, and everything goes black.

**

I'm a snake. Bobbing up and down, up and down. I'm being held by a man. A big strong man. Up and down. Up and down.

My eyes flutter open a crack, and memory slaps back into me.

ake. Greyson, saving me. And now... I strain

o my face. "You OK?"

close of their own accord, a pounding ache

ill. "Will have to get back to you on that."

"I mean it, ʌrley." I can hear the intensity in his voice, even though I can't see it on his face. "You seeing double? You should probably stay awake."

"I... Yeah."

We move along in silence for another minute or so, then I ask, "What happened?"

"Greyson saved you," Samantha says flatly, "Risked his life doing so. Then you ran into a tree and blacked out."

The last she says in the same tone you'd use to tell some idiot, "You tried eating cement and broke a tooth."

Wish it were you, I grumble inwardly.

"But we got some good footage of the snake!" Manuel says, clearly trying to strike a positive note. "After we were all safely out of the way, of course."

"Important thing is that you're OK," Greyson says. "And we're almost back. We made great progress after a shortcut Russel found. May even make it back to the plane today."

His tone is guarded and somehow I can tell there's something else he isn't saying.

"Home tomorrow?" I ask.

"Well..."

"What?"

"You bonked your noggin real bad," Russel s.
"They may not let you on the plane at all."

"I may not let you on the plane," Greyson says. "In fact, ˌ
guarantee that I won't. Not unless it's completely safe."

"Nothing's... ever... completely safe," I grumble.

An example, about how a friend of mine accidentally swallowed a toothbrush while brushing her teeth and ended up in the ER, occurs to me, then drifts away. I can barely form coherent sentences, let alone get on a plane. Maybe it's for the best if I stay here for a bit longer.

But what does that mean? Surely, everyone else isn't going to stick around until I'm fully healed, right?

The question throbs importantly along with the painful pulse in my head, then ebbs away.

The only thing I really feel like or want right now is... sleep. Nice... sleep...

CHAPTER 15

Greyson

"Why didn't you tell her?" Russel asks me in an undertone as soon as it's just the two of us in the lead again.

Not counting Harley in my arms, of course. Despite my efforts, she did drift off. But Jorge has some medical experience and claims she looks to be sleeping peacefully, so I've decided to let her be.

"Don't want her worrying," I tell Russel.

"Worrying." Russel snorts. "If I got to stay at Nayara Springs, the last thing I'd be doing is worrying."

"That's not certain yet."

Russel makes a skeptical sound. "Come on. Our pretty little señorita is out for the count, and we'll reach the plane in under an hour. Ten out of ten says that you two are going to be gallivanting off to Nayara Springs, just like you told me."

"I still don't know why you can't come too," I say.

Russel chuckles. "Oh no, I know what you're trying to do. But I have previous engagements."

"You mean the dates you've lined up with seven different women on Tinder since this morning."

Russel smirks, clearly pleased with himself. "What can I say, I'm a busy man."

"And what am I trying to do?" I press.

"You like her. You're afraid to be alone with her. Why not admit it?"

"I... No."

Russel wags his finger in a teasing motion. "I saw youuu."

I resist the urge to clock him in the forehead. "Russel."

"What?" He looks genuinely stumped as to why I'm pissed. "It looked beautiful."

"It was a mistake," I say firmly.

"A beautiful one, then," he replies breezily.

"I'm her boss."

Russel lifts a small banana he's gotten from somewhere. "And this is a banana, what's your point?"

"My point is, it was inappropriate and I..." I trail off, realizing my words are falling on deaf ears.

"Russel, I'd appreciate it if you kept this to yourself."

"Who, me?" Russel trills. Then he bobs his head as he pats his chest. "Soul of discretion, right here."

"Good."

"But I can't speak for the others. I don't think they know know, but they know, you know?"

I grunt. Trying to delicately say something to them probably wouldn't go over well, either.

"That Samantha woman is still pissy that you didn't go kill that wood snake in her tent while she was butt naked the other night," Russel adds pleasantly.

"That was an actual piece of wood, I saw it and—you know about that?"

Russel wiggles his eyebrows suggestively, then taps the side of his head. "Nothing gets past me, you know."

"Might be best to just leave Harley at the hotel to recuperate. Maybe even fly in her friend to look after her while she gets better."

It's only after I see Russel, looking nothing short of outraged, that I realize that I've been thinking out loud.

"And leave her with the thieving, assaulting louts who pass for hotel staff?" Russel coughs. "I mean, I may or may not have had a stint working as a lowly hotel handyman in Costa Rica a decade or so back."

"Forget it," I say.

Even without Russel's input, I knew full well there was no way I'd be leaving Harley alone in an unfamiliar country when she isn't in her right mind. If only there was a way to avoid her, not see her, while at the same time watching over her.

I'll just have to take it day by day.

By the time we all reach the plane, Harley is still out cold, while everyone else is more than relieved to be getting back to civilization. Everyone says their goodbyes, Russel gives a ten-minute soliloquy on how this trip will never be forgotten, and then, just like that, the plane takes off, and it's me and her, waiting on the SUV to show up and whisk us away to Nayara Springs.

CHAPTER 16

Harley

Fluffy. So comfy.

I peek open an eye.

Greenery meets it.

What the—?

I sit up fast and practically fall over when I see where I am: the most gorgeous place I've ever been in my life.

The decor is boho-chic, although it's the outside that really draws my eye. Jungle-y plants clamor over the sides of a shimmering infinity pool that overlooks a view that can't cost less than $1,000 a pop.

How the hell did I get here? Just as I'm looking around for my phone, the landline on the rosewood bedside table beside me rings.

"Hello?" I say.

"Madame is up, yes?" a cheerful voice asks. "Good! We will be by with the breakfast."

"OK, but how—"

Cheerful voice hangs up and seconds later there's a knock at the door. Luckily, I'm still in my own clothes, so I pad over in the fluffy sandals beside the bed to open the door.

"Madame is well?" a round-cheeked cheerful woman asks, evidently the owner of the cheerful voice. She rolls in a dolly with several layers of covered dishes, then is followed by three more similarly dressed and dolly-pushing women, all smiling.

I have to smile too. Something smells delicious.

"Go on, back to bed with you," the woman orders me cheerfully. "After all, this is the breakfast in bed option."

Which is how I spend a good hour devouring everything from fried plantains to delicious eggs, bacon and some vegetable and casserole mixes that are definitely local, perfectly spicy and even more definitely delicious.

By the end, I'm so stuffed with food that I'm about ready to pass back out on the bed. Except that I still haven't figured out how this is even all happening.

"How did I get here?" I ask the woman as she's almost out the door.

"Yes?"

"I didn't check myself in here," I say. "So…"

"Yes." Cheerful head bob that sets her dark braids jiggling. "Monsieur arrived with Madame, got her nice room."

"Oh." She has to mean Greyson. After I passed out by the plane, he must've taken me here to recover. But still, I could've recovered in a 5-bed hostel. Why take me here? Did he just ditch me here?

"Do you know where he is now?" I ask her.

"If in his room, you have to call 55." She pauses. "Madame need anything else?"

"No, thank you," I tell her, "Though you can call me Harley. What's your name?"

"Maria." She grins, waves as she leaves. "Buenos dias—good morning!"

Then she's gone, and I'm staring at the phone.

"Hello?" Greyson's voice comes over the line groggy and surly after I dial 55.

"Hey. It's me."

"Oh. Great." Suddenly his voice is a whole lot more alert. "How are you feeling?"

"Good, I..." I totter out of bed and stretch experimentally. "Stuffed, but really good. This place is amazing."

I let my gaze trail over to the infinity pool, to find that there's a poolside table with some chocolates and wine laid out already.

"Thank you," I tell him, "but I really didn't need—"

"Important thing is for you to get better. They have a good doctor on hand at this place too, if you need one."

Something about his tone sounds too clipped, abrupt.

"OK..." I say. "Anything else I should know? You already eat?"

"That's about it," he says crisply. "Yes. I have some calls to make, but feel free to wander around if you feel up to it. Just not too far off the grounds. There's bike tours, a spa, restaurants, a swim-up bar. It's all on me."

"I really appreciate this. This place is gorgeous."

"You need anything else?"

Still that tone.

"No."

"Great, I'll check in on you later. Have some calls to make."

"You don't have to stay here, you know," I say. "I'm pretty much better. I can leave later today, tomorrow at the latest."

"I'll book a flight as soon as you're 100 percent," he says, "Enjoy your day."

He hangs up.

"Yeah, you too," I mutter into the dial tone.

Maybe he really did have some calls to make. More likely he's still determined to avoid me. Well, he can be my guest. I'm not about to sit around crying about it.

I shoot off a quick I'm OK, will be back in a few days, will explain later today text to Hannah. Then I do a peer-through-the-bushes visibility test, and finding the pool totally private, strip down and get swimming. The water feels amazing against my sore, dirt-crumbled skin. I sit at the edge of the blue and teal mosaic-stoned pool and look over, delighting in the view.

Wow…

Trees as far as the eye can see, with the odd colorful building or two. There's even a volcano just visible off to my right.

Even the air smells fresher somehow.

I relax my head onto the tiles, luxuriating in how amazing this is.

I've never been to a hotel half this swanky or gorgeous. Part of me always instinctively looked down at people who blew however many hundreds or thousands a night just to get some chichi experience, when you could have fun and adventures just meeting people at any cheap old hostel. But now I get it. Here, there's a kind of calm, peace and wonder that makes any bill seem reasonable.

Then again, I'm not the one footing it.

The thought makes me scowl. Is this Greyson's way of paying me off to stay quiet about our fling? He didn't strike me as that kind of guy, but then again, he didn't strike me as the kind of guy to try avoiding me on purpose, and it sure seems like that's what he's doing today.

Restless, after a few minutes, I leave the pool and open my closet to find my dirty old bag flopped in the corner. My eye is drawn to a gorgeous paisley blue, teal and white bodycon on a hanger in front of me. It still has the tags on and looks to be just my size! But what is it doing there?

Then I glimpse the note. Tell me if it's not your size—G.

My hand wavers out to it, then stops. If Greyson's so fond of me, he can come over here and spend time with me himself. Even if this dress is gorgeous and completely my style (and, by the looks of it, size), I'm not going to spend the rest of the day all cooped up here waiting for him to decide whether or not he wants to grace me with his presence.

That infinity pool romp took at least an hour. If Greyson hasn't come by now or called me to tell me he's on his way over, he probably isn't going to.

I change into some of the least-dirty clothes from my own bag, then set out for the front desk.

"Hey, I'm Harley Davis," I tell a tan man with the most gorgeous skin. "I was wondering what activities you had available today?"

"Room 3B?" he asks, and I nod my head. "Oh. You have a spa session pre-booked for any time today, if you please. We have bike tours every hour on the hour as well. Until 10 PM. At our restaurant, the specials are all seafood. There is also a tour kiosk if you take a right, with tours to the volcano and more extensive tours."

Hmm. Decisions, decisions. I don't know how up I am for an extensive tour to who-knows-where. Then again, until 10 PM is pretty late, and I have an entire day to kill. Plus, after all those days trekking in the rainforest, I still feel a bit tired and grimy, even after that infinity pool swim.

"OK, I'd like to do the spa," I tell the man.

A few minutes later, I'm being massaged by countless hands, glorious-smelling fruity oils, hot stones, serenaded by relaxing violins, with different masks and wraps and scrubs applied to my every part. "The full package," was all the long-eyelashed woman said as soon as she heard my name. Another one of Greyson's pre-booked things, apparently. Calling this a 'spa' doesn't do it justice. It's nothing short of paradise.

By the time I totter out of there, I feel so relaxed and scrubbed and balmed and oiled that I wouldn't be surprised if I oozed into the marble floor of the hallway.

I still want to check out the bike tours.

There's no sign of Greyson, and when I stop in my room to change and grab a small camera, there's no message from him either. So, off on the bike tour I go.

Trees, sloths, the fresh air, glimpses of the volcano—the bike tour is wonderful. So wonderful that I end up staying longer and later to chat with a handsome Costa Rican I've met—Antonio.

By the time we get back, it's late and dark.

"Dinner plans?" he asks, nodding towards the restaurant.

"I..." It feels like a mean thing, ditching Greyson to go have dinner with Antonio. Especially when he's paying for my stay here. Then again, Greyson never out and said that he wanted to have dinner together. Is it really ditching someone if you don't have plans with him in the first place?

"I think I'll have room service again," I tell Antonio.

I should probably check to see if Greyson left a note for me. I have been gone a while, and he might worry. It's the considerate thing to do, with him paying for all this, at the very least.

"Oh no." His forehead creases with disappointment, his eyes shining. "But you will come for the dancing tonight?"

I find myself smiling. "There's dancing?"

"Of course! Starts at 10 PM in the lounge. It's great fun, lots of people come out."

That definitely sounds like my kind of fun. "Alright. I'll be there. Maybe I can even get my friend to come out too."

Antonio kisses my hand. "Till tonight, then, señorita."

"Till tonight," I say, grinning and waving.

Today has been one awesome surprise after another. Except for Greyson being MIA, of course. Then again, maybe he left a note or message in my room.

Once I get to my room, though, there's still nothing from him. I scowl at my reflection.

I should've gone to the restaurant with Antonio after all. Did Greyson really have that many calls to make? A whole day's worth?

I sit down and call Greyson up.

He picks up immediately. "Harley. You OK?"

"Yeah, I... thought maybe you'd be too busy to pick up. You know, with your calls and everything."

Maybe my tone is snarky and I'm being ungrateful, but I don't care. If Greyson wants to avoid me, he should just come out and say it. Tell me that it's over between us.

"If you need anything," he says now, "just tell me."

"Would seeing you be too much to ask? I'm starting to wonder if you're even at the same hotel, or if you just had them reroute this to your cell."

"No, I…" He sighs. "I would never leave you there on your own."

"Still didn't answer my first question."

A long pause. "I don't know if that's a good idea."

"We can't even have dinner in the restaurant with everyone else, like civilized people?"

"Oh. Yes. We can." Still that guarded tone that makes me scowl. "If you want, we can—"

I hang up, glaring at the phone for a few seconds after. We 'can'. If 'I want'.

What happened to the man who took what he wanted when he wanted, damn the consequences? What happened to the guy who just went with things?

"Maybe he was never there at all," I murmur to myself.

My reflection is still rosy after the bike ride, although my eyes are unmistakably disappointed.

"At least there's tonight to look forward to," I tell her.

CHAPTER 17

Greyson

I stare at the door numbly.

What the hell am I doing?

Avoiding Harley like this—what is it supposed to accomplish?

I get up, start to pace.

It's obvious: it'll stop me from getting carried away again. It'll set up some clear boundaries again. Prevent me from messing up again.

I glare at the glimpse of my reflection on the wardrobe door.

Still, what's the point? What was done, was done. Avoiding her now doesn't change what already happened.

Do I really want to, anyway?

I have my meal in my room, chowing down the tropical stew without hardly tasting it, wondering what she ordered. I try calling up my brothers, but none of them answer. I flick on the TV, mindlessly scrolling through channels. I shoot out some work emails, follow-up with the video editor who received our footage yesterday. Finally, I can't take it anymore. I go to Harley's room.

When I knock on the door, though, the maid, Maria, answers it.

"Looking for Madame?" she says, smiling.

"Yes."

"She said she was going to the poolside lounge party. Is great fun."

"Oh, OK."

Before I realize quite what I'm doing, I'm headed there. All the way down the hallway, I can hear the music: loud and saucy and sensual.

I should turn back. I can't.

Inside, the lights are a low red and slant across the dance floor and its sea of bodies. The bar at the far end looks busy. I scan the crowd, looking for her.

It takes a few scans before I see her. Even in the shadowed light, she's gorgeous. Golden waves hanging wild across her shoulders as she moves, turquoise-lidded eyes closed, full hips grooving: she's fully into it. And that dress clinging to her curves, paisley, white and blue outlining every part of her I ache to touch—my dress.

My cock hardens as I make for her.

Only once I'm there do I realize she's dancing with someone.

No.

In a smooth movement, I spin her away, into my arms. Her eyes snap open, her easy smile disappears. "Greyson, what the hell?"

I should be pissed too, and yet I can't be. "That dress looks good on you."

"Yeah, well, thought I might as well get some wear out of it." Her eyes are still narrowed on me, untrusting. "Finally finished with your calls?"

"Listen, I'm sorry, I—"

"No, you listen, if you want to play games, then I'm—"

My lips find hers and our bodies melt together.

There.

The spicy salsa music throbs our bodies on, and our foreheads tip together. She feels so good in my arms, her hips feel so good against mine.

Fuck. I could take her right here.

Our lips peel and remeet, peel and remeet. Christ do I want her.

Her eyes have a question in them when they meet mine, though.

All I can do is tell her the truth: "I've wanted to do that all day."

A smile quirks on her face.

"C'mon," she purrs, leading me by the hand to a bar set into a giant aquarium. "It's on me."

"No." I step in front of her to get to the bartender first. "I'm not letting you pay for a thing here."

She smirks. "Too late. I've already had a drink."

"All the more reason to make it up to you." I place some money on the countertop, catching the bartender's eye. "Two vodka oranges, please."

Almost immediately, two drinks appear. Harley picks up one and cocks a challenging eyebrow at me. "Trying to get me drunk?"

I lean in so that my lips are grazing hers as I speak. "For what we're going to do tonight, I don't need to."

Her eyes widen and yet her body molds to mine as I put an arm around her.

Already, I've lost track of why I tried to avoid seeing her earlier, tried to avoid this. It seems as pointless and impossible as avoiding breathing.

Next thing I know we're both drinking, downing our drinks fast and easy, cheers-ing the next ones, laughing, drinking from each other's drink. All I know is that I want those lips on mine.

I dance us back to the dance floor, back to the sea of bodies.

We pass the man who might've been with Harley before. I don't give him a second look. Harley is mine.

This next song is even faster than the one before it, conga drum beat slamming our bodies together then away, together then away. My cock is hard enough to burst, and Harley's practically panting.

"Now," I kiss into her ear, sweeping her up into my arms.

"Greyson!" she laughs, gaping up at me. "What are you..."

"What I should've done this morning. What I wanted to."

I walk her through the crowd, out the lounge, down the hallway.

"Greyson! Put me down!" she demands, still laughing.

I pause. "Say it like you mean it and I'll be happy to."

"Fine." She bites back a smile. "Put me..." Her voice lowers. "In your room."

My cock twinges. Fuck yes I will.

I grin. "That's not the only place I'll be putting you."

Seconds later, it seems, it's me and her in my room, twining in my bed. The dance continues.

"I can't believe how good this is," I kiss into her lips.

"I can't believe how good we are," she kisses back into mine.

And then we lose ourselves in the sheets and the warmth of each other's bodies. Before I kiss off her dress like I'm burning to, I get one final good look at her in it.

"I knew this dress was you. I knew you'd look fucking gorgeous in it."

She smirks. "Maybe I should keep it on?"

I grab a strap and pull it down, smirking myself. "Not a chance."

Below she's got on a lacy bra that shows off the pink buds of her nipples. My grin widens as I survey her. It really is insane how hot she is. "You brought this for a camping trip?"

Her grin is downright devilish. "What? You never know when you might have to seduce a gorilla to get out of trouble."

I pull down the other strap and bury my face in her cleavage, inhale deeply, then grin up at her, probably like an idiot. "Has it worked? Have you seduced this gorilla?"

She bites her lip, her hands rippling down my body. "Guess we'll just have to see."

As they grasp my boner, she exhales hard. "Wow. Yeah, guess I did."

My gaze is still on her breasts, bouncing their perfect handfuls in my hands. "What happens now?"

As I peel off her bra and rub my lips over her nipples, she moans. "I... don't know."

I lightly bite down on her nipple. "You don't know?"

"I..."

My hand sweeps down and presses into her panties. They're deliciously wet. "You sure?"

"I... uh, Greyson, please."

My finger dips under and inside, thrumming in her wet warmth. "Let me enjoy you first."

All she can do now is moan, her grip tightened on my painfully hard cock. She's wet as fuck, and I dive in to taste it myself.

She gasps, and, seconds later, comes.

And we're only getting started.

**

I wake up cold. It's still dark out, night, but she's gone. I sit up quickly, but I needn't have worried. She's out there in the pool, the clear waters showing off her beautiful naked body.

"Hey," I say, going to join her.

"Hey." She smiles, reaching to pop a chocolate in my mouth. "Didn't want to wake you."

I chuckle as I enjoy the taste. "Earlier today I got so bored I ended up napping for a good part of it. Believe me, the last thing I need more of is sleep."

Her face falls as I pad into the pool. The water is cool, yet perfect.

"I'm sorry about before, really," I say. "I just don't want..."

"What?" Her voice is hard. "To see me after this? To have this continue any longer than it has to?"

"No, I—" My hands find hers. "You don't get it. I've never done this kind of thing before. I always swore I'd never..."

"Get involved with an employee?"

"Yeah. But you came along and—" I exhale. "No. I'm not going to pin this on you. I'm supposed to the producer. I'm supposed to know better."

She's looking out at the darkened horizon, face unreadable. "Can't we just enjoy this while it lasts? And if after, if reality back home isn't... the same, then accept it then?"

She adds a rueful afterthought: "I'm not going to go blabbing to the media either, if that's what you're worried about."

"I never thought that. The others, though... And right now, the company is vulnerable. I'm not my father."

She offers me a tentative smile it takes effort not to kiss. "Maybe that's a good thing? At least if some of the rumors I've heard are true."

"You have no idea." My hands slip around her waist, press her naked soft form to me. It feels so... good.

She doesn't say anything, and though normally I'd leave it there, more words slip out.

"He cheated on my mom. More times than I can count. He was friends with sketchy men I wouldn't even say hi to on the street. And that's only the things that have come out about him. God knows what else there is."

"I'm sorry."

She looks like she means it, so intently that this time I can't help it: I do kiss her. It's a sad, sweet kiss, slow and painstaking. Shit, I don't ever want this night to end.

"My dad cheated on my mom too," she says quietly now, eyes back on the horizon. "I don't think she ever got over it, even now."

"Mine either," I say, my arms around her again.

And we lean there, her and me, cool waters around us, breeze playing with the droplets on our skin. And we say nothing because we don't have to.

I don't know how long we stand there, except that at some point, an orange-yellow stain starts to form on the bridge of the horizon.

"Thank you." She whirls around to smile nervously at me, eyes glistening. "For everything. This place is gorgeous."

"No." I kiss her. "Thank you." I kiss her again. "Let's stay..." I kiss her again. "This has been the best..."

And then our kisses can't stop and it's good, too, because my mind is stupid and ridiculous, and if I didn't know better, I'd think I was going to say: Let's stay a week. Let's never go back.

CHAPTER 18

Harley

Four days.

As my eyes flutter open, I mouth the words to myself, like some crazy secret: "Four days."

Four days of breakfast in bed, dinner in the restaurant, dessert in bed or the pool, and, one night, a surprise visit to a grotto where Greyson had set everything up for a romantic candlelit dinner, just us two.

Four days that felt like four seconds, like four weeks. But now, this morning, the dream has to end. Time to go back to reality.

His strong arms around me make me so safe and cozy that I almost want to drift off back to sleep. But I don't let myself. I want to savor this moment, enjoy it for as long as I can. After all, in just a few hours, we'll be back on a plane, on our way back home. Home, where...

I close my eyes firmly. Let's not think about that.

But now my mind is buzzing and I shift, try to move Greyson's arm off me so I can get up. But even in his sleep, his arm repositions itself around me, holding me more firmly.

When I move his arm the next time, he kisses the back of my neck. "Morning."

I turn to kiss him on the cheek. "Morning."

I slink around so that we're lying down facing each other, nose tip to nose tip. His coal-brown eyes can't decide between being open or closed. Either way, they look happy, a bit dazed—probably how I look too.

"So," I say.

"So," he says.

It's become our thing, our saying, stupidly enough. When we want to leave, stay, or just escape for a quickie, it always starts the same.

"So." "So…"

This time, I don't realize why I said it until I continue, "About today—"

He frowns. We've done a good job at not mentioning it, until now. Now, there's no more escaping it.

"You're right." He shifts his position so he's more upright. "We should get going. I hate being late for a plane, even if we are taking a friend's jet."

"Oh." I grin. "We are?"

He grins, too. "It's an old family friend's. Though he parks it at the airport, and we still have to go through security and all that."

I sigh, mock-scandalized. "Whatever is the point of being a multimillionaire if you still have to go through security like a peasant?"

He chuckles, kisses me on the corner of my mouth.

I steal a kiss, then roll out of bed before he can catch the expression on my face. The thought I haven't dared voice, even to myself: What if we delayed going back? What if…

Forget it, Harley.

"So eager to leave?" Greyson jokes from behind me.

There's something in his voice that makes me turn his way, but by the time I peer at him he's already got his gorgeously broad back to me, pulling on his t-shirt.

The next hour or so is a flurry of packing, dressing, kissing, and nibbling on the final breakfast pancakes and sausages the staff brought us.

"I'm going to miss you," I tell Maria, clasping both her hands warmly.

"And we are going to miss you too!" she says, with enough enthusiasm that she actually seems like she means it, isn't just getting paid to. "You and Mr. Storm are quite the couple."

"Oh." I laugh. "We aren't… It's not…" Seeing her forehead crinkle with confusion, I force a smile. Just end the conversation. "Thanks."

Luckily, Greyson's in the bathroom, shaving and doing who-knows-what-else man stuff.

Maria leaves soon after, with a final hug goodbye, and then it's me and Greyson, in a cab on the way to the airport. Greyson's head is turned to the window. Both of us are silent.

"This was nice," he says quietly, at some point.

"Almost getting killed by a fer-de-lance snake, bumbling around the rainforest after Russel, nearly getting our limbs eaten by a grumpy mother puma." I give a joking sigh. "Ah yes, getting nostalgic already."

He slings me a smirk. "Goof."

I can't resist the earnestness in his eyes, sigh for real this time. "OK. You're right. This was…" I clasp his hand. "Amazing. I definitely haven't thanked you enough. I'm not sure I can. This was the experience of a lifetime. Working with you and the team has been incredible. And this gorgeous hotel, just... Thank you."

Greyson's smile is off, and he peels his eyes away what seems to be too soon. "It's been a pleasure working with you, too. And will be, I hope."

As he releases my hand, I lift my eyebrows. "Is that your way of saying that I'm hired, not just on a transitional basis? Don't you already have a cinematographer, though?"

"Gabriel's been muttering about retiring for years now," Greyson says. "Besides, you're good—really good. You've got an eye for the frames, for pacing. Even watching the shots we got on your camera"—I blush, thinking of the last time we watched them, naked in bed together two nights ago—"I can see they're gold."

"Good, I just..."—How can I say this without it being awkward?—"want to be sure that this isn't... you know..."

The brightness on Greyson's face is snapped out in an instant. "You really think I'm that kind of guy?"

"No, I just—"

"Forget it." His head swings away, his tone suddenly flat. "Either take the job or not. Up to you."

"I'll take it," I say.

"Good," he says.

And the rest of the ride to the airport is in silence. Once we're inside the airy window-walled building, Greyson is all business. We get checked in, go through security in what seems like a couple of well-planned, efficient minutes. Greyson has some frequent flier or premium customer card that gets us through easily.

At Starbucks, Greyson's already ordered his coffee when he asks me, "Want anything?"

"It's fine. I can get myself a peppermint tea."

"One peppermint tea," he tells the barista.

"Greyson," I say, as she walks away to make our orders.

"What?"

"I told you—"

He waves his hand. "It's nothing."

"It's not nothing."

"Fine." He scowls as he eyes me. "I can write it off as a business expense. Happy?"

"It's just that, after all those nights at Nayara Springs, I don't want you to think—"

"What? That you're using me for free peppermint teas?"

"No, I just—"

"I enjoy spending money on you. Nothing wrong with that."

As soon as the words are out of Greyson's lips his eyes widen. Then he scowls. "That came out... Forget it."

Talk about awwwwwkwarrrrd...

"Sure," I say.

Minutes later, as we're sipping our drinks, sitting on less-than-comfy airport seats, he continues, "About before—I overreacted."

"Which time?"

Greyson glances my way, chuckles. "Maybe I deserve that. I was talking about your comment as to why I want you on my team as Storm Media's cinematographer. It got to me." He frowns. "My dad was exactly the type of guy who would hire someone just because they had a thing together. Me, I knew as soon as I saw you behind the camera for the first time out in the rainforest that I wanted you on our team."

"Oh." I sip my tea too fast, burning my tongue slightly. "Good."

"I want you to know that," he says vehemently. "And that, whatever happens when we get back, as long as you want to work for Storm Inc. and show the skill you have this past week, you will."

"No matter what?" I tease him, slurring slightly as I nurse my still-burnt tongue.

"Don't push it."

"Damn it." I sigh. "I so wanted to instate a 'Bring Your Cactus to Work Day'."

His attempt not to smile fails. "One thing at a time, Harley."

I give him an 'OK, captain' gesture. "Gotcha."

He smiles at me and keeps on smiling. I smile at him and keep on smiling. I couldn't stop if I tried.

It's only a half an hour or so later, when we're on the jet, which is as private-plane fancy as you'd expect (the highlight for me is the white leather seats that also happen to be memory foam, perfectly shaping themselves to our butts) that Greyson says, "Good thing you wanted to get home."

"What are you talking about?" I ask.

The look he directs my way is quizzical. "You mentioned how you missed your cousin and ferret at least seven different times. Plus your to-do list of stuff for when you got back." His gaze goes assessing. "You did want to go back, didn't you?"

I turn so that I'm facing the window, glad he can't see how my heart has suddenly picked up its pace. "Yeah, definitely. Of course. Why?"

He shrugs. "Couple times when I was drunk or tired, I figured…" He shakes his head, presses his lips together. "Forget it."

I whirl around to glare at him. "Oh, hell no. You have to tell me now."

"Harley—"

"Greyson. Tell me."

"Can't you just forget it? It's not a big deal."

"No," I sing-song, "Tell me."

"Seriously."

"Seriously. Tell me!"

"Just how nice it would be to stay another week or two, maybe even longer."

"Oh," I say, so I don't say what I want to say.

"Right." He turns to face his window. "Like I said, not a big deal."

"Hmm," I say, so I still don't say what I want to say.

As he drifts off beside me, it takes all the self-control I have not to say 'Me too.'

Although I don't have enough to stop myself from wondering: What happens next?

CHAPTER 19

Greyson

I wake up in the middle of the night. We left the window slot open and I can see murky clouds scudding across a navy sky. Harley's asleep, her head drooped onto my shoulder. I leave it there.

I glare at the clouds.

You're losing it, Greyson.

Although that isn't right at all. I've already lost it. Sleeping with Harley was... not a mistake, but sure as shit not a smart move either.

Staying with her at Nayara Springs days longer than necessary, while dodging calls from my brothers and just about everyone else, then admitting to her that I'd actually considered staying even longer- what the fuck was I thinking?

That's just it: I wasn't.

But now...

My gaze wanders to Harley's sleeping face, her half-smiling lips.

Wonder if the smile would grow if I gave them a kiss...

I grab my phone to distract myself.

On it, there's a message on my voicemail that I got while in the airport but never checked.

"Hi Greyson, it's Madeline. Good to hear you'll be back soon. Just wanted to check in and give you a heads-up on something that's in the works before you get back, if you have a chance. No pressure."

Fuck.

It's the 'no pressure' that tips me off. Despite her chirpy, 'fish are people too' tone, Madeline only uses the expression when things are absolute shit. Which means, on top of everything else, once I get back I'm going to have some sort of shit-storm to deal with.

Movement on my shoulder has me glancing Harley's way. Despite her slight shifting, she's still as contentedly asleep as ever. Somehow looking at her pretty sleeping face is like a visual stress ball: I can't stay frustrated staring at it.

I turn away and try to look to the clouds. There's something prickling at the edge of my mind, something that has to be dealt with, sooner or later.

I leave it for later.

**

When I wake up, it's hours later.

"God," Harley groans, rubbing at her neck. "Is your brain made of stone? I don't know if my neck's ever going to recover from how heavy your head is."

I shrug, smirk. "Didn't know the mystery pillow was your head until I woke up."

"Yeah, well, I wasn't under the impression this was a fair transaction—your shoulder was supposed to be my pillow, end of story."

God she's cute when she's pretend angry. "How can I ever make it up to you?"

"Take me home."

Her words are jarringly serious in our joking exchange. Her mouth falls open, as if she's as surprised by this admission as I am.

"Wow, that came out weird." She laughs. "I just mean—"

"I want to," I blurt out. Then I frown. "I'll make sure the cab gets you home safely."

"You don't have to do that. I don't know why I said that. I think I'm just tired, and half-delirious, and—"

"I want to."

"Greyson—"

"If you keep trying to argue, I am going to buy you four ice cream sundaes in the airport."

"Four?!? Don't be ridiculous. I don't even want one."

I feel like a boy, delighting in her outraged grimace. "Too bad."

"But that's so wasteful! All that trash and the ice cream won't even be eaten—"

I just shrug. "Told you my terms."

"You're a jerk," she snaps.

"A jerk who's seeing you home safely tonight."

"I'm not a damsel in distress."

"Seem pretty distressed right now."

Her hand jabs out to give me a playful slap. I catch it at the same time our eyes catch. "Careful."

Next second, I'm bringing her hand to my mouth, then her head to my mouth. Then I'm undoing my pants, sliding myself inside her…

"Hello, Earth to Greyson, we're supposed to put on our seatbelts."

Harley pokes me again, then juts up her chin in the direction of where the captain probably just gave the instructions I didn't at all hear thanks to my fucking-Harley-on-a-plane-fantasy.

Fuck.

"Right," I grumble, putting it on.

The important thing is: I won. This time, at least.

By the time we get off the plane, out of the airport and outside to the cabs, Harley is already trying to get her own.

"I'm a big girl," she tells me as she jumps inside a cab. "I can make it home by myself. I have plenty of times before."

"It's 4 AM," I tell her as I follow her inside, "I'll see you home."

As the cab pulls away, Harley rolls her eyes at me. "Really, this is silly."

I just shrug.

The cab takes us down streets that are empty and forlorn-looking. Probably I just need sleep. Both of us do.

Back in our bed at Nayara Springs, we did sleep, just... half the time when I woke up, with Harley naked beside me... how the hell was I not supposed to get a hard-on, start kissing her? And when she started nuzzling me back, rubbing herself against me, how the hell was I not supposed to start fucking her?

"Almost there," Harley says suddenly. "Thanks again. I guess I'll... be seeing you?"

At the Storm Media office. Tomorrow. Right.

"Take tomorrow off," I say.

A week would be better, and as much for me as for her. I need to get my head screwed on straight. Give myself a chance to get caught up. But I know Harley. She'll want to get to work straightaway.

"I'm fine," she says.

"Do I have to order you?" I give her a hard look.

"No, boss." Her mouth forms a mocking pout and I have to clench my teeth so I don't give her a punishing kiss.

Even in the dark, the shape of her is like a beacon.

"Careful Ms. Davis," I find myself saying.

"Or?"

Or I'll yank down your shorts and take you, right here, right now.

Fuck if I'm not about to do it, hard-on pressing against my pants, reaching for her...

The car pulls over, and the cabbie says, "This it?"

"Oh." Harley exhales, peels her gaze off me to look at the red-stone building outside. "Yeah. It is."

Her smile is uncertain as she opens the door, riffling through her purse. "Thanks."

"I've got this." I hand the cabbie the money then step out after her.

She's so flustered that she doesn't even notice that I'm out here, carrying her bag, until we've walked halfway to the door.

Before she can speak, I put a hand on her arm. "I meant what I said about making sure you get home safely."

"Please." Harley's laugh is half-hearted, her smile unsure. "The schizophrenic ladybug-killing hobo who lived outside our building moved on, like, months ago."

And then we're there at the front door. And I'm taking her in, up to her room, laying her on her bed, ripping off her clothes, then fucking her, fucking her, fucking her, and it's just as good as I thought, even better, except...

I'm still standing here, looking at her.

For fuck's sake, Greyson, get yourself together!

"So," she says.

"So," I say.

What I should do isn't what I want to.

I give her a quick kiss on the lips, then rip myself away.

As I'm walking away, she says, "Greyson?"

"Yeah?"

"Uh, you're still holding my bag."

Shit. Smooth, Greyson, smooth.

"Right." I go back to her without looking at her. Don't think about kissing her. Don't think about her. Don't think. "Here. 'Night."

As I'm walking away again, she murmurs, "'Night, Greyson."

"'Night, Harley," I say, still walking as fast as I can.

CHAPTER 20

Harley

His kiss tingles on my lips all the way up to my place. One foot in the entrance and I hear scampering.

"Anchovy!" I hiss, seconds before he leaps into my arms.

I let my fingers run along his furry brown back happily as he squeaks happily.

"Shh," I whisper, "You'll wake Han, and you know how she values her beauty sleep."

"I'm awake," Hannah says, snapping on a light.

She smiles vaguely at me, as if I'm the one wearing a furry bathrobe and the furry sloth-head slippers I got her last Christmas.

"I'm sorry," I say, "did we wake you?"

Hannah shakes her head as she comes over to throw her arms around me. "I couldn't miss you coming back. I'm so happy to see you! How was everything?"

I hug her tighter. "I'm so happy to see you! It was... I... don't even know where to begin!"

Anchovy leaps down and races overjoyed circles around us as my bag flops on the floor.

"Begin with your hot boss," Hannah says, with a devilish eyebrow wiggle, "and how everything went."

"Ugh," I groan. "It was... OK, it was amazing. He was. Is. And, he..." I try to bite my lip and hold it in, but this is Han. "He just dropped me off, actually. And kissed me. After we spent four days together in the fanciest resort I've ever seen."

Hannah's jaw drops open and drops even further as I speak.

She grasps both my hands. "Tell me everything." We're halfway to the couch when she pauses. "Shit, you're probably exhausted. Ignore that, you can tell me everything tomorrow. Go to bed."

I go over to the couch and sit down. "No, I'm actually... not super tired anymore. For some reason."

Probably the kiss, but I'm not about to go into how a grade-school-worthy chaste kiss has injected me with energy like a triple-shot espresso.

"OK then." Hannah sits beside me. "Tell me everything, then."

I do. I start at the beginning and go from there. Hannah giggles and groans and 'oohs' at all the right parts, and in the end, she laughs.

"What?" I ask her.

"He likes you," she says simply. "And you actually really like him too."

"Hmm." Patting Anchovy absently on the head, I shrug. "You don't think you might be reading into things?"

Another incredulous laugh. "Reading into things? Harley, you spent a glorious four days with the man camped out in a luxury hotel and, in your words, wanted to spend even longer. If anything, I'm reading too little into things."

"Maybe it's just the opportunity," I continue, "just the excitement of finally nabbing my dream job, meeting one of my film idols..."

Hannah makes a skeptical sound. "Sounds like your delusional self needs some sleep."

I sink into the couch gratefully. "You're probably right—about the sleep part, at least. 'Night, Han."

"Oh no you don't." Next thing I know, Hannah's pulling me to my feet, over to my room. "No way do I want a lecture about morning etiquette because I decided to chew my Shreddies and woke you up. You are sleeping in your own room with the door closed."

"Yes ma'am," I say sleepily as she helps me along.

All at once, the weariness hits me, like a wave that had been sitting placid.

As soon as my head hits the pillow, I'm out, gone and...

**

I wake up to Hannah's "You're still asleep?!?"

I glare at her with my eyes still closed. "You're still here?"

She snorts. "Still here? I just got back from work. Have you really been sleeping all this time?"

"Mrmph," I say noncommittally, although I do open my eyes.

Sure enough, it's broad daylight and my phone says it's 4:37 PM with one missed call.

One missed call from Greyson Storm.

!!!

"Good thing Anchovy still had a crapton of food from yesterday," Hannah says as she comes to my door.

"Are you still just slopping a mountain of minced meat into his food bowl every few days?" I grumble.

"Why not?" Hannah folds her arms across her chest. "He likes it."

"Yeah, and my favorite food in the world is caramel corn. Doesn't mean I should eat mountains of it all day every day."

"Harley." Hannah's giving me her motherly know-it-all look I hate. "Anchovy is a ferret."

"And a damn fine healthy ferret. Who I intend to keep that way."

"Why don't you feed yourself first, then we can worry about Anchovy."

"You were the one who brought it up," I grumble, as I straggle to my feet. "Anyway, you're so bothered, why don't you go escape and have a perfect date with the Most Handsome Man Alive?"

"Because I wanted to spend some time with my grumpy lazy friend."

I crack a half-smile. "OK, sorry. I am grumpy. I think I need some food." Hannah raises an eyebrow. "OK. A lot of food."

We end up whipping up some homemade olive and pepperoni pizza. Once I've eaten and admitted that Greyson called and I still haven't called him back, Hannah shoes me out of there. "Call him!"

"God, it's only been like seven hours since he called, chill."

When I call, Greyson picks up after the first ring. "Hey."

"Hey," I say, "You called. What's up?"

"Just wanted to see how you were doing." His tone is natural, not awkward.

"Great," I say, trying to take the same tone. "I slept in until like 4:30, though. I think I was a wee bit tired."

Greyson chuckles.

"What about you?" I ask, "Tough day back?"

"No," he says. "Surprisingly. Had to catch up on emails and return some calls, but nothing like what I expected. Thought there would be a load of work and problems waiting for me. And I did get a look at our episode."

"Already?!?"

"Our video editors are fast." I can hear the proud smile in his voice, and it makes me smile too. "And good. That's why I called, actually. Thought if you wanted to stop by and take a look…"

"Oh." I frown. "Guess it's too late now."

He pauses. "I don't know. I got the footage on a USB stick, I thought that maybe if you wanted to see it…"

"Of course I do! So, you'll hand it over tomorrow?"

"I can."

This conversation feels like it's going odd. Like there's something I'm not grasping.

"Of course I'd rather see it right this instant," I continue, "But I wouldn't want you to come all this way just to drop it off."

"I wouldn't."

A pause, then he says, "What if we saw it together?"

"Oh." My hand has been tapping a yay-me beat into my leg for who knows how long. I force it still. "I don't know, my place is… Messy? Anchovy isn't great with strangers either. And I wouldn't want to impose."

"I know a place," Greyson says. "If you're game."

"A surprise?" I already like the sound of this.

"A surprise."

"I'm in," I say.

"Great, I'll be there in 10."

"See you."

I drop the phone on my bed and race off. "Hannah, tell me you're still here! Greyson just invited me out and if you still want to hang, I can totally cancel on him. And I have nothing to wear!"

Hannah, on the couch, just smiles. "You go off with Greyson. Roger will be thrilled I can come over."

"You sure?"

"Positive. You and I had our pizza time anyway. We can do girl's night tomorrow? Legally Blonde?"

"You bet," I say, my relief rising and falling just as fast. "But I'm in PJs and my hair is insane!"

"Right." Hannah comes over. "On it."

Fifteen minutes and one slightly untrue 'on my way' text to Greyson later, I'm hurrying into the elevator. I check my reflection with a grin.

Grimly, despite my protests that my hair 'can't be tamed', Hannah calmed its madness into two French braids as I threw some brown eye shadow on as fast as I could without looking like a makeup-challenged hooker. I did a quick hobo shower with my loofah and some almond body gel and then I was as good as new. Or as good as anyone could be when given 10 minutes' notice. I chose a tie-dye lace-up dress that's comfy and sexy, an unusual combination as far as I'm concerned, and now, here I am, ready for my... date? Work meeting?

You don't kiss your boss, stupid.

OK, here I am, ready for my whatever-the-hell, dressed to kill.

Greyson's at the curb in a slick white Mercedes with the top down, staring.

"Too much?" I ask, biting my smile.

"No. You look great."

I get in beside him and we get driving.

"If there's any hair on my dress, it's Anchovy's," I babble.

What the hell is up with me?

Greyson quirks an eyebrow. "Anchovy?"

"Not an actual anchovy." I giggle. "Although that could be a neat pet. It's my ferret. His name is Anchovy."

A smile pricks the corners of his lips. "Of course your ferret's name is Anchovy."

I can't seem to keep myself from smiling either, even though he's teasing me. "What's that supposed to mean?"

"It means that you're a surprise wrapped in a mystery." He slings a gaze my way. "And I'm excited for tonight."

"I would be too," I say, "if I knew what tonight was going to be."

"You'll see," is all he'll say.

And though I want to leave it at that, and should, I can't seem to sit in silence tonight for some reason.

"What if I guess where we're headed?" I say. "Your place, some restaurant, a fancy bar I can't afford... are you even going to tell me if I guess correctly?"

Greyson grins. "No."

I sigh. "I guess I shouldn't complain. I do like surprises."

No point in mentioning how the biggest surprise of all is how I feel when I'm around him. Safe yet dangerous. Excited yet frustrated. Giddy yet earnest.

We get there a few minutes later. Wherever 'there' is. To me, it just looks like a nice but weirdly dark-windowed condo building.

"Are you taking me here to kill me?" I ask as we walk into the lobby. Greyson presses a card to a box and the first set of doors opens up, to show a grand total of nothing.

"Not yet," he says, taking my hand. "Trust me."

"I don't want to be ungrateful, but when you said surprise, I didn't really have in mind some abandoned building," I admit. "Even if it is nicer than any inhabited building I've ever been in."

"It's a condo my dad bought and was about to open for buyers. He died before he could, though. Apparently there's a few electrical and permit issues that he hadn't quite sorted out either—another damn thing my brothers and I have to sort out now." He frowns as he presses the button of the elevator. "Forget it. I didn't take you here to complain."

I give him a cheeky smile. "Don't worry about it. It's nice to learn that rich, powerful people have real-life problems like the rest of us."

He chuckles as we step into the elevator and ascend.

Once we step out in the penthouse, I begin to understand.

"I took you up here to see this," he says simply as we walk out onto an open-air rooftop patio.

"Wow," is all I can think to say.

We have to be hundreds of feet above ground, with a view of the city that must cost millions. All around us, lit-up skyscrapers reach for the sky as the streets below buzz, a grid-work of tiny lit-up movement.

We walk over to the balcony, and as I look out at it all, Greyson wraps his arms around me. "What do you think?"

"I think... good surprise."

I ease my body into his. It feels so good. So warm. So right.

His nearness is making me horny, too. Right here and now, if he just lifted my dress and kissed my neck and even did more, I'd let him.

His breath is hot against my ear. "You hungry?"

Jesus, he turns me on.

But just as I'm burrowing into him further, he steps away. "I got you something."

I resist the urge to sigh. Get it together, Harley, every minute with this man can't be a sex-fest. Even 'I got you something' sounds different on his lips. I've had guys try to impress me by buying me things before and it always left me cold. But with Greyson…

He holds out the bag of caramel corn, and I laugh. "I was just talking about this today. How did you…"

"You were raving about it when we were drunk one night. Nayara Springs didn't have any caramel corn. You were swearing up and down that you would do anything for some, even UberEats some from the US and foot the bill."

I laugh. "Nothing like a good thousand-plus UberEats bill to cancel out a week's salary."

Greyson opens the bag, takes out a handful, and raises one to my lips. "Better late than never."

I close my lips onto a piece, close enough to his finger to suck the tip.

"Harley," he says quietly.

He must feel it too. The sexual charge in the air.

He pries himself away from me and goes over to sit down on a pillowed metal couch I hadn't noticed before. He pats the spot beside him. "StormTV episode first. Then…"

I like the sound of 'then', but I go to sit beside him with just a smile for response. I really am excited to see the show, no matter how distracting he is.

Greyson gets a laptop out of his bag and plugs the little USB stick into the side. Then, we watch.

It's the weirdest thing, watching the episode. The weirdest and best. Of course I've watched my stuff on a screen before, but this is different. The professional editing, the gloss and care taken over every shot—the show looks and feels so, well, good, that I have trouble believing I was the one who filmed these scenes, even though I remember the fear rippling in the pit of my belly as the baby alligator swam towards us and how excited I was to get both of those sloths in the shot.

"It's something, isn't it?" Greyson says quietly, as we watch.

"I can't believe it," I say honestly. "I didn't realize…"

"That you were this good? You are."

"It's not just me," I protest, "This video editor is obviously a pro, and without your direction…"

I trail off, and he just shrugs.

As we continue watching, he says, "With all the stop-starting and change of plans, I didn't expect the show to turn out this good. But it's brilliant. We haven't had a StormTV special turn out this epic since the first season."

Tears come to my eyes, but I blink them back hastily. "I don't know what to say."

"You don't have to say anything." Greyson gestures to the screen, where the credits are going across. There I am: Harley Davis. "This is enough."

Only it's not, not now that it's over and we're sitting next to each other, his leg against mine, his tensed arm beside mine. God, he's so close and so far, and all I know is that, pulsing through me, wild and frissoning and mad is this: I want him I want him I want him.

I grab the caramel corn bag, try a sad attempt at a laugh. "It was so good, we forgot..."

Without a word, Greyson takes a piece and lifts it to my lips. Our eyes lock. My lips suction around the corn, then his finger. Suck.

Greyson's eyes fall to my lips. I swirl my tongue around his finger.

Fuck.

Next second, our lips land on each other's, our hands rippling over one another. Our entire bodies rub against each other. I'm on his lap and he's pulling up my dress. I'm fumbling with his belt. And we're kissing and kissing and kissing. Even with how good it feels, his lips, my lips, his tongue leading mine, his fingertips stroking and caressing me so well I'm groaning down his throat, I know I need more, need him, inside me. Now.

Finally, his pants are off, his erection springing up and ready in his briefs. He snaps the waistband of my panties and I groan. I snap the waistband of his briefs, and he chuckles.

Eyes locked, smirking—you first, no, you—we pull each other's underwear down. Next second, I'm sitting on his erection, and him entering me is nothing short of exquisite.

"Oh fucking yes," I groan as his hardness swells inside of me.

"I've wanted to do this since this morning," he growls. "Since last night."

"Ughhh," is all I can say as his cock pierces deeper into me.

And then he's all the way in me, flexing himself in me, and it's pure ecstasy, his massive thickness filling me utterly.

He gives my ass a little slap and I start riding him. Up and down, side to side, I move my hips onto him, already crazy-close to climax.

My moans have joined into one unending howl, while he grunts with pleasure and exertion.

Up. Down. Side. To Side. More and more and more. Until I'm coming, and he's slapping my ass, slapping my orgasms out of me, one after the other. Until at my final, most intense orgasm yet, I can feel him release inside me, and I lose it.

Everything swirls out of focus as I ride the wave of the strongest orgasm I've ever had. Oh fuck. "Oh yes, fuck, fuck!"

When I come to, I'm slumped on him, and his fingertips are running all over my body lightly, teasingly, almost unbearably. It's keeping my senses hyper-aware, keeping me horny.

Our lips meet and remeet lazily.

"You're a fucking beaut," he says, not that he needs to. The way he's looking at me says it already.

He tugs at one of my waves with a look akin to wonder. "How did I ever..."

"Good looks," I quip.

We crack up, as his gaze wanders aware, off to the city. "It's weird. Like I can't get enough…" He trails off, doesn't have to say more. 'Weird' is the least of how this feels. Normally, I'd be enjoying the ride, mentally trying to come up with an excuse of why I have to go—Sorry, my cousin suddenly contracted diphtheria… My diplomat friend needs me… I have polio. But right now, right here, all I feel like doing is giving Greyson another kiss.

As I do so, I feel something hard poking at my thigh.

Clearly, I'm not the only one finding this all hot as hell.

He picks me up, carries me to the railing and, as I'm looking out at the city, lifts me onto his cock. "Ever been balcony fucked?"

I don't know whether to laugh or cry. Even with the cool railing pressing against my front, right now I feel so fucking good. "No."

"Good."

God, him inside me feels amazing. And how did he get so hard so fast again anyway?

"I want this to be ours," he murmurs into my ear, as he pierces deep inside me. "Ours."

And all I can do, as I come again, is moan.

The night takes us right back to the hotel room: a blur of sex, sleep, holding. Greyson gets a blanket and a mattress he had stowed somewhere, and we sleep under the stars and wake up and fuck and sleep some more. It's like a trance, like two magnets that have found each other and can't pry themselves free. Not that I want to.

By the time the sun crests the horizon, reaching pinky orange strands across the sky, I'm in his arms again.

"It's time," he says.

He doesn't have to say for what.

"You sure you don't want to take another day off?" Greyson asks me.

"Almost forgot—I think I may have to," I remember out loud. "Your assistant sent me a crapload of videos to watch for orientation from home. So I'm stuck home whether I want to be or not."

"She did?" Something passes across Greyson's face. "Oh."

He forces a smile. "You're the lucky one, then. I wouldn't mind another day away from the office. When I'm there, the calm doesn't feel real. When I left, things were one mistake away from shambles."

I pat him. "Give it time."

He rustles my hair. "Thanks, you."

I force myself to an upright position, stretching luxuriantly. Greyson's gaze on my ass feels good. "Well, boss, we've got a full day ahead of us."

I wait for him to give my ass a smack like he wants to, but I just hear a sharp exhale. "Yes. That, we do."

Guess it really is work time.

CHAPTER 21

Greyson

As I walk into my office, I have to pause, sure I forgot something. It takes me a minute to figure out the reason for the missing feeling in my chest: Harley.

It took all my self-control to let her leave my car earlier today, to not suggest a breakfast, brunch, snack, anything as an excuse to spend a few more hours with her, minutes.

But I have a job to get to. I can't shirk all my responsibilities just because I've found something I like doing more. Someone I like doing way more.

Anyway, now that I've been making a lot of the final calls on the new StormTV episode, I've started liking work. Not that the days and weeks ahead will necessarily resemble my first day back, but maybe I can swing it. And more time in the producer's chair too.

No sooner have I gotten to my office and sat in my chair, than a knock has me getting up again.

Opening the door reveals my three brothers all grinning at me.

"Surprise!" Emerson says.

"Why don't you look happier to see us?" Landon asks.

"The only time you guys show up in full force is when there's something wrong," I point out.

"And the only time you call us all to be together is when there's something wrong," Nolan retorts as he saunters in. "Can't us popping in just be for a fond brotherly reunion? After all, word on the street is that we almost lost you."

I step back to allow them in, then shrug. "Being out in the wild has its dangers."

"But you fighting a fer-de-lance snake?!?" Emerson actually looks excited, even though the closest he's been to a rainforest is the Eyewitness books we used to read as kids.

"You know Russel likes to embellish things."

"Huh." Nolan makes a face. "Well, if half what he says about you and that new cinematographer is true..."

I force my voice calm. Nolan thrives on getting to people. "That better not be why you're here."

He eyes me coolly. "And if it is?"

Landon clears his throat. "Guys. Don't be stupid. We're not here to wag our fingers at you for your personal life, Greyson. Although I will tell you it's all over the office, and it doesn't look good."

"It's all over the office?" I say.

Landon's frown is dire. "It's not exactly passed around over lunch, but I've had enough cryptic comments and looks to know that it's common knowledge."

Fuck.

Harley hasn't even gotten back to work yet, and people are talking?

"Maybe I should say something," I wonder out loud, knowing it's a shit idea as soon as I say it.

Landon just shakes his head. "Just lie low and give it time to blow over, and everything will be fine."

"You're probably right. Although it still shouldn't have come to this."

I'm pissed, disappointed—in myself, most of all. What good did I really expect to come out of sleeping with an employee?

"It sure as shit shouldn't have," Nolan mutters.

"Hey," I snap back, "you being publicly eviscerated by a married comedienne you had a fling with a few months back probably shouldn't have happened either, right?"

Nolan sighs, shaking his head. "Greyson, Greyson, Greyson. We expect bad choices out of me. Not you."

I glare at him, but keep quiet. I'm tired of fighting.

"Anyway." Landon squares his muscled physique. "That's not why we're here. I was going to come myself, but as soon as Nolan and Emerson heard, they insisted on coming too."

Nolan smiles wide. "Nothing like some good twin support."

"And just because I don't work at the company doesn't mean this doesn't affect me," Emerson cuts in.

"OK," I say, "so what is it?"

"There's no way around the company's books," Landon says simply. "Dad got away with some serious tax evasion for several decades. It doesn't help that his main accountant died around the same time that he did, the ancient bastard."

"We already suspected that," I say.

Landon holds up a hand. "That's not all. Somehow the media has gotten wind of it, and it's going to be in the papers by the end of the week. Dad's old journalist friend Barry Millow did us a solid and let us know in advance. Said that was all he could do, though. It's a big story."

"Shit," I say. I want to sit down—it's where I think best—but I don't want to be sitting with my brothers standing all around, their uncertain looks drilling into me.

There's no magic fix for this. It's going to look very, very bad for Storm Inc. There's no way around it.

"We can issue a statement," I say, speaking as I'm thinking. "About Dad's tax evasion. Today."

"Today?" Nolan sputters.

"We have to beat them to it," I say. "That's our only play. If an outside source is the first to print this... it's going to look even worse on us. Plus, you know what Dad always said—"

"If you don't like the play, make the play," Emerson says grimly. "I still can't believe..."

"That bastard," Nolan mutters fondly.

"How did he ever expect it to work out?" Landon wonders.

I resist the urge to shrug again. "You know Dad. He didn't think that far ahead. He just took things as they came, damned be the consequences..."

I trail off, realizing what this is making me think of: Harley, and what we have, whatever it is.

"What about the bills themselves, though?" Landon asks. "Paying even half of them could topple the company. We can't afford it."

"This new TV series could give us the boost we need," I say. "But you're right. Even if it's a big money maker, the cash won't come in on time, and we can't afford to delay payment any longer if we're going to make this announcement and make things right. There's no other choice, then. We'll have to sell the music portion of the company. That'll give us more than enough to settle our bills."

Emerson groans. "But my CD…"

"We can have that as a stipulation for whoever buys Storm Music," I tell him. "I'm sorry, but it's the only way."

"You're right," he grumbles. "I just wish there was another."

"So do I," I say, finally sitting down.

Landon looks relieved, but not entirely. "We may just get by with this."

And yet, from the look he and Nolan share, I know there's something else.

"What is it?" I ask them.

"Well…" Nolan begins.

A knock at the door has him practically bouncing over. "Ah, they're here: the donuts!"

I glare at him as he brings them over.

"What?" he says, already biting into one. "C'mon, humor me."

So, I do. I eat my chocolate dip donut, shoot the shit with my brothers, even agree to appear in Nolan's next comedy skit. And then, once that's done, I ask them again, "What is it?"

"It's just…" Landon reaches for another donut, then pauses. "This tax evasion stuff, even with us releasing the information, is bad PR. Really bad PR. Maybe not really, really company-ending PR, but it still looks really bad on us."

"And?"

"And—we can't afford any other bad PR. And I mean any."

He gives me an odd look, and suddenly I understand.

"You don't have to worry about it," I say simply.

"No?" Nolan raises an eyebrow.

"Harley is a professional," I say. "And so am I."

"No one ever doubted that," Landon continues, "but if your relationship gets out, and worse, if it continues and that gets out…"

I rise. "I told you. You don't have to worry about it."

"It's over, then?" Nolan asks.

I clench at the edge of my desk. "You're overstepping, little brother. Don't come in here and tell me how to run my life."

"You're not Dad," he snaps back. "You can't just bang whoever you like and get away with it."

"He's right," Landon says quietly. "Times are different, too."

"You two have no idea what you're talking about." I turn to face the window, take a breath. "You can leave now."

No one moves. The gilt gold clock on the wall ticks and tocks and ticks and tocks.

Finally, Emerson heads for the door. "Just—consider what they said. They're only trying to help."

Nolan and Landon leave after him.

I stare at the window and the cityscape beyond for a very long time.

For whatever reason, I couldn't say it, tell them what I needed to: It's over.

CHAPTER 22

Harley

"You OK in there?" Hannah asks, poking her head into my room.

Slumped on my stomach in my room, aimlessly scratching Anchovy under his little chin, I shoot a glare at my laptop and mutter over the announcer chirping about workplace safety, "No."

"God, it's been like five hours." Hannah comes in to sit beside me, her blue eyes wide with astonishment. "The videos are still going?"

"They're still going," I intone, hardly believing it even as I'm saying it. "Before, I thought I'd do anything for this job, but this… is literally the most pointless thing ever. These training videos are from the 80s, and they're just talking about how not to pour poison on your arm and BS like that."

"These are mandatory?"

"I didn't even know about them until yesterday when Greyson's assistant sent them." I sigh. "Thought I'd be going into my first day of work at the office today."

"Well…" Hannah's clearly trying to find a positive side of this, and having trouble with it. "At least you're getting paid for this?"

"Sure. And I did get some sleep in an hour or so ago, so that was good."

"Why?" Hannah's smile my way is knowing. "Didn't get much last night?"

I can't stop my grin. "You know it."

"Ready to admit it now?"

"Hannah."

She sighs. "Fine. Though if you ask me, you should just call up Greyson and sweetly ask if there's been some kind of mix-up. Maybe he doesn't even know about the videos."

"You just want me to call him," I say.

"No, I just want you to stop groaning and eating all the apple chips," she says, leaving and taking the bag with her as she does so.

I glare at my phone for a minute or so, give Anchovy a good little belly rub, then finally cave and call up Greyson.

"Hey," he says. "How are you?"

"Sleepy but good," I say.

"Good," he says. "Finished the videos?"

"No, there's still three hours to go."

"Oh?"

"I've been watching for five hours. I don't want to be rude, but could there have been some kind of mix-up? These things are from the 80s and pointless as hell."

"Five hours? Shit. What are they even about?"

"Workplace safety, and... I honestly fell asleep." I sigh. "Sorry, I probably sound like a terrible employee. I shouldn't have called."

"No, you were right to. I haven't even heard of these."

"So I don't have to watch the last three hours?"

"No. I'll talk to Madeline."

"OK, thanks."

"No problem."

It's weird. This whole conversation has seemed flat, completely neutral. Like I really was just talking to my boss.

"So, Greyson, about last night…"

"We do have to keep it professional here, you know," he cuts in.

"Exactly what I was going to say," I say coolly. "That it?"

"Yes."

"Great. Goodbye."

He starts to say something just as I hang up. I toss my phone aside with a frown. Anchovy scurries away.

Not that I meant to hang up right as Greyson was saying something, but if it's that important, he'll call me back.

I slap my laptop closed, balling some duvet in my fist.

What was up with his 'keep it professional' comment? Just because I smoked pot that one time at camp, and our whole affair happened, doesn't mean I'm some idiot airhead who has no common sense when it comes to work.

I thought Greyson knew that. Just what does he think of me, anyway?

"Screw it," I say, lying down and going under my covers. "At least I can get some sleep now."

CHAPTER 23

Greyson

I make sure to get to the office early to talk to Madeline without the risk of being interrupted. Our talk shouldn't take long.

"You look good," I say, taking in her rosy cheeks and usual vigorous walk with relief. She looked well yesterday too, but she was so busy I hardly had a moment alone with her. "I was worried."

"My family have always been quick healers." She gives her tightly honey-bunned head little laugh. "I'm a bit surprised I got sick at all. It's good to see you too, Mr. Storm. Everyone loves the new show, too."

"Let's hope the public agrees. I wanted to thank you for everything you handled while I was gone. I've been surprised how little there's been for me to do now that I'm back."

She grins. "Just doing my job."

"About the new hire, Harley," I continue, as her grin wavers almost imperceptibly. "Any reason why you had her watch eight hours' worth of 80s videos for an orientation day we don't normally have?"

By now, Madeline's kindly milkmaid features could be carved from stone. "No. No reason. Just thought since she's so young, going above and beyond as far as training goes wouldn't be amiss."

"Right."

I eye her, trying to decide how to phrase the next part. It was one thing for Landon to claim the 'whole office' knows about me and Harley based on some cryptic comments, but Madeline would definitely know if anyone does: she's the eyes and ears of the place.

"About Ms. Davis…" I continue.

"Don't worry," she cuts me off with a crisp red-lipped smile. "I have her cubicle on the opposite side of the floor. Near the coffee machines. Far from yours." Her chin lifts. "Since Gabriel was so happy to retire, and we have no back-up cinematographers on hand, I've also prepared a folder of resumes of potential candidates, if it should come to it."

If it should come to it. Huh.

Again, that smile annoys me instead of reassuring me like it usually does.

Maybe because, without a single word, Madeline has made herself clear: I know, and I've handled it.

Problem is, have I 'handled it' on my end?

"It won't come to that," I reply. "Ms. Davis is very good at her job."

"Excellent," Madeline says. "Better safe than sorry, though. I left the folder on your desk. Is that all?"

"Yes, it is," I say. "Thanks again."

And then she's left, leaving me with my thoughts. There's still an hour before Harley's set to arrive. She doesn't have that much to do here; even Gabriel moaned about the pointlessness of spending time in the office, filming the odd PR short or rewatching his old footage to improve his cinematography. I could easily make an excuse about why Harley would be better off working from home for the time being. Or even taking a break until the next StormTV shooting. It's not like she didn't make enough to tide her over for several weeks at least.

Then again, I have to film that announcement today. Ever since we released the statement about Dad's tax evasion yesterday, online SJWs have been screaming about the need for me to make a public statement myself on where Storm Inc. now stands and our plans for the future. So I will need Harley after all. At least, at 3 PM, when I have my time slot with her booked.

The next few hours, I fritter away. That's the one thing I can't get used to about being president: while on paper there's a lot more you're supposed to do, in reality, you're in charge of finding the right people to solve the right problems. Once that's done, there's not much more to do, other than answer the odd email, and schedule meetings no one really wants to go to.

I visit Landon to help with the specifics of putting Storm Music on the market, his new job now that he isn't bogged down with the impossibility of Storm Inc.'s books. I eat lunch in my office. I return calls.

And then, at 3 PM, I go over to Harley's desk.

"Hey." She brightens at seeing me.

"Hey," I say. "You look..." I catch myself just in time to growl, "professional."

That was close—too close. Telling your employee she looks 'good' is a fast track to a harassment suit. Inappropriate.

But she does look good. Hot as hell, in fact. Her pencil skirt shows off her trim middle and generous hips, while the tie of her high-neck, slightly sheer teal blouse is beckoning for me to untie it, rip it off to see what's underneath.

"Thanks." If she noticed my almost-slip, she's giving no sign of it. "You look professional too. Is it time for us to film?"

"According to the schedule," I say.

"How long do we have?" she asks.

She seems so casual. Isn't she finding it insanely hard, keeping this space between us that feels intrinsically wrong? All I want to do is take her in my arms and see if she can keep that cool, devil-may-care tone any longer.

"Nothing scheduled after this," I say, "We can take as long as we need."

"Oh." She grins. "Good. Since I'm a perfectionist."

"You're going to have your work cut out for you. I'm useless in front of the camera."

"Don't worry," she says easily, "I'm good at coaxing the best out of people."

I'll bet. As for what I'd like to coax out of you...

"Great," I practically choke out, tearing my eyes off her so my brain can have some chance of focusing. "Let's go."

Once we're in the film room, I can't help but heave a sigh of relief.

"Tired of being under scrutiny 24/7?" Harley jokes.

"That's not it," I say, even though it is part of it.

"OK."

The clock in this room is loud, each tick echoing around the high ceilings. The whizz of an overeager fan isn't helping either.

"You're right," I finally admit. "It just comes with the job: the expectation that I'm some kind of man-God. Even though I'm no role model."

Harley's looking at me with something that, if I didn't know better, I'd say was admiration. "The best ones never think they are."

God, what the steady hazel gaze of hers does to me...

"Right." I make for the green screen. "Let's get this over with."

"Sounds good to me."

Harley hefts her camera on her shoulder. "Who knows, maybe it'll be good the first take. It does happen."

Not with me, it doesn't. Talking to the camera feels like talking to my dad when he was in one of his stubborn moods, or even my batty old Grandma Josephine, who would as soon pat you on the head as chuck a slipper at your face screaming about elder abuse and demons in the Honey Nut Cheerios.

I take out the notes Madeline made for me and get reading. "This is Greyson Storm. As you may have heard recently, an unfortunate truth has come to light regarding my father, the late Collin Storm's, tax evasion..."

Harley yawns loudly, mouthing: Bo–ring.

I glare at her, falling silent. So much for a perfect first take.

She shrugs. "I'm sorry, but come on. There was no point in going on like that. The normal Greyson Storm is a thousand times more interesting than whatever that was, trust me."

"That's how I am in front of the camera."

"Not with me you aren't," she says. "Why don't you ditch whatever pre-made script your assistant made you and just say what you really think?"

"That's not what the public wants."

"You might be surprised what they want."

All I know is that I want you, I think but don't say.

A strand has come loose from her pulled-back bun, and it seems almost unbearable that I can't walk up to her, real close, and tuck it behind her ear. Then tip her chin up and...

Focus, Greyson.

"Try it," she says. "For me?"

The last words crossed some invisible boundary, but I don't care. The next thing I know, I'm tossing Madeline's notes aside, and starting:

"You all know who I am. Why I'm here talking to you like this. I'm as sad and disappointed and angry about this whole tax evasion thing as you are. My dad was supposed to be an all-American, one of the good guys. He was supposed to be the one who not only made his own rules, but also didn't break the intrinsic ones. But I'm not here to bash on my dad, whatever his faults. I'm not here to talk you out of thinking that Storm Inc. is a corrupt company, or even tell you that we're a company that can change, come back and be ethical again. That's for you to decide, based on the actions we'll take over the next few weeks and months. I just wanted to be the one to tell you that we'll be paying our debt in full. More than that, we'll be running a lottery to pay off the debts of some of our most loyal viewers. And we want to hear from you. How we can do better. How companies around the world can. It's not going to happen all at once, but I can promise that I will do everything in my power to put Storm Inc. back on the map for all the right reasons. Starting now. Thank you."

I only realize I've stopped talking when Harley bursts out, "Wow! That was amazing! You were..."

"That was easy." I can hardly believe I'm saying the words. "I just…"

Everything that happened still doesn't feel real. Guess I signed up Storm Inc. for a new charity too. Clearly, selling Storm Music was the right—and only—choice.

I walk up to her, still stupefied. "You're magic. Did that just happen?"

She laughs, looking so genuinely surprised and delighted and amused that before I've thought about it, I've kissed her.

It's like coming home. Our bodies meld together.

She tastes like coffee, and I'd never have thought coffee could be a turn-on but I'm as hard as ever. Something's nagging in the back of my head, something important, but I can't remember.

Not with her here, taking over every one of my senses. Her arms are soft as hell, her clothes too. Her mouth knows just how to take and give, follow and lead. Fuck, I want her.

I want her bad.

I kiss the words out of her: "But… Greyson…"

And then I remember. We pull away at the same time.

"Shit, sorry, I…" I trail off.

She's breathing heavy, her gaze still stuck on my lips, me.

She looks over at the door, then at me. I understand without a word.

I go over there and lock it. When I turn around, she's sitting on a table, legs swinging. "So."

I don't move.

I can feel it, the last of my self-control dissolving the longer I'm in the room with her. When it's gone, there'll be no turning back.

"So," I say.

This is risky and I know it and yet, with her there in front of me, tangible and sexy and irresistible, 'risk' seems like the most abstract concept in the world.

"Greyson—" she says.

"Harley," I say, not moving.

I should leave. I need to stay.

"We shouldn't," she says simply, correctly interpreting my pause. "Tell me to leave. Look at me, and tell me to leave."

She knows I should. I know I should.

It's the right thing to do. The only thing.

I swallow. I have to do this.

"Fine," I say hollowly, turning away.

"Go on," she urges me. "Tell me. Say it."

Next thing I know, I've strode right up to her, taken her face to mine and kissed the words right out of her mouth.

Our tongues tangle, lips snag. She knew I was hers as soon as she sat on that table and started swinging her legs.

I kiss her to the table so she's sitting on it again, undo her blouse, the mocking blue tie that was made to be untied.

"We shouldn't do this," I growl, kissing at the newly bared skin, lapping my way down, sucking a nipple into my mouth.

"We shouldn't," she agrees, hands gliding over my pants where my erection is.

The slightest of nibbles, and she squeals. My gaze swings up to find her mouth a sexy 'O'.

"Then stop."

She grabs my dick and strokes it, hard. "You first."

My hand drops to her skirt, then up it, pressing into her wet panties. "You."

She unbuttons my pants, rips down my boxers, grabs my cock, and, with hungry eyes, hisses, "You."

My 'you' turns into a moan when she clambers her body to mine. What follows is pure instinct.

I grab her and turn her around so she's on the table, pussy and ass raised to me. I rip off her panties, shove myself inside.

And finally—finally, finally, finally—everything is as it should be.

There's no more words—there's no need for them. Just me and her. In and out. My cock reveling in her perfect, tight slit.

In and out, deep and deeper. Her wet warmth is enough to bring me to the edge already, except that I want to hear her moan my name first. I want her to come for me.

The table scrapes across the floor as I pound her, but I don't care. All I know and need is what I'm buried in, right here, right now.

I slap her ass, and her groans get more harried. "C'mon. Come for me, baby. I want to hear you moan my name."

She's reduced to monosyllables now, her whole body shaking, pussy clasping hungrily at my cock with every thrust.

It's so hot, so fucking hot that I can't take it. Can't take this. Her.

"Grey-son, oh Grey-son, oh yes Greyson!" she shrills, taking my hand and slapping it over her mouth to muffle her cries as she comes, over and over again on my dick.

Seconds later, I'm losing it too, exploding into her. Fuck. Fuck yeah. Uh…

We sink onto the carpet, half-entwined, limbs akimbo.

I'm mumbling nonsense, holding her not because I want to but because, for whatever reason, I can't seem to let her go. "My Harley, my girl…"

Her eyes, when they open, are the happiest I've seen them. Sleepy and happy and surprised. A little worried, too.

"God," she murmurs, "You take a sex god course or something? That was amazing!"

"How'd you guess?" I yawn, and find myself dabbing a kiss onto the tip of her nose.

She giggles. "You into my nose now too?"

"Hell yeah. That light sprinkling of freckles. The Seussical slope shape. So hot."

Her grin warms me.

"I like you," she declares.

"And I like you."

It feels more intimate and real, those three words, than anything I've ever said to any other girlfriend or lover, words uttered just to meet milestones, expectations.

Harley is, being with her is… different.

A knock on the door has us sprawling apart.

"Fuck," I mutter, clambering into my pants.

More knocks follow.

"Mr. Storm?" Madeline's officious voice drawls. "Are you in there?"

"Yes, Madeline!" I say, in my most normal voice. "Just finishing up the final cut. Can't be disturbed. Will be out in five."

"Well." I can almost hear the gears grinding in her head. She knows. "It is pretty urgent."

"Five minutes," I snap, and then, thank fuck, hear the angry clack of her heels against the floor as she leaves.

"I could've been ready in like two, maybe," Harley says, grinning lopsidedly.

I take one look at her and bust out laughing. "What... Why?"

Somehow, she's gotten her bra looped around her head, her blouse bunched up at her stomach.

"I panicked." Her smile is helpless and adorable and makes me want to kiss her. "I just... can you help me?"

I chuckle as I go over there to help undo her bra. "Don't know how much help I'll be. Women's clothing isn't exactly my expertise."

"Nah, women's pleasure is." She winks at me, and this time I can't help it: I do kiss her.

The just-a-second kiss extends into a drawn-out lip-lock, then a series of them. Then my hands are re-finding her breasts and she's pulling away, half-moaning but also saying, "Greyson."

"Shit." I rip myself away. "Sorry."

She adjusts her clothes and smooths her hair. "Do I look OK?"

One look and again all of me is clenching to hold in what I want to do to her.

"OK isn't the word, but you look presentable, which is the important part, I guess."

"You guess?" she teases.

I say nothing, because anything more and my cock is going to get even harder.

"It's time to go," I say coolly.

"Read my mind," she returns easily.

We leave the room separately. I don't look back.

The rest of the day is a dull blur, brightened only by my glimpses of her and the cold hard knowledge that this is how things have to be.

CHAPTER 24

Harley

"OK, Anchovy, I know you aren't crazy about the long grass, but I promise, there are no snakes here. This is Toronto, not Alabama."

Anchovy responds by flopping on his belly and not moving. I give his avocado-print leash a little tug to no avail.

"You goon," I grumble. "C'mon, I need this. Hannah's on a date with the Most Handsome Man Alive, and I'm tired of hopping every time my phone goes off."

It wouldn't be such a bad thing if the text I was expecting actually came through. The text from Greyson, that is.

Instead, I've run across the room and snatched up my phone for such important notifications as:

a) A pleasant memory of Anchovy frolicking in the sand two years ago

b) Some misplaced, misspelled spam for Viagraa

c) A Nigerian prince offering me $1,000,000,000,000 if I would only give him my bank account information, seven Google Play cards and my grandmother's address.

It's stupid. I know how this can go. Greyson is my boss. Nothing can happen.

And yet, so much has happened already.

Part of me was sure that our exotic, crazy-hot affair was linked to the exotic place we were in, that it'd fizzle out once we got back here. But the hot sex and sweet night we had on the rooftop, the wild sex and chemistry we felt in the office—I feel more attracted to him now, if anything.

Ugh! Why is it the one man I want is the one I can't have?

I'm about to sit down in frustration when I notice that Anchovy is pulling on the leash, apparently now finally ready to get going on our field romp.

"About time," I mutter.

I'm glad for a distraction, and Anchovy is probably the cutest distraction alive: the way he bounds down the pathway happily, stopping every so often to scrutinize an odd-shaped rock or a tasty-looking ant. He's so distracting that I only realize on the third ring that the ringing is actually coming from my phone. I get out my phone just in time to see the call end. The call from Greyson.

"Shit."

Next second, though, he's calling again.

"Ooh, two calls in a row, is this an emergency?" I joke, picking up.

"Depends on your definition of emergency."

"What's yours?"

"I want to see you. Now, if you can."

"What—I'm supposed to drop everything and come to you? You gave me quite the brush-off today, in case you've forgotten."

"Is office sex your definition of a brush-off?" he asks drily.

"No, you know I meant after."

"I'm sorry," he says. "Just that close call with Madeline rattled me. And I knew if I spent any more time in that locked room with you, I wouldn't be able to help myself again."

"Fine," I say, pretending like his answer hasn't made my smile as big as I am.

"Where are you?" he continues, "I can come meet you."

"What if I have plans?"

"Tonight can work too."

God, this man is insatiable. But in a good way.

"Sorry," he says. "Forget it."

"What?"

"I'm being pushy. You have your own life. You don't owe me anything."

"OK..."

My gaze wanders to Anchovy, who's currently amusing himself with a spiky stick.

"Well?"

"Well what?" I ask.

He takes a breath. "Let's start over. I'd like to see you now or later tonight. Or later this week, if you're free. Does that work for you?"

I pretend to think about it, although I'm smiling, ready with my answer all the while. "Hmm... let me see... how about: yes, yes and yes. Does that work for you?"

"That works great for me." The smile in his voice makes me smile bigger. I feel like an idiot. A silly-stupid, crazy-happy idiot. "Where should I meet you?"

"Well," I say doubtfully, "I am walking Anchovy right now..."

"Sounds good. Where?"

"We're in the middle of Bynaural Park, but we'll probably stop by the rest station for Anchovy to get a bite to eat in about 15."

"I'll meet you there in 30."

Although he really gets here in 25, with a wicker picnic basket to boot.

"What's this?" I say with a little laugh.

He's dressed in a fitted plain black t-shirt and jeans, and he looks just as handsome as he does in a suit.

"I figured since it's almost dinnertime, and the caramel corn was on sale, why not have a picnic?"

I tip open the lid of the basket. "You didn't…"

He did. Three bags of delicious-looking caramel corn, and what looks to be a fresh baguette, with ham, cheese and a fresh basket of strawberries too.

Right now, Greyson's attention is otherwise occupied, though. Crouching down, he's trying to get the attention of Anchovy, who's currently gobbling down his favorite meat snack that I bought him.

"Believe me," I tell Greyson, "Nothing short of his tail on fire will distract my little furry friend when he's in Food Heaven."

Still, Greyson gives Anchovy a little pat with the pad of his thumb.

"Are you trying to ingratiate yourself to me through my ferret?" I ask.

Raising himself upright, Greyson just smiles. "Is it working?"

I give him a quick kiss. "Maybe."

The next few minutes go by in a whirr: our hunt for the perfect picnic spot, Greyson finding it right beside a tranquil pond and a massive willow. Next thing I know, we're sitting, eating, passing the baguette back and forth, while Anchovy gobbles up our crumbs.

Afterwards, I lie down with my head in Greyson's lap, watching the willow undulate in the breeze overhead.

"Thank you," I say.

"Thank you," he says. "And for your help with my PR segment. Apparently, it's already a hit."

"Knew it," I say. "I've never claimed to be a PR expert, but I do know truth when I see it. It's refreshing. No wonder you're a hit."

"It's not me, exactly. And compared to my dad..."

"What?" I sit up to give him a hard look. "You're not as adept a liar? I don't get why you keep comparing yourself to him."

His look back at me is just as hard. "He was Storm Inc., Harley. Even if he did a lot of shit I'm not proud of."

"I'm sorry, you're right. I... I'm in no position to judge your father. We don't know his side of things, either."

"Don't be sorry, he was a dick in a lot of ways. Though you're right, sometimes I wonder if I ever really knew him. And my mom and him, I think they just stuck it out for us kids. I'm not even sure if I was planned myself, or if it's my fault that..."

I touch his arm. "Don't say that."

"It's true. Maybe. They weren't suited, my father and mother. She was too demanding, and he bucked at any whiff of control. He never liked sticking with things, either." He looks at me again, although this time he isn't really looking at me. "Even this whole 'love' thing people always talk about. Sometimes I wonder if it isn't just another socially acceptable addiction. If it isn't... Because I haven't ever felt..."

Something thumps in me and I look away.

Why does it matter, that he's said that? Why do I care?

The wind rustling the willow sounds like water. But the water not moving sounds like silence.

"You've really never been in love?" I finally ask him.

"No. You?"

"No," I say. "But that doesn't mean... Hmm. I mean, I've never met a couple who I knew well that I wanted to be, whose relationship I wanted to have. Only old couples on the news for 50 years together that I don't really know. What do I know, the old woman could secretly be beating the poor husband with her cane when he forgets to pass the salt."

A stunned silence, then Greyson laughs loud and hard.

"You're dark, you know that?" Another laugh. "I like it."

I make a grimacing smile. "I'm glad someone does."

"You're right, though," he continues. "Long-term love seems like the hardest thing in the world, the most impossible. Anyway"—he clears his throat as he gestures around—"this has raised picnics considerably in my estimation."

I have to laugh. "Meaning?"

"The only other picnic I've been to was a family shit-show."

"Then why try again?"

"Because..." He trails off, eyes narrowing at whatever he's thinking. Then he gives his head a little shake. "Forget it."

"Greyson."

"Really, it was nothing."

"Liar."

I sit up and look at him right in the eye. "Tell me."

"Harley."

I move my face even closer to his, so our lips are nearly brushing. "Tell me."

"You," he says, and takes my chin in his hand and presses his lips to mine. Warmth and electricity rocket through my body.

When we finally manage to pull away, he wraps me in his arms. "Just because I had a feeling that being with you would make anything good."

Whoa. First he says he doesn't believe in love, then he says that?

"Greyson, I—"

Already, his stony cold expression is back in place. "I meant what I said before: not a big deal."

"Fine," I snap back.

Maybe it's even better, me having to pry the words out of him with a verbal crowbar. Makes it clear he isn't just trying to butter me up. No, I know he's saying it—doesn't want to say it—because it's real.

My gaze is caught in the undulations of the willow overhead, my mind in wondering how long this will last, can last, why I even care at all. This can't last.

And yet, right here, right now, Greyson and me, Anchovy and the crumbs, the willow and the water scented ever so slightly with the evergreens on the far side of it, all this, it's enough.

CHAPTER 25

Greyson

By the time I've dropped Harley and her ferret back at her place, and gotten home, it's late. Late enough and dark enough that as I step into my condo, I don't notice anyone's there until someone says, "Imagine seeing you here."

"Nolan." I'd recognize that voice anywhere. "What are you doing here?"

"Good question." Nolan's tone is firmly playful. "What are you doing here?"

"This is my condo."

Nolan chuckles. "Ah, so it is. I ate all your kale chips, by the way. Hope you don't mind. Who knew something so healthy could actually taste so good? Maybe I'll include them in my next skit, just for an excuse to eat them again."

I head over to flick on the light switch. "Why are you here?"

Not that Nolan showing up here unannounced is unheard of, but it's no weekly occurrence either.

"You weren't missing your beloved younger brother?" he asks.

"Cut the shit." We both know he didn't show up here just for us to bask in each other's presence.

He frowns. "You still making an appearance on my special at the Grange tomorrow?"

"Yes," I say.

"Good."

"Nolan."

"Alright. I came here to tell you I got you a last-minute talk with The Reginald."

"What?" I growl.

"C'mon, you should be psyched!" Nolan's tone is psyched enough for the both of us. "How much shit did The Reginald get Dad out of? He's Storm Inc.'s best lawyer!"

"What shit do we need to get out of?"

"What shit don't we need to get out of, am I right?" Nolan chuckles, although his face goes serious after a half-second. "Seriously, Greyson. You don't want to miss this."

"My PR talk about the tax evasion was a big success," I point out. "I've already made our first big payment of the back taxes and set up that charity. What more is there to do?"

Nolan just smiles. "Come now, Greyson."

I glare at him.

"Can't you just go and trust me that this is in your and Storm Inc.'s best interest?" he continues.

"Not until you tell me what the fuck this is all about. There's no reason you wouldn't unless you knew it would piss me off and I wouldn't go if I knew."

He throws up both tan hands. "Whoa, cool it."

"Right." I go to my fridge, rip open the door. Maybe if I find something yummy to bribe Nolan with, he'll go away. "I've had enough of this."

Nolan trails behind. "I just thought, right now, with all that's going on, some advice..."

"Is this about Harley?"

Nolan's grin falters. "I mean, it's not not about Harley."

"You fucker."

"No. Fuck you, man." Nolan slams the fridge door shut. "You want to date your employee when Storm Media is in a literal bad publicity shit-storm, that's your business. But you go talk to The Reginald too, at the very fucking least. He knows his shit. You know he does."

"I've got it handled."

"Do you, though? Greyson, do you even have a plan if this gets out, if your little cinematographer squeeze decides to get pissed at you for cancelling a date and goes public?"

"Don't call her that."

"Well?"

"She wouldn't do that."

"You know that."

"Yeah. I do. Now back off."

"So, you won't see him?"

"Will you get off my case if I do?"

Nolan takes a few steps back, lifts his hands. "Consider me off already."

I eye him. "When is it?"

"That's why I came here—it's tonight. As soon as you can make it."

"And if I have plans?"

"Dude, you don't even have food in your fridge, let alone plans."

I eye him for a minute. Part of me wants to make up some bullshit and send him on his way, just to screw with him. I've never liked people interfering in my life. But another, stronger part of me wants to send him away so I can call up Harley, see what she's up to, maybe even set up another date.

Maybe Nolan has a point. Seeing The Reginald can't hurt. And I can always walk out if I don't like what I'm hearing.

"Fine," I say. "And I assume you'll want to come with me since you don't trust me to be able to walk into the big scary office all by myself..."

Nolan barks out a laugh. "Actually, I have... other interests there."

"Other interests?"

"It's not always all about you, you know."

Another glance at my brother and it hits me. "You're an idiot."

"What?" Nolan's already making for the door, his smile unmistakable. "She's hot."

I head after him. "If The Reginald finds out, you're toast."

A flat look. "Jenny is his secretary, not the mother of his children and love of his life."

"Let's just get there."

Nolan, having insisted on being the one to drive, jokes and fiddles with the radio all the way there. I resist the urge to call up Harley and call off this whole stupid thing. Instead, I shoot her a text:

Thinking of you.

A few seconds later:

—Good or bad?

Why not both?

—Ooh now I'm intrigued. How can it be good and bad at the same time ;)

Guess I'll have to show you next time I see you.

—Why not now?

Oh, fuck me. Now I have a hard-on.

—You can tell me, if it's easier.

Vaguely, in the background of my consciousness, I can hear Nolan humming something. A glance out the window finds us still a few blocks away from Reginald's office. I've got time.

I text her: You and me. On the floor of my patio. Outside.

—Ooh I get to see your place?

I freeze. I don't invite women to my place. We go to theirs or I get a hotel room. It does not happen.

But right now... my slip-up isn't seeming like so much a slip-up as an actually decent idea. Why couldn't Harley come over? Just for one time, to see how it would be. Maybe I could even find her a big sweatshirt she could take home...

What the fuck, Greyson?

But I'm already texting her: Tomorrow. I want you there.

—Oh yeah?

I want you everywhere. But there is good. For now.

—Call me. Now.

"Finally. I must've hit every red light in the city," Nolan grumbles, oblivious.

My hands clench as my erection throbs. Fuck me. We're here.

Nolan's already halfway out of the car. "You coming?"

No way am I admitting what just happened to him.

"Yep," I say, leaving the car, and shooting off a final text: Can't. Sorry. See you tomorrow.

Inside, The Reginald is ready to see me, while Nolan starts chatting up his admittedly hot secretary. Jenny's got a good figure, but this time for some reason, it appeals to me less than usual. I mean, compared to Harley...

Focus, Greyson.

"Greyson, wonderful to see you," Reginald booms, both freckly tanned hands coming to clasp and shake mine. "Sorry we had to see each other last time under such... unfortunate circumstances."

He's talking about the funeral, which was a convoluted media and family affair so stupefying that I barely had time to be sad, let alone get my wits about me.

"I am too," I say. "It is a great loss, but we're doing the best we can."

"Of course, of course." Reginald bobs his salt and caramel haired head, then opens the door and gestures inside. "After you."

Huh. I'd forgotten how wood-filled his office is. Even smells like wood. Wood and competence, that is.

Reginald goes over to sit on his army green embossed chair, his small too-light eyes taking me in. "Storm Inc. hasn't had it easy lately."

I try to smile blandly. This chair I'm sitting on is too comfortable. I need to stay on edge, on my A game. "That's one way of putting it."

Reginald barks out a laugh. "Your dad's tax evasion, the debacle of your first TV crew in Costa Rica—that's the only way of putting it."

"OK."

"OK." He assesses me with cruelly amused eyes. "Well, you're no idiot, Greyson. I suppose you know why you're here."

"My brother thinks I could use your advice."

"Damn right he does, and damn right you can. You've handled the tax evasion coming to light beautifully, so I've no advice for you there. As for the other… issue, I understand that you may not want to take my advice, but at least hear me out. I think there's some information you're better off knowing."

I fold my hands together. "I'm listening."

"How much do you know about that new fling of yours, Harley Davis?"

"She's not a fling," I growl before I can stop myself.

His eyebrows fly up. "Oh. So, then you must know quite a bit about her."

"I know some."

Another infuriating head bob. I don't know why I'm so pissed off right now.

"Of course. Then what I'm about to show you should come as no surprise."

Reginald opens a yellow file folder, then slides a sheet of paper in front of me. I gape at the face that's eyeing me mockingly.

It's a mugshot of Harley. That ironic glint to her eyes, a fuck-you kissy face, it's her alright. There's no mistaking it.

"I assume you're going to tell me what this is for?" I ask him.

"Nothing that serious, admittedly," Reginald says lightly, although judging by his expression, he thinks differently. "She was arrested for protesting in college. Apparently, she was quite the radical."

I slide the sheet of paper back to him. "OK. Now I know. That it?"

"No, actually."

"OK. What else?"

"I don't suppose I need to point out that right now Storm Inc.'s public image is shaky at best."

"I'm aware."

"And that any new misstep could undo all your hard work. Could make it look like your latest talk was just bullshit."

"Just say it."

"If your relationship with Ms. Davis came to light, it would look very, very bad. And if she gave even the slightest hint that you made some sort of power-play to make it happen—"

"That's not what happened."

"Doesn't matter." Reginald's voice is quiet, forceful. "Doesn't make one iota of a difference, to be honest. If that girl gets it into her head that she wants to screw you and Storm Inc. over, she has all the power to do so right now. That's the climate post-#MeToo. People are actually believing women now."

"But—"

"I'm not finished. Even if that doesn't happen, it seems like your team didn't do their due diligence when it came to a background check on Ms. Davis."

I shuffle in my chair. Truth is, my staff didn't have any time to do any 'diligence' at all for the background checks. We even had a real live paranoid schizophrenic in for an interview before we realized what was going on.

"Go on," I tell him.

"Harley Davis was charged with tax evasion two years ago."

"No," I say.

It doesn't make any sense. Maybe she pushes the envelope of the law when it comes to minor stuff, like pot and protesting. But actual tax evasion? That's not her.

"Let me finish," Reginald continues. "The accusations were later retracted, for whatever reason, and nothing substantial came out of it. But still. The very existence of these allegations is enough to cast serious doubt on her suitability as an employee, especially at this vulnerable time for your company what with your father's tax evasion recently being revealed. That, plus her night in jail, and your relationship... this is a perfect storm, Greyson."

I return his concerned look blankly. Reginald's right. I know he's right. He's telling me the exact thing I'd tell any one of my brothers if they got it into their dolt head to fall for some bad-news girl. And yet, as he speaks, all I can do is stare deeper and deeper into the wooden map of 18th-century England on his wall.

"All it'll take is one ambitious journalist to do a little digging—finding all this out took me minutes, by the way—and you'll have another perfect storm to dig the company out of. If you can even manage it again. There's only so many scandals the public can stomach from your company before they start to lose trust for good. And once it's gone, there's no getting it back. Not ever."

Not ever.

Storm Inc. ruined... Landon and me out of a job. My dad's legacy gone. My mom's fortune... gone. All Dad left her was the company, after all. Same with the rest of us. He always believed in pouring most if not all of the profit back into the company, so that it was always growing, expanding.

"Don't take my word for it," Reginald's saying now, "look at American Apparel, McDonald's. Big companies that got hammered by bad press and nearly destroyed because of it. Sure, McDonald's bounced back—but is Storm Inc. as much of a superpower as McDonald's?"

We aren't. Of course we aren't.

I'm standing now. I can't bear to hear any more of this.

"I need... to think," I tell him. "Talk to Harley, too."

Reginald's look on me is stern. "Make sure you do more thinking by yourself than talking with her." He sighs. "I know business can be hard and cutthroat, Greyson. But you really have to cut out your weaknesses before your enemies can use them against you. For all your father's faults, he was always good at that."

Don't I know it. He never hesitated to miss one of our birthdays, or blow off a date with my mom for wining and dining some top exec. But he grew the business—by leaps and bounds—made profits that his competitors only dreamed of. There's no denying that.

"Thank you," I tell Reginald at the door.

"Don't thank me unless you listen to me," he says sternly.

"You don't know her," I say without thinking.

Seeing his face, it's clear that he doesn't understand. I'm not sure that I do either.

It should be clear, what has to be done. But it's not.

"So," Nolan says, once I'm in the waiting room. "How'd it go?"

"I need to talk to her," I say.

"That's it? He didn't show you the... and the..."

I glare at him as we go into the elevator. "He did. Anyway, I'm going to go over there right now and—"

"Now?"

I check my watch. It's 11 at night.

"Remind me why this meeting couldn't wait until tomorrow?" I ask him.

"Because this is the only time Reginald could fit you in," Nolan replies, "Plus my comedy show is tomorrow—unless you've forgotten."

"I haven't."

By the time we're in the car, I've made up my mind. There's no point in going over to Harley's with my head all messed up. I need to sleep on this. Think about it. And then, decide what I'm going to do.

CHAPTER 26

Harley

"Second day of work, second day of work, I'm going to my second day of work," I mutter-sing to Anchovy as he picks his way about the weeds outside of our building.

If he keeps taking his sweet time to poo, I'm going to be late for my second day of work.

"C'mon, little guy, let's do this thing," I urge him.

Sure enough, he finally does his thing, and I hurry him inside.

"Aren't you late?" Hannah asks helpfully as I'm rushing around to jam everything I need in my messenger tote and also throw on something at least halfway acceptable looking.

"Aren't you late?" I shoot back.

"Yep," she says, grinning. "But I stay late at work and Marjory loves me, so I'm good."

"Marjory loves everyone," I mutter with a sigh. If only I had enjoyed working at that chichi nursery as much as Hannah does. Of course, Hannah is the vice-manager and gets paid $30 an hour to sit on her ass and smile at flowers. I, on the other hand, was so bored that I was driven to strange and unfortunate plant experiments: pairing cacti with random trees (I figured the change in company might encourage them to make odd babies), propagating every succulent limb I found in a massive bin called 'Succlandia', trying to upsell the customers from one or two plants to ten. Needless to say, I was fired after a month.

"Don't be nervous," Hannah says, as I race for the door. "They'll love you."

"I'm not nervous." I hike my messenger bag higher on my shoulder. "Even though they don't love me."

"Huh?"

"Half the women give me the evil eye, while the others pretend they can't see me at all," I admit.

"They're just shy?"

"Hannah." I frown at her. "That's what you said about Mallory Robinson, right up until she dumped that coke on my head."

"Well, her boyfriend was hitting on you."

"Yes, even after I told him that I could only ever view him as a turtle and nothing more."

We giggle.

"Well, they just don't know you yet," Hannah assures me. "As soon as they do, they'll love you."

"Hopefully. Worse comes to worst, I can print out a life-size picture of you and keep it in my office at all times."

"Please don't do that."

"Yeah, I don't think I'll do that."

We laugh, and I glance at my phone. "Shit! I really am going to be late—byeee."

The drive there is thankfully fast and warm. With the windows down and the radio playing—"Hey Jude, don't be afraid..."—and glancing at Greyson's morning text—Can't wait to see you—I'm feeling pretty good.

By the time I get to my desk, I'm gasping for air, having run up the stairs once it was clear the elevator wasn't coming any time soon. I collapse in the chair and mutter "woo-hoo" under my breath, since I'm either not at all late or hardly late.

"Oh." The clack of high heels and then a woman with an unimpressed heart-shaped face stops by to eye me critically. I'm pretty sure it's Greyson's secretary, Madeline. "You decided to join us. I should let you know that we take our jobs very seriously here at Storm Inc. Tardiness is not tolerated. At all."

"Oh, I'm really sorry," I say, but her shoes are already clacking away.

I take out my phone and gape. One minute late, seriously?!?

This is your dream job, I remind myself. Your dreamy dream job.

It would've been nice, too, if Miss Manners Madeline had also graced me with the knowledge of what exactly I'm supposed to do today. According to my schedule on the computer, there's a big fat load of nothing.

Still, at some point, I'm bound to see Greyson...

Even thinking his name gets my heart hopping. Our quick text exchange last night got me hot and excited. And he did invite me over for tonight, too. Better that than another office encounter. Yes, it was crazy hot and totally worth it. But way too risky. Better to do it in his bed, or mine... or ours.

Ours... Where did that thought come from?

I set it aside as another series of clomps announces another presence.

It's Samantha, striding by with her gaze fixed so firmly ahead that I'd almost guess she was paid to assume that position.

I sigh. Well, here goes my day.

The rest of the morning isn't completely uneventful. A feisty young fly escapes my attempts to kill him no less than eight times. I manage to organize my entire email folder. I text Hannah a picture of some whale socks I'll probably be buying my mom for Christmas. I resist the urge to text Greyson—he's probably busy with work.

Lunchtime I escape to wander the nearby neighborhood, finally finding a nice tree to sit under and dig in. As I do, I spot some familiar faces at a picnic table nearby. Lucky me: I've had the good fortune to sit in full view of Madeline, Samantha and the rest of the Harley-does-not-exist crew, which makes up most of the office. One icy look my way, one unreturned wave I attempt, and they're finished with me.

"Jerks," I grumble, wandering off to find a better lunch spot. Not that I don't enjoy being iced out and all.

I finally find a nice grassy hill that I plonk down on and get eating.

I check my phone to find a text from Hannah:

—You OK?

Not really, I reply. No one will even look at me, let alone say hello.

—You think they know about you and Greyson?

Maybe.

—Maybe just give work your 1000%.

I would, except there's literally nothing to do! I'm sure it'll get better though.

—Fuck those bitches. We'll sic Anchovy on them.

Somehow I don't think that'll improve my reception, I text, grinning.

—Well, you know I love you. Legally Blonde tomorrow tonight?

Third time's the charm!

Since the last two times we've had to reschedule.

I finish my sandwich quickly enough, then return to my desk. Greyson has texted me by now, too:

—Where are you?

Was outside. Am back now. You?

—Outside. Figured you'd be outside with everyone else—Madeline planned a sporadic Staff Picnic outside. Must've just missed you. I'll try to get away.

Don't worry about it.

I bite at my lip. There's probably no point in mentioning my reception to Greyson yet. Maybe the other employees really do just need to get used to me.

I try to use the next few hours productively. I watch a documentary on cinematography, make notes, and drink a crapton of water. I try to pretend not to notice how half the people I say hi to pretend not to hear me, while the others give me such blank, hateful stares that I stop dead in my tracks.

It shouldn't matter, anyway. As much as I'd prefer to be on cordial, even friendly, terms with my coworkers, I'm here to work, not to make BFFs.

I'm just finishing up watching the documentary when I sense someone nearby. It's Greyson, smiling oddly. "Got a minute?"

"Yeah, sure, of course! Not much to do right now."

"About that: sorry. We're just scrambling to get this new season up and out, and figure out ads and... we should get on the planning stage for the next episode soon, and you'll be one of the first people I consult."

"Oh. Really? I'm just the cinematographer, though."

"You have a good, fresh perspective. Even better, you're a fan. I'd love to know where you'd want us to film next."

"Like now?"

"Why not? I mean…" Greyson pauses, remembering we're still at my cubicle, in the middle of the office. "How about we go to my office first? There's something else I want to talk to you about first."

This 'something else' seems serious for whatever reason, but I can't get the memo to the rest of my body: I feel tingly, light and silly with Greyson so close. Like even if, improbably and inappropriately, he swept me up in his arms and spirited me away to his office, I'd only be able to laugh and laugh and laugh.

"Follow me," he says, his hand slipping easily in mine.

He freezes. Drops my hand.

"Sorry, I—"

"It's fine," I say, although my heart rate's doubled.

We both take a circumspect look around, but it doesn't seem like anyone else has noticed.

In his office, Greyson closes the door, then sits down. "So."

"So"—I break into a smile: there's our word again—"why not Australia? I've heard kangaroos can be neat, although a pain in the ass if you're not careful. Plus, out in the desert there's no forests for us to get lost in."

"You hated getting lost so much in Costa Rica?" he asks, smirk teasing.

"Not with you," I blurt out unthinkingly.

He tries to fight his growing grin, fails. "Wasn't so bad."

"You loved it," I accuse him. "Admit it."

Still that smile. "Nope. No can do."

Although his gaze dips to my lips, peels away. Heat prickles between my legs.

Jesus. Every time I'm alone with the man, my hormones take over. It's all I can do not to grab him, kiss him hard how right here and now.

Greyson swallows, places something in front of me. "This is for you."

"Me?" I say blankly. It's gorgeous, an adjective I never thought I'd use for a water bottle, but here I am. It's pink-to-blue ombre exterior also shows off an adorable watercolor sloth.

"I noticed yours had a crack in it," he explains. "This one is really good, too: includes a filter, is recyclable and biodegradable, the whole shebang."

"You..." Do not hug him, do not kiss him. Do not. "...didn't have to."

"I wanted to. But there's something else." Again, that change to stern tone that doesn't seem to register for me.

He got me the cutest, fanciest, most environmentally friendly water bottle ever!

"I went to see a family friend, a lawyer, the other day, and he told me—" The door opens.

Clack-clack-clack

"Oh, I'm sorry," Madeline says, firmly not looking at me. "Just, Greyson, we wanted to get your take on something before the ad is released this afternoon."

"Can it wait?"

"Mmm... unfortunately not. I hate to break up this... meeting you had planned. But it really is urgent."

"Fine." Greyson's tone is flat. He clearly has no other choice. What did he want to talk to me about, anyway? "Harley, it can wait until tomorrow." He leaves out the door, throwing me a wink.

I get up and leave too. No point in sitting around here for no reason.

And that wink—it meant we're still on for tonight, right? My lips compress together. I've never been in a 'secret' romance before, and I'm not sure I like it. Not that Greyson and I should be flaunting whatever we have together in the office. That would be inappropriate. But still. I don't know.

When I check my phone a few minutes later, Greyson has texted me:

—I want to see you tonight. I'll pick you up at 6 for CANOE, then we'll see where the night takes us?

CANOE fired Hannah after her first shift back in the day, I text him back. You know you don't have to take me to the classiest place in town.

—Alright. Rosalinda is probably more your style. Next time, Opus though.

I grin. I've never been to Rosalinda, but Opus is definitely fancy. What is it with Greyson and feeling like he has to treat me? Not that I'm complaining.

Sounds good to me, I text him back.

Guess even if the rest of this afternoon is a snore, I have something to look forward to, at least.

**

The end of the afternoon can't come quickly enough. More documentaries, more go-die stares, and by the time the clock ticks to 5 PM, I'm practically bounding out of my seat.

At home, after losing track of time in the latest Kate Morton novel and ending up with just minutes to spare, I yank on my blush half-crochet dress, slip on a beaded headband, call to Hannah, "There's leftover spaghetti in the fridge!" and run out the door to meet Greyson.

"Sorry I'm a bit late," I tell Greyson as I get into his car.

"Good thing you look good," is all he says.

"And if I didn't?" I tease.

His gaze glides over me for a nice long while before he starts up the car and gets driving. "Impossible."

"You should see me when Hannah and I do mud masks."

He chuckles. "Still not buying it."

"What if I spontaneously developed a second nose?"

Stopped at the stoplight, Greyson turns to look me over, his gaze lingering when it meets mine. "Beautiful. End of story."

And then he kisses me.

It's a soft kiss. One that knows what it wants and is in no hurry to get there. It's the kind of kiss that I'll recap to Hannah tonight, relive when I go to sleep later on. The kind of kiss that takes your breath away. That you remember until the day you die.

And then a car speeds past us and, realizing the light has changed, we separate.

"What was it you wanted to ask me, anyway?" I wonder as we continue along.

Suddenly, Greyson's jaw tightens. "Not now."

"OK..." I say, and, for some reason unable to shut up and shake the sense that it's something serious, continue, "Because I promise, I let my crazy friend use my laptop a few years ago, so any Google searches involving pipe bombs was totally not me."

Greyson swings an amused look my way. "What makes you think I know about your Google searches?"

I crinkle my nose. "OK, maybe not you. But the government, maybe."

Still amusement, touched with the slightest amount of suspicion. "Why would the government care?"

"Because I'm a criminal, of course."

I expect him to laugh, but he doesn't.

"What?" I tease, "Think I'm a criminal?"

"Are you?"

I stare at him, waiting for the crinkling in the corners of his eyes to show that he's joking.

"I mean, I got arrested for protesting once," I admit. "Spent a night in jail and even got a mug shot, but..."

I stare at his neutral yet still gorgeous side profile. "Why am I getting the feeling that this isn't a surprise?"

"Is that all?" is all he asks.

OK, now I'm getting pissed off.

"What does that mean, is that all?"

"Just that."

"What, am I supposed to tell you every bad thing I've ever done or thought of doing? What's gotten into you?"

"I told you. I talked to a family friend. A lawyer."

"And he knew about the arrest."

"He knew about a lot more than that. Something about tax evasion?"

"Oh, that." I almost laugh. "I was just an idiot and let my sketchy cousin Terry do my taxes. Turns out he didn't, just took the money for doing it from me and some other people and disappeared to Hawaii without telling anyone. That was when I first got into film school, so I was working my ass off so much that I didn't even realize what Terry had done until a year later when the tax people got on my ass. The woman they assigned to my case was a complete Nazi, tried to make the case I did this all on purpose. It was ridiculous. I paid the money and they threw her case out of court." I swing him a sidelong glance. "Is that what this is all about?"

Greyson's eyes are on the road, his mouth set. He looks like a stranger.

"It's a big deal," he says quietly. "With my father's tax evasion coming out how it did, and all the damage control I've had to do because of it, if it comes out that an employee of ours was involved in anything even remotely linked to tax evasion..."

"Anyone who knew the first thing about it would know it's complete BS!"

"But that's just it!" Greyson growls. "The media doesn't look into things, it thrives on misinformation. One shitty article and the general public's mind turns like a teeter totter."

"In that case, there's nothing we can do about it," I argue. "They could post a bogus article claiming either one of us is some Satanist and people will buy it."

Greyson says nothing as I scrutinize him.

"That isn't what you're worried about," I say flatly, realizing it as I'm saying it. "It's us getting out, too."

"Both."

He pulls into a parking spot. I stare out the window.

"What?" he snarls finally.

"I just—I thought you were better than this."

"Better than what, worrying about my own company? The company that my whole family's livelihood depends on? It's a big deal, Harley."

I turn to find him looking at me. I look back at him, hard. "I never asked you to sacrifice anything for me. You want to fire me, fire me. You want to end things, end them."

"I never said I wanted any of that."

"So?"

"So." He tries to smile. "I just—we need to be careful, with this. With us. I don't want your reputation getting dragged through the mud, either."

"Having dinner together in a public restaurant isn't exactly keeping things on the DL," I point out.

Greyson's hands are clenched on the wheel. "I'm not giving up whole parts of my life to mitigate risk. I just—needed to know."

"I get it. I'm sorry, for what it's worth. I never intended to imperil your company."

His hand finds mine, encloses it. Squeezes it. "I know."

With a kiss on my forehead, he pulls away, exhales. "We better have dinner before I forget all about it and kiss you how I want to."

I giggle. "Sounds good to me."

From the outside, the restaurant is nothing special: just a colorful shiny banner reading Rosalinda's set onto a window-covered cement block. But inside, I'm craning my neck every which way. The place is exquisite, brimming with light and plants of all sizes. It's got a cool boho vibe, with a big crimson Persian rug on the floor and yarn tapestries dangling off the walls.

"I've got a reservation," Greyson tells the maître d'. "For the top floor private patio."

"Ah." The man nods. "Right this way, then."

I tuck my hand in the crook of Greyson's arm. "You're right, this place is just my style. Low-key."

"Low-key, gorgeous, fresh," he corrects me.

"If I was a blusher, I'd be blushing," I say with a little laugh.

The private patio is nothing short of an urban jungle. Vines and palms and monsteras of all sizes and shapes drape around us, so that we have complete privacy, while small lit candles add some romance.

"Talk about a rainforest throwback," I say with a little laugh.

"My first choice was CANOE," Greyson reminds me.

"And you get second dibs for Opus," I point out.

"Good."

"So," he says, once we've gotten drinks and wandered out to look across the sunset spilling over the city, making even bland skyscrapers into beauties, "how's work going?"

Hmm.

"There's not that much of it, to be honest," I say.

"Madeline hasn't been keeping you busy?"

"She was supposed to?"

Greyson frowns. "The other day, I thought it over and realized there are actually a bunch of small projects for you to get started on. She was supposed to pass that on to you, give you the preliminaries. I'll have to have a word with her. She's been acting off all week."

I stay quiet for a minute or so, but when he doesn't change the subject, I say, "What a view, eh?"

What a fail at a subject-change.

"Harley." Greyson turns to face me head-on. "What are you not telling me?"

"It's nothing," I say. "I just think my coworkers aren't used to me yet, is all."

"What makes you say that?"

"It's probably just in my head." I force a laugh. "You know, new job jitters."

"No. I don't know. My team has always been really friendly to all new employees. Are you saying—"

"I'm not saying anything. Can we forget it, please?"

"Harley—"

"I'm not saying it again."

Greyson shuts his mouth, looking away angrily. Maybe he's thinking about how we've already fought twice in the past half hour.

But I'm not about to create some work drama prematurely. Plus, Greyson getting involved would probably just make things worse.

Our meals are served a few minutes later, and we eat in silence. It's deliciously spicy Mexican food, but if Greyson's enjoying it, he's giving no sign. The three furrows in his forehead and two staring eyes indicate he's deep in thought. Finally, he says, "Don't worry about it. I'll talk to them."

"Please don't."

"Trust me, Harley. I know how to handle this."

"I don't doubt that. But I don't think there's anything you can do to help. You really think the other employees will be receptive to you calling them out on it?"

"Yeah, I do. My dad and I hired them not just because they're good, but because they're willing to grow."

I nod dully, and almost don't say it until I do: "I think that, whatever their beef is, it has to do with us. Don't you?"

Greyson swirls his fork around his plate uselessly, takes a sip of water. Until he can't avoid it anymore. "It might be."

His mouth has become a snarl, his eyes frustrated and narrow. "I haven't told anyone, though. My brothers guessed, but that's it, and they wouldn't spread it around."

"I haven't told anyone either," I say. "Except for my cousin Hannah, who wouldn't tell anyone and doesn't know anyone from the office anyway."

"Probably was Samantha," Greyson growls. Then he sighs. "What's done is done, though. If only there was a way... Maybe if we cooled things off for a bit, waited it out."

"Yeah, that might be best," I say simply.

I should leave it at that, but I can't. "Might be best to cool things off for good."

Greyson's look at me is abrupt. "What?"

"I'm a detriment to your company, your image, your employees. We don't even know what this is—is it really worth risking everything for it? Maybe it's best if I stay away from the office, and you call me up next time you go to shoot another episode. Or you can even find another cinematographer if you think that'd be easier."

I can't believe I'm saying this, virtually giving up my dream job. But it's the right thing to do. I can feel it.

The last thing I want in the world is to hurt Greyson.

At the end of the day, I'll still have Storm Inc. on my resume. And as for Greyson and I...

"Why are you saying this?" he asks hoarsely.

I find that I'm rising to leave, done with my dinner, done with tonight.

"I'm tired of pretending like we're a normal couple one minute, then hiding away the next. I'm tired of you putting off the inevitable. I think you have some hard decisions to make, Greyson. And me being here isn't making them any easier for you."

Our eyes catch. I could kiss him now, so easily. Let him kiss me back. I could let the kiss make everything OK. Turn logic into feeling, impossible into possible, make everything right—for now at least. But it would only be a temporary distraction from the shadow hanging over all this.

"Goodbye Greyson," I say, as I leave.

The next second, he's by my side. "Harley. Don't go. We can figure this out. I can figure this out."

Don't look at him, don't you dare look at him... or notice how good he smells... or how much you want him...

As I tear myself away a second time, I choke back my next words: "I'm sorry."

And then I'm hurrying through the restaurant, down the stairs, down the street to get away. Until I spot a cab, and then I'm in there, going home, and it all feels unreal. So unreal. Like this is something I've concocted in my mind back there at the restaurant. Like Greyson may lean over and kiss away the trouble any second now.

CHAPTER 27

Greyson

I sit there for a minute, maybe more. Wait for her to come back, to change her mind. To sweep towards me and change this all with a smile, a kiss.

She never comes back.

I call her, but it goes straight to voicemail.

The worst part is that she's right. The company will probably be vulnerable for another year, at least. Can we really lie low that entire time?

And people aren't so easily swayed by what their boss tells them to do, especially if they've lost respect for that boss based on his actions. While I'm sure talking to my staff will get them to straighten up, part of me wonders if it will be enough, if it isn't genuine. Harley hates fakeness, won't like it, will see right through it.

Maybe the Storm office isn't the place for her.

But I can't let her go.

My phone goes off, and I answer it without looking.

"You coming?" Nolan asks. "I got the kale chips."

"Oh, right." I'd forgotten all about the comedy act I agreed to participate in. Almost missed it. Damn, I really am slipping. "Now's not really the best time."

I've got the beginnings of a pounding headache, and I'd like to try giving Harley another call.

"Dude, save the jokes for the stage!" Nolan's voice is incredulous. "I had the graphic designer put your face on the poster—you can't bail now!"

"You know you're fine without me."

"Yeah, I'm fucking hilarious without you, but not hilarious enough to cover the big gaping absence of your face. Come on."

I rise from the table. "Fine. I'll be there in 15."

"That's the reliable big brother I know and love."

I get there in 10, trying to call Harley on the way. But it's no dice. The only part of her I have now are her words, echoing with a truth I don't like. A truth I can't accept.

Maybe we don't know what this is, but that doesn't mean we can't make it work.

The comedy club is packed, and my brother waves me over. "Just the man I was looking for! Look at the two lovely ladies I have with me."

He's gesturing to a redhead and a raven-haired woman, both wearing badges that say PRESS. Behind them, Nolan winks at me. I've got his message loud and clear: This is our chance for some more good publicity for Storm Media. Though I'm not at all in the mood.

We exchange pleasantries, then it's time for my brother's show to start. As usual, he's whip-crack smart, hilarious, jumping amidst different current issues, joshing certain people in the crowd. Then it's my turn.

As soon as I get up on stage, I know it's all wrong. I miss Harley, and I don't want to be here. Still, I stick it out, trying to match my brother's gregarious high energy when he's in his absolute element, trying to joke back.

By mid-time, my brother gives me a pat and a concerned look. "You good?"

"No."

"Yeah, I can tell. It's OK, though." A winning smile. "They paid to come here for me, remember."

We chuckle and he shoos me away. "Thanks for coming out, anyway. You can go off to your girl if you really want to now."

"OK."

But as I'm leaving, one of the press women pulls me aside. "Can we talk?"

"Sure."

We go into a hallway, and her tiny magenta lips compress together. "I probably shouldn't tell you this, but I really liked what you said about your dad's tax evasion and how you stepped up with the charity and all that." She leans in. "The Star is going to be publishing an article about you and your employee's relationship."

"What?"

"Right now, it's all hearsay, but as soon as the other media outlets pick up on anything substantial, you could be in for a full-on scandal."

I eye her blankly. It's all happening so fast: worry about the worst-case scenario, then the worst-case scenario itself.

"I've seen how these things play out. They're going to eat Storm Media alive if you don't beat them to the punch."

I've been watching her big horse teeth move numbly, hardly aware of the words coming out and what they mean. "What are you saying?"

"You have to fire her. Maybe not for good, but—"

"Why are you telling me all this?" I ask.

"I told you, I liked your talk, plus I'm a huge fan. I don't want to see Storm Inc. go down over this."

"You won't."

"OK."

We stand there for a few seconds, awkwardly.

"Thank you," I tell her. "But I have to go now." And then I leave. I call a cab numbly, pacing, hardly thinking.

Once I'm in the cab, the gears in my head grind around it: Harley. Tomorrow's article. Madeline. Harley.

Finally, I call up Madeline. "I've heard the Star is about to publish an article with some gossip about me and an employee. Can you see if you can get in touch with them and have them pull it?"

"Sure," she says in a clipped voice, before hanging up.

I'm at home a few minutes later when she calls me back. "Sorry. No dice. They're running it."

I lean back into my recliner and groan.

"It's fine," I say, with more confidence than I feel. "I'll figure it out."

"Boss, if you want my take—"

"I don't," I snap, hanging up.

It's obvious to anyone with half a brain what I have to do: give up Harley. For now, maybe even for good.

Not just for the company's sake, but for hers. The Star is half trashy gossip anyway, but if anyone else catches us together and decides to pick up the story and run with it... we're both done for.

Plus, what kind of relationship could we have if we have to duck and hide for months, maybe even years? Take-out every day, movies every night... Harley deserves better than that. She deserves to be shown off like the prize she is. I won't let her agree to something substandard just so we can be together a bit longer.

I go out onto my roof to call her up. Maybe the clear night air can clear my head. "Hey."

"Hey."

"So."

She tries to laugh, but it's not much of one. "So."

"I'm sorry," I say.

"Don't be sorry. This is for the best."

"Let me explain. They're running a story about us in the Star tomorrow. I don't think we have much of a choice at this point... maybe at some point in a year or so..." I trail off.

"I get it," she says. "You have to fire me too."

"I don't have to—"

"Yes, you do," she says sadly.

Up above, the stars are nearly invisible from the light pollution. It seems like my night with Harley, looking at the stars, is years away.

"You won't get a better reference than mine," I find myself saying. "I have friends in the business who would love to work with you. I'm not going to have this screw up your career. I'm not going to rest until you get an even better position."

Her voice is hushed, sad. "OK."

"I'm so sorry." My words fall flat. What the fuck good does my 'sorry' do her, really?

"Don't be. We both knew this was over before it really started."

"Still, I should've protected you better."

"I'm sure you did your best."

Her words slay me. Anger, blaming, all that I expected and could deal with. But this quiet, fair acceptance... I can't take it.

"I tried to get the story pulled, but they won't budge," I find myself rambling. "And this is only the beginning, if we keep going on how we have—"

"I know how scandals work," she cuts me off. "I know we have to do this."

"Doesn't make it any easier," I say miserably. "If I could just see you one last time..."

We both let my words trail off. We know we can't. The last time would invariably lead to the next, and then the next after that. Even now, it's taking everything I have not to urge her to come here, now. To be with me.

"Thanks for everything," Harley says quietly. "Goodbye."

Seconds after she hangs up the phone, I realize it, what this foreign feeling inside me is.

"I love you," I say into the silence.

CHAPTER 28

Harley

"Har?" Hannah says tentatively from outside the door.

"Yeah?"

"Don't want you to take this the wrong way... But why are you sitting in the bathroom with the lights off?"

I blink. "Huh. So I am."

"Can I come in? I need to brush my teeth."

"Sure," I say. "I'm just sitting on the edge of the tub anyway."

I honestly can't even remember coming in here in my sad stupor, but I'm not about to admit that.

"Is everything OK?" Hannah asks, flicking on the light and reaching for her purple toothbrush.

"I... Yeah?"

She pauses, gives her head a shake to throw her light brown bangs out of her face before shoving her toothbrush into her mouth. "You don't sound very convinced. And didn't you leave your date with Greyson way early?"

I clamp my lips closed firmly, but that doesn't stop it from bursting out of me: "Greyson broke up with me."

Hannah drops her toothbrush. "He what?"

"The press found out about us. Storm Inc. can't afford any bad publicity right now."

"But..." Hannah trails off, her mouth working soundlessly.

I rise, touching her arm. "It's fine. Really. There's no way this would've worked long-term anyway. He's my boss."

Hannah bites her lip, then, halfway to reaching for her toothbrush, gives it a kick instead. "You know what? Screw bedtime and tooth-brushing. We gonna party."

At her last statement, uttered in a 'gangsta' voice, I giggle. "Oh yeah?"

Hannah grabs my hand and marches me out of there. "Hell yeah."

In my room, she flips through my clothes until she gets to the tightest, shortest, reddest dress I own. "Let's go, sister."

I chuckle as I take it off the hangar. "As you say, cousin."

She grins, giving me a side-hug. "Seriously, though. I've got you. Remember how you threw me a surprise party, then a birthday vacation to England after that asshole player dumped me via Snapchat?"

"Of course," I say, side-hugging her back. "How we got a picture of him and burned it in that forest after too?"

Hannah sighs wistfully. "Oh yes, the craycation."

"I could really use a vacation right about now," I murmur, half to myself.

Hannah snorts. "You came back from Costa Rica literally a week ago."

I wave my hand dismissively. "Details, details. Aren't you supposed to be getting ready too, or am I hitting up Coda alone?"

"Who said we were going to Coda?"

"Where else do we go when we want to dance?"

"Point taken." Hannah smiles. "Give me 10."

Ten minutes later, we meet in the hallway.

"You look hot," I tell her. "Is that the dress from—"

"The Most Handsome Man Alive?" Hannah nods. "You bet. Although I don't know how much he would approve of its intended use tonight. We're gonna get crazzyyyy!"

I laugh. While Hannah and I actually have gotten into some shenanigans while drunk, including climbing an interesting and tall fountain and attracting a small crowd to cheer us on, I have a feeling that tonight will be a little tamer. Sadness isn't exactly an upper for me, even if I do get wasted.

Still, I don't want Hannah to feel obligated to go out, either.

"You don't have to come," I tell her, "Really, it's fine. I'm not even sure I should be going out at all."

"You're right." Hannah nods her head in faux agreement. "Sitting around at home always makes me feel better after a breakup... not!" She grabs my hand. "Now let's get going, hot stuff."

I smirk. I'd forgotten how good this dress looked, how each of its bandage strips was basically painted on. "I'm ready when you are."

The Uber ride to the club is quick, but once we get there, the line-up is snaking around the door.

Hannah marches us right up to the bouncer. "My friend just got dumped," she tells the no-nonsense-faced doorman with a head like a bald pale battering ram.

"And I can do a pirouette," I chime in helpfully.

The guy recrosses his arms, looking the textbook definition of 'Don't Fuck with Me'. "Oh yeah?"

I do the world's worst rendition of a pirouette, then shoot the guy a winning smile. "Hell yeah?"

He chuckles, showing off painfully white teeth with a shake of his head before waving us inside. "Alright, alright. Just don't do that again."

I do another horrid pirouette once we're inside, although the doorman's attention is already elsewhere. Not that it really matters. I can already tell that it's going to be a good night.

House and techno music blasts any stray thought out of my head, while the crowd looks more cool than douchey.

Hannah gets us some Caesars, and I down mine almost immediately, hardly tasting the tomatoey goodness. Tonight, I'm not drinking for the taste, after all.

She gives me a sympathetic side-eye. "That bad, eh?"

"I just…" I can feel the words bubbling in me, floundering angrily. "I didn't see it coming, is all. I mean, I did and I didn't."

She nods sagely. "I understand perfectly."

I have to laugh. "No, you don't."

She laughs. "No, I don't. But Greyson is a jerk, whatever you think."

"He's just trying to protect the company—and me. If other media outlets pick up this story and it goes viral it could ruin my reputation and career. With me fired, the small story will probably blow over. I could still have a fighting chance. Greyson at least said he'd give me a glowing reference, recommend me to his friends." Seeing Hannah's dubious look, I shrug. "It's the smart thing to do. What was stupid was for me to hook up with him in the first place."

"You're talking all logical, but looking all miserable," Hannah says sympathetically.

"My head's all sorted out," I agree. "Now, if I could just get my heart on board…"

I get us a few more drinks and sip mine, shaking my head. "I'm just disappointed in myself, I guess. I thought I was this strong person who could just march through life without being thrown by anything. But how all the other people at work were shunning me, and now this, how hard it's hitting me… it's making me rethink all that. Maybe I'm not as invincible as I thought."

Hannah's hand on my shoulder is light yet reassuring. "Hey. None of us are as invincible as we thought."

I sigh. "I know, Han. But it's me—I mean, remember how I went toe to toe with Annabelle Leigh in front of the entire class, and just laughed when she and her bitch friends tried to get me back by flushing my student card down the toilet? Remember how many guys I've dated and dumped or who things just didn't work out with and I didn't give a damn? Remember how many parties and guys and opportunities I sacrificed to be the best at what I do? And now, what it comes down to is this: I threw away my dream opportunity because of some hot guy."

"Some hot guy you have a crazy connection with," Hannah pipes in.

"Not crazy enough to try and make it work," I murmur, shaking my head. "I just—I guess I'm worried I'm not that person anymore. I mean, it sounds conceited, but I've never been dumped before, Han. Never been fired. Of course I've had people dislike me, but… this feels different. I just can't get my head around why I risked everything to be with this man. This man who wouldn't do the same for me."

"Stop," Hannah chides me. She puts her hand to stop my glass from making it to my mouth. Clearly, she sees how I've been drinking not just to get drunk, but to get obliterated. Not that it's really helping, so far. "You couldn't have known how things would turn out."

I look at her head-on, moving my hand so I can down the rest of my fruity drink. "Come on. I knew how this would end. Bosses don't end up with their employees. End of story. Relationships at work just make everything messy. Everyone knows that."

"You did it and it's done," Hannah says. "What's the point of beating yourself up about it now?"

Putting down my cup on a nearby ledge, I throw up my hands, glaring at the disco ball overhead, which is currently throwing an annoyingly vibrant blue beam into my eyes every few seconds. The air smells musky, human, and even, if I was in the mood, sultry. I am not in the mood. I don't want to be here.

I turn to her. "Because I'm trying to figure it out. What made Greyson so..." Ugh, I hate the word, but it's coming out whether I like it or not, "Special. I've dated other guys who are hot, funny, fun, rich. Guys other girls would kill to date. And sure, Greyson is an amazing catch too. But still. Why risk it all on the one guy who it can't work out with? It doesn't make any sense."

"Love never does," Hannah says simply.

"That's not... we weren't..." How I felt in his arms. The glint in his eyes when he was looking at me, a second before he looked away. I had a feeling that being with you would make anything good. I shake my head. "It doesn't matter, anyway."

Hannah's looking at me with a look I haven't seen on her before, a look I hate: pity. I'm not the weak one, the one who gets hurt. That's not me.

"C'mon." I take her by the hand and pull her after me onto the dance floor. "Let's dance."

In the middle of the dance floor, I let the beat take over. Groove my limbs into motion, roll my hips side to side, bob my head back and forth.

God, it's such a relief. The music. The all-encompassing feel of the place: the lights, the people, the pounding bass. Yes, all there is room for here is being here. Now. Yes. Yes.

The next song is "Smells Like Teen Spirit", and Hannah and me jump around, faux angsting and yelling along to the lyrics.

A few more songs, and we goof off, do the chicken dance to some rap song, laughing our heads off.

A man comes and goes, another.

One takes my hand and spins me. He's handsome and looks like an artist and yet I spin away just as quickly.

Suddenly, I can't take it anymore. Can't bear being here for another second.

I pull Hannah outside.

"What's the matter?" she asks me.

"I can't," I say simply. "I can't be here and pretend I'm up to meet another guy or dance. Or anything really."

"Hmm." Hannah's head bob is pure understanding. "Need a good cry?"

I sigh. "Think so."

"Well, we got a few good songs in there." She's already taking out her phone, ordering us an Uber. "Plus, you're probably right. Holding it all in won't do you any good—unless it does."

We both chortle at that. Our Aunt Beatrice has a philosophy: "Emotions never did nobody any good." She seems as blissful as a sloth whenever we visit, even after her beloved canary Bella died, though for all I know she could have a punching bag in the basement.

When we get home, Hannah gives me a big hug. "You sure you just want to go to bed now?"

"No," I say truthfully. "I want to hop on a plane—any plane— and just see where I end up. Forget all this. Get away. But for now, I think I just need some sleep."

Hannah yawns. "Yup. Sleep sounds good to me. I'm really sorry, Har." She hugs me again.

"I am too," I murmur. "I am too."

CHAPTER 29

Greyson

"Why you looking so Grey, son?" Landon chides me as I walk by his office.

"Not now," I tell him.

I'm surprised Nolan hasn't thrown his quintessential 'Grey, son' joke at me lately. Then again, a lot of shit has been going on. So far, I've managed to avoid checking the papers today.

There's one waiting on my desk.

STORM PREZ'S STEAMY AFFAIR WITH TEENAGE INTERN, the headline reads. I roll my eyes. To be fair, the assholes got 2/4 of the facts correct—probably a new record for them. Not that anyone ever reads the Star for its stellar journalism, but still. Part of me had hoped that last night's warning was baseless. That this morning I could call up Harley and tell her I made a mistake.

Clearly, that won't be happening.

Clack-clack-clack

"Good morning, Mr. Storm," Madeline says, pausing in the doorway. "So, you've seen it?"

"I've seen it," I say gruffly.

"Ah." An inclination of her strawberry-blonde head. "Well, it's certainly not my place to tell you how to run your business, but—"

"Ms. Davis has been let go," I say. "That should satisfy the gossip mill—in the media and in this office."

Madeline almost beams before recovering her composure. "You've done the right thing, sir. I know everyone in the office would agree."

I give her a cutting glare. "I know how fond you all were of her."

It occurs to me that I've never really disliked Madeline—or any of my employees—until this moment.

I thought they were better than acting like a bunch of bitchy high school girls against a new employee. Then again, if I'd known, maybe I could have put a stop to the bullshit. It's too late now, anyway.

As for Harley, it's only 9 AM and I've already had to stop myself from calling her up several times. Mostly for mundane bullshit excuses, like if she wanted her desktop ivy plant brought to her or donated, or what she thought of the weather on this fine day. But there are some actual legitimate things I need to know, like whether she wants me to get her a new position with a friend ASAP or give it some time, and which qualities she wants me to emphasize in my reference.

Spectacular. Gorgeous. Funny. Daring. Unprecedented.

Fucking focus, Greyson.

Madeline, apparently, has decided to pretend that she didn't hear my earlier remark.

"I think Mr. Landon wanted to see you," she says, heading for the door.

I say nothing, sit down when she leaves.

Maybe I was a bit hard on her, but too fucking bad. Her and the rest of them should've known better than to take out petty gossip on Harley. And if she thinks I'm going to pretend to be happy when

I just made the hardest decision of my life... then she's fucking delusional.

I manage to stay seated for another few minutes before another excuse to call up Harley—check in, make sure she's OK—drives me to head over to Landon's office.

On the way there, my phone rings. It's Maurice.

"Hate to be the bearer of bad news, kiddo," he says.

It's always caught me off guard how my accountant sounds like an Italian mobster with a mouthful of food, but he does the job damn well.

"What do you mean?" I ask him.

"These taxes you sent me that your brother tried working on," he rasps. "Is the boy mentally handicapped or what? I don't know what the original documents were like, but whatever he's muddled with and you've sent me is complete shit. And I mean complete shit."

I groan. "You don't mean—"

"Hell yeah you'll have to send me the original documents. In full. Can't be more of a shitshow than what I have in front of me. It'll take some time though, for sure. Gonna cost you a pretty penny too. I'm going to slash my fees in half because you're like a son to me and there's no better lingonberry pie than the one your mama sends my family every year for Christmas, but damn, Greyson. You better get that brother of yours straightened out. I could've made more sense out of shredded scraps of seven different translations of the Bible than this shit."

I clench the phone harder. "Got it. I'll have the files sent to you this week. Thanks."

"Ah, it's what I do. You take it easy, kiddo. And be careful, these young lionesses can eat you for breakfast if you aren't careful."

I suppress my next groan. "You mean you—"

"Saw the papers this morning, afraid so. Not to say that I trust the Star more than my klepto aunt after she's visited and I've some missing silver and she claims to know nothing about it, but still. Talk travels, and people often don't give a rat's ass about 'The Truth'."

I exhale. "True. Thanks again, Maurice. Time for some major damage control."

"Amen," Maurice says. "And tell that dipshit of a brother of yours to come see me if he wants to learn how to decode figures and numbers the right way, instead of throwing them around like Jackson Pollock paint on a canvas."

"Will do," I say, hanging up.

When I knock on Landon's door, I find that my fist is pounding with way more force than necessary.

"Whoa, try to bash in my door, why don't you?" Landon says with an easy smile as he opens it.

"Maurice called," I say. "You fucked up."

Landon's face clouds over. "That's what you're opening with, really?"

I stride in, spinning around to face him. "You had one job... and you not only royally fucked it up, but you cost the company precious time and money by doing so."

Landon lifts his chin to jeer at me. "Hold up—I cost the company precious time and money? How about your little tryst with the cinematographer girl? You think it looks good having

Storm Inc.'s name in the tabloids after all the drama we've had about Dad and his tax evasion?"

"That situation is dealt with," I say tersely. "Right now, we're talking about you."

Landon throws up his arms, his muscles showing through tensed and huge. "You weren't here, Greyson. I got lost, I'll admit. Transferring all the info to the computer and trying to make sense of everything, I took some liberties I probably shouldn't have. But you weren't here. You went gallivanting off to Costa Rica, having fun at playing the producer and banging some chick, while the rest of us were stuck here without a president."

I open my mouth, then close it.

Fuck. Landon's right.

All of me is raging and I want to pound the walls, his desk, take him by the shoulders and shake him until he shuts the fuck up. But he's right. I have failed him. I've failed everyone, Harley most of all.

"Maybe I wasn't there how I should have been," I admit, "but still, you were supposed to be the president while I was away."

"Me, right." Landon barks out a laugh. "The guy who was maybe open to the position but knew next to nothing about it, and who was already bogged down with the full-time job of muddling through the company taxes. Shocking I fucked that up."

I stand there, glaring at him, unsure what to say. I just want to yell. At someone, something, anything. I just want her back.

"And this scandal..." Landon continues, shaking his head.

I shake the thought out of my head, force my voice to a measured tone. "That situation... is dealt with. She's been fired."

"Oh, has she then?"

"She has. And Maurice will fix the taxes while we repay what we can. The crisis should blow over."

"Good," Landon says, sinking back so he's sitting on the edge of his desk. "Just don't pin this on me. You were supposed to be here."

With his words, the last of my anger seeps out of me. Suddenly, I'm incredibly, incredibly tired.

"You're right" and a sad nod is all I can manage. "I've been failing a lot of people lately."

Although the only one my thoughts keep circling back to is the last one I want to think about right now.

"Hey." Landon raises himself to give me a pat on the arm. "Don't sweat it. It's a high-stress time right now for all of us. But we'll get through it. Storm Inc. always manages to."

"Thanks." I smile at him, rearrange my features into a cool expression.

As president, that's my job: keep up morale, even when I'm not feeling it myself.

Back in my office, I sit down at my computer, check my emails, then check my phone. I got a call while I was talking with Landon and had my phone on silent.

When I listen to it, chills go up my spine.

It's Harley: "Greyson, hi. I... don't want to disturb you. I just—I have to talk to you. Right away. It's urgent."

What strikes me isn't how something in me aches at her voice, or how I have no idea what this 'urgent' thing could be. Or even how, now, finally, I have a legitimate actionable excuse to call her up.

It's what was in her voice, what I've never heard there before: fear.

CHAPTER 30

Harley

A Few Hours Earlier

Ugh. Mornings.

My stomach gives a dismal lurch, and I groan.

Thank God I don't have to go into work today. I'm not normally one for epic hangovers, but this morning I feel like death if death were a half-smushed pigeon trying to eat moldy scrambled eggs.

Ugh!!!

I lurch from the bed to the bathroom so abruptly that Anchovy lets out an angry grr and races to the main room, probably to unleash his fury on my favorite decorative pillow. Oh well.

Knees against the cool tile, face precariously close to the toilet, I dry-heave a few times before hot liquid pours out of my mouth into the bowl.

"Oh, blessed mother of... ugh..."

Ladies and Gentlemen, I give you The Exorcism of Harley Davis.

When I'm finished, I have just enough energy left to totter back to bed and collapse there.

Is sadness barfing a thing? Maybe that's it.

I check my phone, but of course there's no text from Greyson. Just like there was no text from Greyson last night. Just like this morning, at whatever random way-too-early time I woke up, there was no text from Greyson. Just how tomorrow there will not, in fact, be any text from Greyson. Not ever again.

"He dumped you, idiot," I grumble at myself. Which prompts my stomach to lurch precariously for no discernible reason whatsoever. Unless... sadness barfing?

I grab at the glass of water beside my bed and gingerly lift it to my lips. The cool water feels glorious going down my throat, not so much once it's in my actual belly.

"Damn it," I mumble as I stagger back to the bathroom.

An hour of back and forth bathroom trips later, and a terrible reply to Hannah's text of How you feeling?, and there's a knock on my door.

"Go away," I groan, then, "What are you doing here?"

"Dear Lord, you look like a corpse," Hannah says sympathetically. "Hangover that bad?"

"I don't know, I never get hangovers," I groan. "And who gets hangovers where they keep barfing and can't stop?"

"Oh," she says, sitting on the edge of my bed.

"What does that mean, 'oh'?"

"Just..." She looks away. "It's probably nothing."

I dab at my face with a wetted face cloth. "I swear to God, Han, if you know something..."

"I'm just being paranoid."

I glare at her. "Tell me."

"No. You just need rest, and—I should go."

I lurch upright then, half-up, totter with a whimper. "Hannah..."

"Get back into bed!" she snaps.

I don't move, glaring at her, stomach doing strange contortions I didn't know it was capable of.

"If I tell you, will you?" she persists.

"Sure thing." I flop back on my back, exhaling in blessed relief, although I still feel like crap.

"It's just... I'm going to go to the drugstore to buy you something. It's probably nothing, but you did mention you skipped a period the other week, and now that you're barfing like crazy—"

"Pregnancy test," I garble out, horrified. "You think I'm pregnant."

"No. I mean, just to be sure..."—reassuring not-a-big-deal smile that fails miserably—of course this is a big deal!—"...before we take you to a doctor..."

I chuck a pillow at her. "No doctor! Not pregnant! My Allenia pills haven't failed me yet!"

She doesn't have to say it: All it takes is one time.

Anyway, Hannah's already out the door with a cheery wave and "See you soon, Har!"

Apparently, I manage to doze off because the next thing I know, she's back, drugstore shopping bag hooked on her arm.

I glare at her and gesture to myself weakly. "No barfing. Look, I'm better."

Although only if 'better' means I still feel like deep-fried death.

She takes out a pink box that my first instinct is to chuck at the wall and stomp on. "Come on. Humor me."

"No."

"Harley."

"I said no."

She crosses her arms across her chest. "You know I'm going to stand here until you do it."

"I'm too tired," I whine.

She doesn't budge, gives me a hard look. "Scared, more like."

"Go away."

"C'mon." She comes to the side of the bed and helps hoist me up. "Either we're going to do this together, or I'm going to drag you there."

"Can't it... wait?"

Hannah gives me an even harder look. "You really want to wait on this."

I sigh. She's right. Of course she is. No way can I relax with the thought of oh-my-Lord-do-I-have-a-baby hanging over my head. "Fine."

I snatch the drugstore bag from her arm and hurry to the bathroom. Inside, I close the door and look at my bedraggled expression.

Jesus, this is it. This is really it.

After this...

Don't think about it.

I take out the applicator, go over to the toilet, pee on it and toss it into the sink.

"No, no, please God no," I mutter as I wait.

This can't be happening. I take my birth control pills religiously. Same time every day. I've never even had a pregnancy scare before. This can't be happening.

"Har, you OK?" Hannah asks from outside the door.

"Yeah," I say, "Don't worry, I..."

I fall silent.

No. Fuck no.

"Harley?"

I can't speak. I can hardly breathe. There, in the sink, is the applicator. With two thin but unmistakable blue lines.

I'm pregnant.

**

"I'm sorry," Hannah says a few minutes later, after I've cried and sobbed and blubbered about it.

"Me too," I say miserably, for probably the fifth time. "Jesus Han, what am I going to do?"

"I don't know," she says, "There's always..."

I shake my head immediately. "That feels wrong. I don't know, doesn't mean it is wrong, right?"

My sidelong look at Hannah just makes her shake her head. "You know I can't answer that for you."

My gaze droops dully to my ugly orange and pink patchwork quilt, the one my mom made. God, Mom. She's going to be so disappointed in me. I'm disappointed in myself. A week ago, I was on top of the world: dream job, dream guy, and now... Now there's nothing left.

Nothing left other than the unwanted little being in my belly.

"Jesus," I groan, "and what about Greyson?"

"Don't you worry about him," Hannah says firmly. "First you look after yourself."

"He has a right to know," I say simply.

"But not to make the decision for you."

"I know," I say. "He probably doesn't even want to hear from me."

Hannah pats me. "I think you should lie low for now. Rest up. Figure out what you want to do. You've got enough going on without involving Greyson right now."

I lean back into bed, onto the pillows Hannah propped up for me. "You're probably right. Thanks."

Another one of those reassuring smiles, though this one works a bit better. "Later, we can watch some Charlie's Angels too, if you're up for it."

"Thanks." I yawn, my eyes closing. "See ya."

She leaves and, while I should be fast asleep, all I do while I lie there is cycle through the same thoughts.

A baby—God, what am I going to do? How could this happen to me? What am I going to do? Why does everything keep going wrong? What am I going to tell Greyson? What am I going to do? What the hell am I going to do?

I toss and turn, and groan. I still feel like crap, although thankfully I don't feel like barfing anymore.

Finally, I can't take it anymore. I sit up in bed, grab my phone and dial Greyson's number.

I can't be strong right now, sick and pregnant. All I can be is weak.

Anyway, I need to tell him. To hear his voice. Might as well get this over with.

Of course, he doesn't pick up.

"Idiot," I mutter to the disappointed twist in my gut. "He's not going to be overjoyed to pick up a call from his ex-employee/hookup."

I can't help but leave a message, though. Then, I sink back into bed. At some point, finally, sleep comes.

Then, my phone rings.

CHAPTER 31

Greyson

"Seriously Harley?" I grumble as I listen to her voicemail message for the second time. "Why call me and then refuse to fucking pick up?"

Yeah, I ended things with her. Yeah, she was 10/10 pissed with me. But then why call at all?

The next few hours at work, I hammer the tasks on my to-do list like my life depends on it. I need all the productive distractions I can get.

By the time the work day is done, I should be satisfied, only I'm not. Can't be.

Not with Harley's call still in the back of my mind. She hasn't responded to my calls or texts. Is she messing with me?

Finally, I call her one more time, before I get in my car.

I start driving, foot goading the car faster and faster. It's only once I turn onto the street her building is on that I realize that's where I've been heading.

Maybe not the best idea, but fuck it, she sounded really upset. Maybe she needs me.

I know I...

Just stick to the plan, Greyson.

That's the problem, though: I don't have one.

It takes me staring at her building's buzz pad and firmly locked set of doors for me to remember that I don't even know her room number. I badger the man at the front desk through the glass until he grudgingly allows me to look up her name and buzz the room number.

"Be right down," someone says over the line when I tell her who I am.

A woman with light brown hair eyes me appraisingly as she steps off the elevator.

"Is she here?" I ask, then, seeing her scowl, add, "Sorry, this is Greyson. Her... work colleague."

The last part comes out wrong and awkward.

"I know who you are." Her glare indicates that she has no illusions about me being Harley's 'colleague'. Is this the cousin Harley told me so much about? "And she can't see you right now."

"She's OK?" I ask. "She called me saying that she needed to talk to me. Are you sure she won't?"

"Yes," she says firmly. "Although I'll tell her you stopped by."

"Good. Thank you."

We stand there, eyeing each other for a good minute.

"I really think I should see her," I press. "She said it was important."

"You can't now."

Another minute, an exchange of glares. All of me is burning to shove past this woman, demand to see Harley, talk to her face to face.

"Why not?" I snap.

"She's sleeping, wasn't feeling well earlier," she says. And here I thought her glare couldn't get any fiercer. "She doesn't want to see you. Did she ask you to come here?"

"No," I admit. "Just..." I trail off.

Pushing this much to see Harley, I'm not doing it for her. I'm doing it for me. To see her, to know she's OK. To see her smile just one more time.

But that's not fair to her. I was the one who ended things with her, even fired her. The least I can do is respect her wishes now.

Even though I don't like it. Not one fucking bit.

"Alright," I say. "Just tell her... I'll be waiting for her call. Whenever she's able to."

"I will," she says.

And still, I can't seem to force my dipshit feet to take me away. What am I expecting, Harley to come skipping out of the elevator, wearing that great big grin of hers that always melted my heart?

With a normal person, hell no. But this is Harley, who defies convention and any state of normalcy. If anyone would do it, show up when least expected in the wildest way possible, it's her.

But the elevator doors stay closed, and finally the woman turns to leave.

"Wait," I call after her.

She pauses. "What?"

"Are you Hannah?"

She nods.

"Can you... can you tell her, just that I'm sorry. That I care about her a lot."

Her face remains stony.

"I know what you must think of me," I say. "Just... Yeah. I'm sorry." I turn to go.

"Greyson," she says.

"Yeah?"

"If you really care about her, you'll stay away from her. All you can do now is hurt her."

I gaze at her steadily. She's right. I've done nothing but hurt Harley, after all this.

"I can't make any promises," I tell her. Not with Harley working like a magnet on me hour in hour out, even now. "But I will try."

Her smile is sad and she wants to say more, but she only nods, turns to go. "Goodbye."

"Goodbye," I say hoarsely after her.

As I walk away and out of the building, down a street I don't know, and then another, away from my car, towards I don't know where, it occurs to me. Harley is the only woman I've ever known who could bring tears to my ears when she wasn't even there.

At some point, I make it back to my car, and my phone goes off.

This time, it's Nolan. "You can't avoid me forever, big brother."

"Avoiding you?"

"Yeah. This is the tenth call, but I'm not going to give up that easily."

"This is the first call I've gotten from you."

"What?" A pause. "Shit, ha. I was calling the wrong number. That explains it."

"OK."

"Don't you want to know what it's about?" he continues.

"I assumed you were going to tell me."

"Oh, Mr. Bigshot Greyson Storm. Always knows the who and why of it all."

"Except for this time."

"Alright, alright—I thought I'd let you know: I'm ready for us to go out. I know I bailed last time—my hot ex Sammy called—but this time, we're a go. For real. A hundred percent."

"And if I'm not feeling it?"

Nolan barks out a laugh. "What's there to feel? I'll ensure we have enough drinks that we don't feel anything we don't want to."

"I don't know—"

"Ah, but I do." My little brother used to be a salesman, and it shows: he excels at pushy good humor more than anyone. "Drinks, hot girls, drinks, deep fried pickles, more drinks. I've already booked us a table."

"You're not taking 'no' for an answer, are you?"

"Nope." Nolan's clearly pleased with himself. "Besides, I just received some good news."

"Oh?"

"A certain company president just made the right decision with regard to a certain employee—who will remain nameless, naturally."

"Careful," I snap.

"What?" His tone is indefatigably good-humored. "I can't congratulate you on a decision well made?"

"Push it," I find myself snarling. "See where it gets you."

Especially since I am just now driving away from Harley's place, wishing for nothing more than to have seen her.

"Forget it." Nolan knows when not to push his luck. "You coming along tonight. I'll take it. I'll come over to yours and we can cab together?"

"Sure," I say, just to get him off my back.

It'll beat sitting and having Harley hammer at the sides of my skull all night like she has been all day, anyway.

At my place, while waiting for Nolan to come over, I throw a panini in the oven. I place a couple of stray dishes in the dishwasher, refill the Brita. Anything to fill the extra seconds and minutes that teem with her. A call is so easy and fast these days...

Stop it.

I grab the panini out of the oven early, start chowing down on its lukewarm goodness. Maybe a night out will be good for me. Get my mind off her.

Within seconds of Nolan arriving—"Hey there, brother man"—we're ordering a cab.

Less than a minute later, my phone rings.

It's Emerson. "What would you say to two tag-alongs?"

"Do I have a choice?" I ask.

"Landon says he's forgiven you, by the way," Emerson pipes in.

"Wonderful."

"Great, so we're at your door."

A knock, and I hang up, going over to the door and opening it.

"Couldn't you just have knocked instead of calling?" I ask them.

They just smile placidly.

"Woo-hoo," Nolan says behind me. "Another Storm Night of Brotherly Shenanigans."

"Thought we couldn't afford any more bad publicity," I point out.

Landon grins as he saunters in. "A couple of parkour stunts won't hurt anybody."

"Don't worry," Emerson says, following in behind him. "I'll keep them in check."

I shake my head. "That's my job."

The cab arrives shortly after, and we all pile in.

"Heard the good news," Emerson says to me once we're in Royale, at our table. "Think this calls for shots."

"Many, many, many shots," Nolan says with a devilish smile.

"Drop it," I growl, although they're already on their way to order at the bar. Apparently, table service isn't fast enough for them.

Several shots later, we're on the dance floor, on the prowl.

Nolan and Landon have already found their ladies for tonight, while Emerson and I are getting chatted up by two stunners. When they leave for the bathroom, Emerson turns to me, excitement glinting in his eyes. "You want the blonde or the brunette? Damn, I can already tell, this is going to be an epic night!"

"Sure," I say.

He tilts his head and gives me a gentle smile. "Don't sound so excited."

"Think I'm just tired."

"Boo," Nolan says in passing, as his girl tugs him along to who-knows-where. "Have another shot."

So, I do. I don't feel much different, though. My phone is still empty. Harley still hasn't called. Not that she would. I'm the one who would. Should.

I'm being stupid.

"Want to come over to our place?" the blonde says to us. "We're just here for the weekend for work, but they got us this sick room at the Harbor Hotel."

"Hell yeah!" Emerson enthuses.

"What about you?" the brunette asks, hand going to my chest.

I stare back at her blankly. I feel nothing.

She's hot as hell, got a body like a porn star and a face like a model and... I feel nothing.

"Greyson?" Emerson says.

"I have to go," I say. "I'm sorry."

There's something I have to do.

CHAPTER 32

Harley

"Remind me why we're watching this?" I ask Hannah.

"Because you wanted to?" she says, pausing the movie.

"Because I'm an idiot," I conclude.

Only an idiot would think that watching Knocked Up on the day she found out she was, in fact, knocked up, was a good idea.

I check my phone again, glaring at the empty screen. Of course Greyson isn't going to call me again, after he called and texted several times, and even showed up here.

"I can't avoid him forever," I say softly.

"Harley, listen to me," Hannah says in the no-nonsense voice she uses with underlings at the nursery who don't water the plants properly. "You just found out about this. You don't need to tell him right away."

"I know, but I think it's best if I just get it over with. Otherwise it's going to keep nagging at me like this."

Just then, my phone lights up. My heart leaps. It's Greyson.

"Don't," Hannah says, but it's already too late. I've picked up.

"Hey," I say.

"Harley, thank God," he says. "Are you OK?"

"Yeah, I'm... fine."

"What was that other message about? Why haven't you been returning my calls? You weren't feeling well before?"

His questions hit me rapid-fire, and suddenly, a wave of fatigue settles over me again. Oh God, how am I going to tell him?

"I just… I'm sorry."

"Don't be sorry," he says, "see me. I'm coming over now."

"Now now?"

"Yeah, the cab will drop me off in five."

Shit. Shit. Shit. Shit!

"Harley?"

"I just—I don't think you should come."

"What the hell should I do, then? You won't pick up when I call and—what was so urgent anyway?"

"We shouldn't…" I realize it halfway through saying it, laugh bitterly, "…do this over the phone."

"Great. Then it's a good thing I'm almost there now."

A small, childish part of me wishes that if I stay silent, he'll go away. Too bad that real life isn't like that.

"Listen," Greyson continues reasonably, "I know that I've been a dick to you, and I am sorry. But I have to see you. Something's up, I know it is."

I say nothing.

"Harley," he says.

There's nothing to it. No excuse to make. Nothing to say, except: "OK."

"Great. I'll be there in two." He hangs up.

I rise, feeling Hannah's worried eyes on me. "He's almost here now."

"Oh, Har. Do you want me to send him away again? I know, last time you were asleep, but I can just say that you changed your mind." She scowls as she rises, hands on her hips. "What the hell is he doing anyway, coming over here at one at night?"

"It's fine." I rise, shaking my head. "I have to do this. Better to just get it over with."

Hannah's gaze goes incredulous. "In those?"

I look down and, remembering what I'm wearing, laugh. "Guess my moo-moo PJs are as good as anything."

They are, after all, my comfiest ones, even if they're covered with peacefully slumbering pink cows and artfully written purple MOOs.

I'm at the door when my phone goes off. It's Greyson: Here.

We meet outside.

He's wearing a purple shirt and black pants and of course I want to kiss him. If I didn't know any better, with the way he's looking at me, I'd say that he adored me.

His gaze strays to what I'm wearing, and his eyes crinkle. "You look... cute."

I resist the urge to turn on my heel and hurry to escape. No matter how cute Greyson thinks I look now, what I'm about to tell him will change everything, maybe even his whole view of me.

"Thanks." I force a chuckle. "Wasn't exactly expecting company, but these'll do."

He smiles, but it doesn't reach his eyes. He's worried and... holding back. Maybe wants to kiss me as much as I want to kiss him.

It doesn't matter.

"There's a creaky old picnic bench in the back," I tell him. "We can talk there."

We sit down at the creaky old picnic bench in the back, look at each other. The sky is cloudy and only one star shows through. The moon is nowhere to be seen. The air is both cool and clammy. I don't want to be here. I don't want to do this.

"I'm glad you're OK," he says.

"I'm glad you're OK," I say.

"So," he says.

"So," I say, tears coming to my eyes.

This may be the last time we say that to each other. God, everything feels the same and I'm going to ruin it. I have to ruin it.

Jesus, Harley, just tell him. Just get it over with—out with it. Bam, done, finito.

"Listen," Greyson says, taking both my hands in his, "about what I said, I—"

"I'm pregnant," I burst out. "It's yours."

His hands drop mine. He stares at me, blinks a few times.

All around us, crickets are chirping laughter. A car whizzes somewhere. The air is even cooler, prickly now too.

"Oh," he finally says.

"I haven't decided what to do yet," I say. "Though I'm not sure I could bear..."

I trail off into silence, then more of it.

"Oh," he finally says again.

He doesn't have to say any more. His face says it all: shock, puzzlement.

When his eyes finally do meet mine, they're narrowed. "If you want... compensation, like child support, of course I'll meet my obligation, but—"

"That's not what I want," I say, surprising myself. Up until now, I didn't know I wanted anything. And yet, even though what I want is impossible, even though saying it aloud will only drive him farther from me, I finally know what it is I want.

I look him straight in the eyes and say it: "I want you to own up publicly. To our affair—and our baby."

He blinks. His mouth falls open. Just then, at his moment of utter rejection, he looks almost painfully beautiful: sculpted cheeks, tousled hair, dark eyes. He looks away.

God, have I been an idiot.

What am I thinking, asking him to put Storm Inc. on the line like that? How could I be so selfish? This is his life and family we're talking about.

"Forget it," I say quickly. "That was unfair of me."

I rise.

Now that I've told him, I have to let him go while I can still bear to. Maybe Greyson hasn't given me a real answer, but he doesn't need to. His face has already said it all.

"Don't feel like you owe me anything," I say coolly. "I'd still like that glowing reference, but that's it. I can handle myself from here on out."

"Harley, wait," he says.

I pause.

"I..." He swallows. "Can I just have some time to think? This is all so sudden. And I..." He exhales. "I don't know what to do."

"Of course," I say, already walking away. Greyson isn't uncertain—he's buying time. Time to figure out a delicate way to say that the only involvement he wants is a check to soothe his guilty conscience. I saw his face. The last thing I want to do is to guilt him into anything he doesn't want. "It's fine, really. You go live your life. I'll go live mine. Just thought you should know."

And then I keep on walking away.

"Harley," he says from behind me.

But I don't stop. Can't.

If I stop, it'll all spill out, all the unfair and ridiculous hopes I have that somehow we can still be together, make this work without toppling his company. That he'll choose me.

But I can't stomach rejection again, not after my deepest wish got nothing more than a stunned blink in response. If Greyson was going to choose me, us, he would've done so in the first place, back before this pregnancy was even a thing.

He's already made his decision.

Back inside our place, I sink onto the couch and look at Hannah.

"That bad?" she asks quietly.

Even Anchovy is curled into a sad ball on the armrest.

"Yeah," I say, not letting the grief settle, not letting myself curl on the couch beside Anchovy in my own sad ball. I force a smile. "I have an idea."

CHAPTER 33

Greyson

What… just happened?

I came here, excited and worried and frustrated, expecting… I don't know. Not that. Definitely not that.

If I closed my eyes, I could still see her face perfectly clear: makeup-free, gorgeous beyond all reasonableness, sad. As if we'd lost each other again.

With how she walked away just now, have we?

I stare at the picnic table's scratchy grain, trying to get my head around it all. A baby.

Her and my… baby. And her idea of what I should do: leave the company. Then backtracking. It was too much to process right then.

All I knew was that as soon as I'd seen her, seen that she was OK, something inside of me relaxed, warmed.

And now all is tense and cold again. I hurt her again, I could see that.

I get out my phone, ready to call her up, tell her to come back down, talk this out with me. I pause.

That would be a very bad idea. My head isn't any clearer than it was when we were talking.

This has all been too sudden. I need to sober up, sleep. Get my head straightened out. And then, when I'm ready, I'll go to her.

After I call up the cab, it comes quickly enough.

Back at my place, Nolan and his date are already passed out under a blanket on my wraparound leather couch. Landon's muscular physique is just visible at the microwave heating up... an entire tin of apple pie?

"Want some?" he asks, as if this is a perfectly natural thing to be doing at two in the morning.

"No?" I say.

In bed, I lie there, eyes closed, fatigue closing on me like a vacuum. Sleep doesn't come.

Only the scraping certainty that I've failed Harley yet again.

**

I awake to the serene sounds of a burbling brook.

"What... the fuck?" I grumble.

Landon smiles. "Rise and shine, brother. We have work to get to, remember? Isn't the alarm I set for you nice?"

I swipe at my phone, glare at the time I see. "It's 5 AM for fuck's sake!"

He nods, straightening his tie in my mirror. "Thought I'd wake you before I headed out for the gym. Nolan pranked your phone by changing your alarm to 'Who Let the Dogs Out' for noon."

"Fucker," I mutter.

Guess waking up at 5 AM beats waking up at noon. Although I feel like shit.

"Everything OK last night?" he asks, his eyes meeting mine in the mirror.

"Meaning?"

"You jetted off—probably to see that cinematographer I'm assuming?"

When I don't answer, he continues, "Then you came back looking like absolute shit."

"Don't worry about it."

"I'm not," he says smoothly.

"Good."

"Good." Landon heads for the door, throwing me a wave. "See ya."

I glare at his receding back. Trust him to throw salt in a wound that I didn't even know I had. Not that I thought things were at all OK after last night. Just—I don't need any more reminders that things are fucked. Royally.

I sink back into bed, eyes closing even though I know it's pointless. There won't be any more sleep for me. Not until I've called up Harley and told her.

I sit up and stare into the mirror. Told her what, exactly? That I was an idiot to break up with her in the first place? That, screw the consequences, we should be together?

She's probably already past that. I've let her down too many times already. Why the hell should she trust me again?

Halfway to reaching for my phone, I pause.

I'm not exactly in great shape to call her right now. This pounding headache isn't showing any signs of going away anytime soon. Maybe popping a couple Advils and getting some work done in the office will put me in a better mood.

A few hours and Advils later, I'm at the office. The headache is gone, my mood is still shit. Not that I really expected it to be any different, with what happened last night. Clearly, the ball of tension in my upper back isn't going to go away until I get it over with. Call her up. Tell her what I have to. Whatever that is.

But it's break time, and part of me is still certain I'll find the right words if I wait a bit longer.

So, I prowl the office, scrutinizing all the productive workers, the small cogs that make up Storm Inc. I eye the employees, the best of the best my dad narrowed down to work for him. I catch a glimpse of Landon, excited with the new project he's working on.

I glare at my reflection in the bathroom mirror.

I can't figure it out. Whether I would really risk all this just to be with her. Whether it could still be the right thing to do even if it ruined her dream career and reputation too.

"Look at this." Landon saunters into my office a few minutes later, waving several newspapers triumphantly. "What do you see?"

I peer at the headlines. "Economy's not doing as well as expected?"

"No." He eyes the heavens like I've just called a dog a cat, then gives the papers another shake. "No scandals about Storm Inc. or you. Even the Star has moved onto an alien sighting in Mississauga. You know what that means?"

"What?"

"We're scot-free."

"Scot-free," I repeat numbly.

"Yeah, no big deal," he quips. "It's not like our entire company was in peril."

"I... think I'm just beat."

"Right." Landon heads for the door, still grinning ear to ear. "Anyway, just thought I'd share the good news. Nolan is happy enough to go camping."

"You say it like that's a good thing."

"To be fair, no one could've foreseen that leaving the marshmallows out would attract so many bears last time."

"Yeah, yeah."

Landon gives me a final wave. "Keep at it, President."

"Thanks," I say.

And then I sit there. It occurs to me that I can't put this off any longer. I have to talk to her. Even if I don't have the slightest idea what I'll say.

One call, three rings. No answer.

I call again. And again.

"C'mon," I mutter, clenching the phone. "Not this again."

But my next call goes unanswered, and so does the next.

"What the hell," I snap to myself.

What the fucking hell does Harley think she's playing at? She blindsides me last night, gives me no time to do anything other than be fucking shocked, then won't answer my calls?

At the next call, I leave a message: "Hi Harley, it's Greyson. I want to talk to you. Pick up."

The next call is answered.

"Hello?" an unfamiliar voice says.

What in the hell?

"Is Harley there?"

Silence.

"Well?"

"She's sleeping."

I look at the clock. It's 2:30 PM.

"No, she's not. Put her on."

"Yes, she is," the phone woman snaps back. Probably the cousin who was such a bitch to me last time. "And you're in no position to be making demands."

"I'm the father of her child," I snarl. "I have every right."

"Oh yeah?"

"Yeah."

For a second I'm sure the bitch is going to hang up the phone, but then she sighs. "She said you were a piece of work."

"Oh?"

"Affectionately, though." Another sigh. "I'm Hannah, Harley's cousin."

"Hello again."

"Hello again. But I'm telling you, she doesn't want to talk to you. I just picked up to ask you to stop calling."

"How do you know she doesn't want to talk to me if she's asleep?"

"Because she seriously considered putting her phone in a blender this morning before I talked her out of it."

"Oh. Still."

"Now's not a great time, anyway."

"So she's not going to even give me a chance to respond?"

"From what I heard, you had your chance. Unless you're calling because you know what you want?"

"If I could just talk to her—"

"Let me rephrase: Now's a bad time. It's almost time for us to board. The last thing she needs is you showing up and making everything more complicated."

"Board." I rack my mind stupidly for what she's talking about. Not board a plane, can't be. "Board what?"

"We're taking a last-minute trip. We've been wanting to go to Thailand for ages, so we figured, why not now?"

"A trip," I say, as if the words could have a different meaning if I say them right. "How long?"

"Haven't decided yet. A month, maybe a few. She'll come back to have the baby, of course. Harley doesn't have a job, as you know, and my job loves me so much they'll let me have all the time off I want. There couldn't be a better time than now."

"A few months?" I snap. "OK. You really have to let me talk to her. This is all happening so fast, for Christ's sake!"

"I know." Her voice is sympathetic, but firm. "And the last thing Harley ever wanted to do was to pressure you. She feels like she overstepped herself last night. She doesn't want to be a burden or to endanger your company."

"She…" I fall-sit onto my office chair, stare at the door. "Hannah, listen to me. Just put her on—or I swear to God, I'll come there myself—"

"You don't know what gate we're at," she points out cheerily, "but fine, I'll ask her and see what she says."

Muffled voices. I twist back and forth in my chair, back and forth, back and forth.

"Greyson?" Sleepy voice. Sad? Happy?

"Harley, hey, I… you're really going away?"

"Yeah. Now might be my last chance, before... well, you know."

"I wanted to talk to you. See you."

"Well. We're talking now."

"What if I wanted to try it?"

Her pause is too long to be promising. "It?"

"Us."

"Greyson, don't say things you don't mean."

"How do you know I don't mean it?"

"Because it's not something that takes almost 24 hours of thought! Either you know you want to be with someone or you don't. It's that simple."

"Maybe it's not like that with everyone."

Another pause that makes me want to chuck my phone at the wall. "Greyson, I saw you."

"What do you mean you saw me?"

"I saw your face when I told you. There was no excitement, no happiness. You were just stunned, scared."

"Of course I was. This is a fucking baby we're talking about. Being a father is a big fucking deal. Of course I was scared—am scared—aren't you?"

"Yeah, but... you already ended things with me, OK? I don't want you being pressured into getting back together with me just because of this. Let's not make this harder than it has to be."

"Why can't you believe me when I say that I want to be with you?"

When she finally speaks again, her voice is a teary whisper. "Because I don't think even you knew what you were going to say until you called me up. I think you waited this long because you couldn't decide. I don't think you know, even now."

"Harley…"

"Not wanting to lose someone isn't the same as wanting to be with someone," she says.

"Goodbye Greyson," she says.

"I wish you nothing but the best," she says.

And then, she hangs up.

I sit there, staring at the wall.

Not wanting to lose someone isn't the same as wanting to be with someone…

Goddamnit.

That's what it was with my dad and mom, by the end. He didn't want to be with her, not really. All they did was fight and criticize and make up for half an hour, if that. But when the prospect of losing her arose, he did everything in his power, fought tooth and nail to get her back. Only to mistreat and cheat on her, often in the very same week.

He didn't want to be with her, but he didn't want anyone else with her either.

Is that what this is about? Have I become my dad? Do I not want Harley, I just don't want to lose her? I already gave her up once, why should this be any different?

I've never particularly wanted one way or another to be a dad. Only, when I'm with her…

Time ebbs away. Things just work. I smile so big I feel like an idiot. I forget everything I'm supposed to do.

I get up from my chair. I know what I want to do. I know what I have to do.

Too bad they aren't the same thing.

CHAPTER 34

Harley

"Flight 45 to Bangkok is now boarding. All passengers in Aisles A-H, please line up immediately," the grouch-faced stewardess intones overhead.

"Almost time." Hannah nudges me with a grin.

"Yep," I agree.

"What do you think Anchovy is doing at Roger's right now?" she asks.

"Honestly?" I say. "Probably revenge pooping all over that poor man's house."

"Good thing he loves me," Hannah says with a small smile.

"And is joining us in a few weeks," I add. "Annnnd has a sister who actually likes ferrets. I just wish we could've taken Anchovy with us."

"No, you don't." Hannah wags a stern finger at me. "Even on road trips, Anchovy's MO is to start projectile vomiting everywhere."

"Little ferret vomit is actually cute?" I try.

Hannah just shakes her head, and we chuckle. I lean my head on her shoulder. "I'm just glad you're here. I can't believe you actually agreed to this."

"It was a pretty crazy idea," Hannah agrees. "But this might be our last chance with the little one on the way."

I smile, even though it hurts. "Did you always know I would keep it?"

She nods.

"How?" I ask.

She shrugs. "I just did. I'm so sorry about... you know."

Up until now, we've successfully avoided taking about it—the whole Greyson thing. At the mention, something twists in my stomach.

"It's OK," I say, even though it isn't, at all. "Better we're honest with ourselves now then months or even years down the road. I don't want to be with someone who isn't a hundred percent in it. Plus, he already chose the company over me." I exhale. "Not that I blame him."

Hannah gives my arm a squeeze.

I give my belly a pat. "And now I've got a bun cooking in the oven."

Hannah glares at me. "Stop."

"What can I say," I continue, smiling evilly. "I've got a bat in the cave. I'm in the pudding club. My tin roof's rusted. I've got a pea in the pod."

Hannah groans. "Help me, Lord."

I pat her. "Just think of the feasts we'll have! Now that I'm eating for two."

"Let's start with plane food," Hannah says eagerly. "This is the one and only time I'm A-OK with eating obscene amounts of Pringles."

"Yeah, let's drink our faces off and—" I freeze, realizing it at the last second. "Oh."

"Drink apple juice for two?" Hannah tries.

I force a laugh. "Really, it's fine. I just have to get used to it. This. Me and my little something something."

"That's not even a saying," Hannah declares with an eye roll.

I sniff. "That's what you think."

"Flight 45 to Bangkok is now boarding. All passengers in Aisles I-P, please line up immediately," the grouch-faced stewardess intones overhead.

Hannah and I exchange a glance. "That's us."

We rise.

"Harley!" someone yells.

I freeze. No way.

"Harley!" the familiar voice yells again.

I turn around. Holy fucking hell. Yeah way. It's Greyson, racing towards us.

"I... you..." he wheezes. "Don't go."

I gape at him as he skids to a stop right in front of me. "Please. I need to... talk to you."

"OK." I stand there staring at him. This doesn't feel real.

"I'll give you two a minute," Hannah says. "I can probably get the stewardess to give us an extra minute or two."

"Thanks," I tell her, before turning to gape some more at Greyson. "How did you even find us?"

His eyes feel like they're boring into me, they're filled with such intensity and adoration. "A friend... Harley, you have to listen to me. Last night was a shock, but I've been thinking. I don't want to be without you. I want us to work. Without you, my work is nothing. My life... please. Harley, I want to be with you."

I stare at him. How is he managing to say just about everything I longed to hear?

"But last night..." I say. "And Storm Media, how can we..."

"Screw Storm Media, screw everything." He seizes both my hands, brings them to his chest, his eyes going tender as they meet mine. "All I know is: every one of the happiest days of my life has been with you."

I peer at him. He's still catching his breath, but those eyes—invigorated, excited, happy, scared—say it all: he means it. Every word.

"Still, though." It can't be this easy. "You have responsibilities. People who count on you."

"I've stepped down as president," he says. "It was never what I wanted, anyway. Landon is more up to the job, has always been a better leader than me. I can mentor him until he's ready."

"OK," I say. "But the trip... we've booked our tickets. And I just feel like this is so sudden. How do I know you aren't just trying to do the right thing by me because of the baby? Because if so, that's not what I want. At all."

"Harley." Greyson forces a miserable smile. "I was away from you for 24 hours and it was pure torture. You calling me up gave me an excuse to reach out to you. I would've cracked in a few days, tops. I'm an idiot." Another one of those grimace-smiles I want to kiss away. "A complete idiot. The kind of idiot who only realizes what he has once it's gone, but—I'd rather that than be the kind of idiot who lets the best thing that ever happened to him leave. Harley, I want you to be my girlfriend. I want to date you, I want to name our child together. When I'm with you, for the first time, I finally get what all this 'love' craziness is about." He exhales, looking as surprised at the words coming out of his mouth as I feel. But the craziest thing of all is that they're true. They're really true. "You're it, my it."

I don't realize that I'm crying until he presses his lips to my tears. His eyes on mine are hopeful, questioning. "So?"

I giggle. "So."

"I said it first."

"Well, I... have a trip to go to."

His hand finds mine. "Then so do I."

CHAPTER 35

Greyson

Two Months Later

"You were right!" I yell as Harley and I sit on the hill and take in the sight before us. Disco lights paint the mass of dancing bodies bright green, crimson and turquoise. Giant glittering yellow banners and massive flaming torches and bonfires are lighting up the sky. Some Calvin Harris song that makes me want to dance even though I'm sitting down and not big on dancing. Maybe it's just that punch I drank. "This Full Moon Festival is amazing."

"Course I was." Harley plants a kiss on my cheek, then leans her head onto my shoulder. "Mama Har can't be wrong." Another grin. "Although the internet did help. Who knew they had a whole island dedicated to this thing?"

"Even if this place has a lot of horror stories," I say contemplatively. "Robberies, kidnappings, injuries—do you know hundreds of people get burned on the fire jumping ropes every year?"

"Drunk people and flaming jump ropes don't seem like a wise combo," Harley admits with a giggle. "Now, do you have any other uplifting observations to make?"

One look at her in her metallic pink dress and I have all the material I need: "You look hot as hell."

Harley laughs and hides her face with her hands. "Anything not obvious?"

I reach over and give her butt a little whack. "Oh, somebody's humble."

Harley giggles. "What can I say, I come by it honestly."

I lean over to whisper in her ear. "If our kid looks anything like you, they're going to be beautiful."

She steals a kiss. "If they look anything like you, they're going to be beautiful."

I grin again, so big and wide my mouth is almost sore after all the grinning I've been doing. Being around Harley does that to me. "Guess the odds are stacked, then."

"Guess so," she says happily, then, "Ooh!"

"What?"

"Look up."

I do. I crane my head back to stare and keep staring. "Wow. It's easy to forget how many stars there are."

"There's no forgetting now," she says softly, then, "Kiss me."

I do, peeling myself away with difficulty. "Stop it, you."

Her grin is downright devilish, sending a twinge right to my cock. "Or what?"

My lips lap at her ear as I answer, "Or I'll make you regret it."

She lunges another kiss at me, this one with enough tongue to make my cock instantly hard. "Something tells me I won't regret it one bit."

"That's it," I growl, pinning her down onto the grass. "Don't say I didn't warn you."

Our mouths remeet and our tongues entwine. She tastes like the caramel corn I bought her minutes ago. She twists her mouth against mine with a passion that drives me mad. My hands twist in her hair, shove her lips back to mine when she tries pulling away.

"But Greyson," she giggles.

"Don't start what you don't intend to finish," I murmur, pulling her back to me and sucking on her lower lip.

She groans. "What are you trying to do to me?"

I grind my pelvis into hers. "What we both want me to."

Partway through another groan, she manages to shoot me a teasing smirk. "That so?"

I press my fingers into her panty-covered pussy. "You tell me."

Another glaring moan. "You ass."

"You like it."

"Oh yeah?"

I kiss her, hard. "Yeah."

I take her chin in my hands, but still she's pulling away. "What about... we're right in the open. Anyone could come..."

She's right, reasonable, logical. Problem is, with the lust sparking in her eyes and her lips pouted with want, I can't calm down. Plus, there is no one around right now.

"I won't tell if you won't," I say, as my fingers slip inside her.

"Ooohhhh, that's so... ohhh... Good." She bites her lip.

Inside, she's even wetter than I expected.

"That's it, baby." I smile over her. "I love seeing you all hot and bothered."

Her eyes close and her back arches. "Just... please. More."

I peel down her blue satin panties, growling in appreciation. "The ones I bought you. Good."

But she's too deep into her pleasure to answer now. Fuck, she's hot. Just seeing her like this, dress bunched up around her legs, gorgeous slit bared to me, throat up, I'm close myself.

Hot as fuck.

My fingers jam into her as my other hand caresses the soft flesh of her ass, enjoying its fullness.

"I love you like this," I murmur.

"Huh…"

My lips find hers. "Mine."

Hers kiss mine back hungrily. "Yours."

And then I pick up the pace. Already, she's squirming, my fingers working her expertly. I dip my head down and lap at her upper thighs, around her opening. Her pelvis twitches as her moans rise a pitch.

"You gonna come for me?" I croon, right before my lips land on her clit.

"Uhhh yess!" she shrills.

I lap my tongue around her spastically at the same moment I start finger-banging her fast and hard.

With that, she loses it, letting out a loud wail. As she comes, I lap and finger-fuck her mercilessly—watching as she comes once, and then again, and then again. As she's shaking, I hold her in my arms.

"That was… you were…" she murmurs sleepily, snuggling up to me.

My boner hasn't gone anywhere. God, she's so hot and pretty and amazing. Carrying my child. The perfect woman. My perfect woman.

My lips find hers again and I press my body to hers. She finds my erection quickly enough, her hands going to my pants and stroking.

"Oh yeah?" she says saucily.

"Yeah," I growl, giving her ass a nice smack and then a squeeze.

She clambers on top of me, grinding her hips into my painfully hard cock. "Let's see what we can do with this."

"Think we need to be closer," I say, peeling off her dress and tossing it aside. Underneath, she's naked, tan, fine as fuck. My lips lock over one of her nipples and her head falls back with a croon.

My hand strokes along her head. "That's what I like to hear."

She shakes me free. "No, it's your turn."

I stroke her breast, pressing it further into my face. "This is for me."

With the lightest of pressure, I bite down on the tip of her nipple and she yelps with pleasure.

I smack her ass and she groans, fumbling with my jeans buttons. "I need... please."

I press the flat of my palm into her chest firmly. "Whose pace are we going at?"

She exhales. "Yours. But Greyson, please..."

I undo my jeans and she grins, biting her lip. We move onto our sides and I take off my pants and briefs, my cock springing up eagerly.

"That what you want?" I ask lightly.

Seconds before her lips suction around my cock, she purrs, "Want isn't the word."

As her mouth glides all the way to the base of my dick, I understand: 'need' is.

Tongue and lips working in tandem, she sucks me like a pro. As my cock jams the back of her throat, it takes all I have not to come on the spot.

Jesus, she's good. So hot. I love her so goddamn much.

Her hand pumps me further into her mouth, her tongue swirling around my shaft. She sucks extra hard on the head as she comes up for air.

"So," she says, with an evil smile.

"So," I say, breathing heavily.

"See ya," she says, diving back for my dick.

Never have I cracked up during a blowjob, but then again, with Harley a lot of things are new. Like how right now I'm coming within minutes of her going down on me. Like how, in this most random of all times, I can really see myself spending the rest of my life with this girl.

Even as I come, she doesn't let up one bit, so my climax is crazy-hot and intense.

Afterwards, we're holding each other so tightly, it only occurs to me slowly: with her naked gorgeous body in my arms, I'm getting hard again, my cock instinctively edging for between her legs.

This time, we go slow. I explore her body with my fingertips, my lips, my tongue. I can't believe how her soft her skin is, how good her curves feel. I could get off on massaging them alone. It's like a meditation to me, hearing all her little groans and pleasured sounds.

"You're hot as fuck, you know that?" I growl, as her lithe body clasps against mine.

Finally, I can't take it anymore, I slide my cock inside her. Just the tip, though. I want to savor every second.

Like her long-drawn out, "Ooooo". How her body breaks into shaking.

I slip it in a bit more—her back hikes up, the groan moves down her throat.

I slip it in a bit more—her pussy clasps against my cock eagerly.

I slip it in all the way—pleasure spikes through me, and she comes, twisting on me.

"Oh Greyson," she moans. "Yes."

I slip it in and out a bit faster. "More?"

Her lips lunge for mine, peel away. "More."

And I give it to her. In and out, painstakingly slowly. She comes so many times I lose track. It's my most favorite sight in the world: my girl climaxing on my dick.

I draw it out, enjoy it. Until finally, I can't take it anymore and my climax explodes out of me at the same time her latest and greatest does.

As we twist together, pleasure exploding back and forth, something bursts out of me: "I want you forever—my sweetie—my wife—my Harley."

And then it throws us out and we collapse, utterly spent.

Although I can't relax as much as I normally do. I want you forever—my sweetie—my wife—my Harley—what the actual fuck was that?

Do I actually want that, or was that the orgasm talking?

I peer down at Harley, in my arms. One look, and I know. It's right. We are. She is.

We've been travelling for two months now, after I managed to snag that last-minute ticket, and never have I thought twice about it. I barely remember there's a home.

"Greyson?" Harley says with a tentative smile.

"Yeah?"

"About what you said…"

"Forget it," I say. "I mean, not for good. But for now."

I have an idea. If I'm going to propose to her, it can't be anything less than perfect. Not for my girl.

"Oh?" Eyes closed, I can hear the smile in her voice.

I kiss the top of her head. "Just… right now is perfect as it is. Isn't it?"

"It is," she agrees. "We are."

EPILOGUE

Harley

One Year Later

"Who loves you?" I coo at the baby in my lap. "Mama loves you."

The chubby little boy in the cow PJs (a joke gift from Hannah, of course) with Greyson's dancing eyes and a curl of my wavy blond hair giggles, delighted.

"Are you sure about this?" I ask Greyson as I eye Janie critically. She has become a close friend recently and has always been amazing with little Dakota, but still. Every time I have to be away from my little boy, there's a pang.

"It's just for an hour," he assures me, crouching to give our son a kiss on his fat cheek. "And we'll be less than twenty feet away. I told you: I'm not missing date night with my fiancée for anything in the world."

I can't quite hold back the smile forcing its way onto my face. "Oh, alright. But just an hour."

Greyson's hand finds mine. "And not a minute more."

Outside, the plains spread before us, wild and dusty. I sneeze.

"Do I get to find out what the surprise is?" I ask, peering around. I can't see anything but desert and tents.

"Just a bit farther," Greyson says, leading me along. "And then..."

"Surprise!"

I gape as people burst out of a tent I thought was suspiciously large. First up is Hannah and Roger. "But… how?"

Hannah's beaming as she holds out the lace and macramé dress we picked out together a few months ago. "You're getting married!"

"Now?" I turn to gape at Greyson.

He just smiles. "Now. You said you wanted it to be a surprise and in a wild location, remember?"

"Yeah, but…" I laugh, surveying the endless-seeming plains. "This is perfect."

Twenty minutes later, after Hannah helps me get my dress on and my hair and makeup nice, we come outside to see that the team Greyson hired has set up the lily flower hangings, a golden lily-twined archway and the chairs. Russel is the first to sit down, wearing a mustache that looks recent, bushy and hilarious, throwing a wink my way.

"I always knew you two were soulmates," he says lugubriously. "Just like me and my Esme. We will find our way back to each other, somehow."

Another mystery is how they got Anchovy here. He's scurrying around everything delightedly while Hannah tries to chase him down. She pauses to smile at me. "You look gorgeous."

"Thanks. I… this is crazy."

"C'mon everyone!" Greyson says, hurrying everyone along. "I told my bride one hour and I intend to keep my promise."

And, the wildest thing of all, he does. The ceremony is quick: my dad walking me down the aisle, the priest having us say our vows. When Greyson says: "I want to spend the rest of my life with you. You are the best thing that's ever happened to me. You have made me into the man I am today," I know he means it, has as little doubt about it as I do. Together, we're just right.

And then we kiss, and then it's done. We are husband and wife.

It's weird, all this. I never cared much for the institution of marriage, but with Greyson, it just feels right. Just how it felt right the second time he proposed to me, on one of the Aeolian Islands he'd booked just for us, with a candlelight dinner under the stars.

The food is delicious, the highlight, of course, being the caramel corn. Landon has to step out to call a lawyer he's setting up a meeting with, but he gets back in time for his speech. He and the rest of Greyson's brothers deliver speeches that get everyone laughing. Hannah delivers a toast so good that I tear up and we hug for a long, long time.

And then Greyson and I dance, chest to chest, as Elvis Presley croons, "Can't help falling in love... with... you."

Partway through the song, Greyson catches my eye. "Hey."

"Hey," I say.

He brushes a tear off my cheek. "What's up?"

"Just—all this, it's so perfect that it's beyond belief. Landon being great as president. You getting your old job as producer back, me as a cinematographer. The new series being a hit. This amazing wedding with all our family and friends. Our son being beautiful and healthy."

Greyson's grin is enough to get me grinning too. "You forgot how we're here for a documentary on the lions of the Kalahari."

"How could I forget," I say, right before I kiss him.

"How could you," he says, kissing me right back.

"So," I say.

He laughs. "So."

I bring our clasped hands to my lips, kiss them. "This."

~The End~

If you LOVED First Comes Love, be sure to check out Enemy's Secret!

It's a fun and flirty hot romance read filled with page melting heat, lots of teasing, drama and some sugar sweet moments guaranteed to leave you with a very satisfying happily-ever-after.

https://www.ashleepriceromanceauthor.com/product/enemys-secret-an-enemies-to-lovers-second-chance-romance-love-comes-to-town-book-2/

Ashlee Price Merch – First Comes Love Tote Bag, Throw Pillow, and phone covers:

https://www.ashleepriceromanceauthor.com/product-category/ashlee-merch/

ENEMY'S SECRET SNEAK PEEK

She's the one I broke up with.
My first love now turned into a sworn enemy.
They say time heals all wounds.
I say it ripped me a new one.

I can't blame her for wanting to tear me and my company to the ground.
I deserve her wrath.
I was all she ever wanted.
Then I broke her heart into a million pieces in front of all her friends.

With those pouty red lips and bedroom voice.
Strutting into the courtroom with more confidence than I can ever remember.
She has the judge eating out of the palm of her hand.

Kyra is the kind of woman every man wants.
Beautiful. Smart. An incredible mother.
To a daughter that sure does look and act a lot like me.

But I'm no longer that young punk.
We deserve a second chance.
This time I'll make it right.
This time I'll make her mine.

Chapter 1

Landon

They say time heals all wounds, but I'd say it just ripped me a new one. Over a nine-year-old scar.

Kyra Fucking Masterson.

Same inky hair, Snow White skin, same pouting red lips. Is that why I'm getting a hard-on just from a glance?

Granted, her tight little body looks hot as hell in that two-piece grey pinstripe suit, and the hard wooden surface of the stand would be perfect for bending her over and...

Not now, Landon.

But I can't peel my eyes away. Shit, everything about her looks the same, but... better somehow. Different. I can't put my finger on it.

"This is why, your honor, we are here today to discuss the plagiarism charges against Storm Media," Kyra says in that same throaty voice I had grown so used to. Although right now there's a sharp edge to it that will allow nothing but agreement. "Because there's more than enough evidence to warrant it."

My lawyer, Dirk, states some kind of defense, meant to shut this all down. With the shit-show going on around Storm Media already - we're getting audited by the IRS thanks to Dad's shady finances - the last thing we need is Goldtree Inc. getting dirt on us too. With Greyson's latest TV series, we've managed to avoid the red, but another scandal - or worse, a big payout - could put us right back there. Not that Dirk is coming cheap.

Nevertheless, as much as I hate to admit it, I'm actually slightly enjoying this. Seeing Kyra in her element. Sure, I'm focused more on the appealing way those pouty lips are moving than on the actual words coming out of them, but still.

"We will continue to examine the evidence brought before us over the coming weeks," the judge is saying now. "Court dismissed."

Outside the room, in the lobby, I call up Nolan.

"Did we win?" he asks.

"Dude, it was the first day."

"Well." He sniffs. "Maybe we got lucky. I am a lucky person, you know."

"Course I do. You got to be my brother, after all."

Nolan snorts. "Also, just an FYI, your dog shit on my rug."

"It was an ugly rug," I say blandly. "Anyway, you have to listen to this - "

"Hello? Did you not hear me? After I did you the hugely awesome, major favor of babysitting your psycho stray mutt, he goes and lets a big one loose on my sustainably-bred alpaca fur rug! Now, I don't know what could be more important than that, but - "

"I saw Kyra."

"Oh." I can almost see the smile creeping over Nolan's face. "The Kyra?"

"No, one of the many Kyras that inhabit our city. Yes, of course it was the Kyra!"

"Where'd you see her?"

"Get this: she's the lawyer for Goldtree Inc."

Nolan laughs loudly. "Well, you're done for. Remember how much she studied in school? Seemed like every time I saw her she had her nose buried in a book."

"Glad you're so optimistic about our chances," I say drily. "Anyway, book smart does not a good lawyer make."

"Hmm," Nolan says blandly.

"Alright, she's amazing in court," I say. "And hotter than ever."

"Too bad you screwed that thing up," Nolan says meditatively. "Now, I bet all the Storm charm in the world wouldn't make that right. Mind if I step in?"

I know he's just messing with me - not dating each other's exes is one of the basics of twin etiquette - but still, I snap: "I bet I could win her over if I wanted to."

"Nah." Nolan chuckles, and if he were here, he'd be shaking his head. "No way."

"I did it once," I say. "Can't be so hard to do it again. Plus, it would help get the case against Storm Media thrown out."

"Dude," Nolan says. "Last time you saw her, you - "

A tap on my shoulder. I turn around.

"Got to go," I tell Nolan, hanging up as soon as I see who it is.

There she is: dark long-lashed eyes narrowed, pretty lips curled into a sneer, arms crossed over her chest.

"Word to the wise," she says. "Don't talk about someone when they're in the same room."

God she's pretty. Plus, there's this edge about her now that's driving me wild.

"Kyra, hey." I smile. "Imagine running into you here."

She doesn't smile. "I heard you, you know."

"Huh?"

"Don't act dumb. 'I bet I could win her over if I wanted to.' God, you haven't changed one bit."

"Listen, it's not what you think - "

A sharp bark of a laugh. "Oh really? So it wasn't Nolan you were bragging to?"

I pause, deflated. "OK, so maybe - "

She heads off. "Forget it. I've got to get home."

"Kyra," I say, following her. "Just hold on - it's been good seeing you, even under the circumstances."

The look she gives me manages to be both bland and hateful at once. "Wish I could say the same." Eyeing me, she shakes her head. "God, you really think we're back in college, don't you? That I still can't resist you."

I try to smile. Since apologizing hasn't been working, maybe a bit of humor? "Well, you were crazy about me."

"Key word being were. Now?" Her chin lifts. Her eyes flash. "I hate you."

"Whoa there, hate? That's a bit much." I try to smile, but find that I can't. The way 'hate' rolled off her tongue so easily shook me.

"Not really," she says with a light eat-shit smile. "Anyway, I'll be seeing you."

"No, Kyra, just hold on a second." I move to block her path. Shit, why can't I just let her leave? "You don't really hate me." Why do I even care?

"Yeah, I really do," she says. "Think about it, Landon - there aren't many things worse than seeing your ex again." Her eyes narrow with thought, then her head tilts to the side. "OK, maybe getting a lobotomy, having your pants rip in the ass, and your dad and best friend getting married, but since I've been lucky enough not to experience those - I'm going to go."

She storms away, then pauses. "Oh, and Landon?"

"Yeah?"

"If it wasn't clear before, I still hate you. After that stunt you pulled back in college, I'd rather drink bleach than go out with you again."

God, talk about a psycho. Maybe I was a dick when I pulled that 'stunt', but still.

I find myself snapping too. "Good, because I hate you too."

Whoa - what now?

Her sculpted eyebrows arc. "Good."

"Good."

"I'm leaving now."

"Good."

"We're going to win this case and take your crooked ass down," she snaps.

"Yeah, you go and try that," I snap back.

And then she's gone and I can't seem to pry my eyes off her ass.

Where the hell did that come from? Obviously, I don't hate Kyra, even if she is being a major bitch. Then why blurt it out?

Maybe her saying she'd rather drink bleach than go out with me brought it on. Or how she kept saying 'I hate you' like it was a saw that could cut through me. Or how, despite all of this, I've got a hard-on that says she's hotter than ever.

Fuck it, I have to get home. Break the news to Greyson, then figure out what to do myself. Something tells me that Kyra and Goldtree Inc. aren't going to back down easy.

"Landon, glad I found you." It's Dirk, his face as impassive as ever.

"Haven't been hiding," I reply.

"Maybe you should." The crack of a smile that doesn't reach his eyes is the only indication that my lawyer just told a joke. "I don't want to worry you, but they have a good case. A damn good one."

"Good enough to not get thrown out of court," I say neutrally.

"Listen," he says. "Your dad has already had his name dragged through the mud this past year. Accusations of this kind aren't seeming as far-fetched as they once did."

"Accusations of this kind..." I shake my head, scowling. "My dad was a lot of things, Dirk, but he didn't copy other companies. He didn't need to."

"I know. Thing is, this Goldtree has quite the case. That doesn't mean they're going to win, though."

I eye him. "What's your point?"

"My point is that it's going to be a close one. So don't go pissing off Ms. Masterson."

"We were just talking. Why does it matter, anyway?"

"She's well-known around here. Killer at her job." Dirk's eyes narrow significantly. "And apparently even more killer when she's upset. She's credited with single-handedly revamping Ontario's hunting laws after a family member got hurt by a hunter. So don't piss her off."

I shrug. "I think that ship has sailed."

"Then don't piss her off further."

I glare at him. "Really? That's our game plan: don't piss off the opposing side's lawyer? That's what we're paying you for?"

"Careful," Dirk says quietly, rubbing his temples. "I'm doing this case partly as a favor, a thanks for all the times your father had my back. We both know The Ronald refused to touch this case with a ten-foot stick."

I grimace. It really is a measure of how low public opinion of Storm Media has sunk that even Ronald flat-out refuses to represent us - he almost represented O. J. Simpson, for Christ's sake.

"I will be careful," I say smoothly, turning to go. This conversation is long past its expiry date. "And we will win."

There's no other option. Although, as I'm leaving the building, it's not our win that's clogging my head. It's her.

Kyra.

Smiling that hateful smile.

Vivst my website to get Enemys Secret

https://www.ashleepriceromanceauthor.com/product/enemys-secret-an-enemies-to-lovers-second-chance-romance-love-comes-to-town-book-2/

GET MORE FROM ASHLEE PRICE

Amazon lists millions of titles, and I'm happy you discovered this one.

But if you'd like to know when I release a new book, instead of leaving it up to chance, sign up for my newsletter.

I'll send you an email when my latest release goes live.

https://www.ashleepriceromanceauthor.com/signup/